On Guard

J.R. GRAY
ANDI JAXON

Cover Image: Michelle Lancaster
Cover Model: Thomas Jamezz
Cover Design: Kerry Heavens
Editing: Candace Royer-Love
Proofing: Michele Ficht
Formatting: GrayBooks and Andi Jaxon

Selling my virginity wasn't how I saw my first week of college going.

But after my parents cut me off, an offer from a gorgeous rich stranger doesn't sound so bad.
It's only twenty-four hours and I'll never have to see him again.
Wrong.

Much to my horror, the stranger is Oliver Godfrey, the captain of my fencing team.
And as if that isn't bad enough, his parents own half the city.
There is no escape from him or the way he makes me feel.
He's everything I don't want.
And everything I need.

A playboy like him shouldn't look at me twice, so why is he ruining my life?
But what Oliver wants, Oliver gets, and he wants me.
He's arrogant, possessive, and infuriatingly obsessed with me.
This can't work.

His parents want him to marry an heiress so I can't keep him.
All I can have is stolen moments hidden in the dark.
He's going to break my heart and I'm going to let him.

TRIGGER WARNING

Skip for spoilers.

Religious trauma and homophobic parents
Degradation and power exchange

To all the people hoping this is dino porn— it's not.

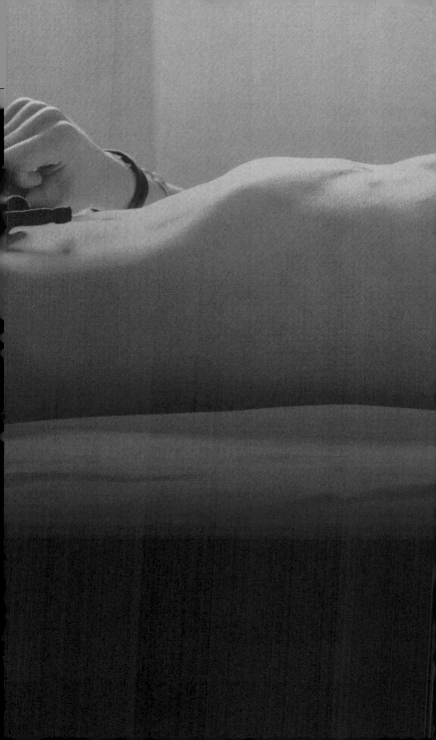

Prologue

Isaac

T he hot August night sticks to my skin as mosquitos bite every inch of exposed flesh they can find.

"Come on, babe," Tim whines. "It's been two years, and I leave for school next week. We aren't going to get any more chances."

With my wrist trapped in his grip, he rubs my palm against the bulge in his jeans, and I jerk back.

"Stop it. I'm not ready." I wrap my arms around myself, clutching at my ribs like it'll stop him from reaching for me again.

I hate how he's pushed this since we graduated a few weeks ago. Like there's a time limit on our virginity, and we have to have sex right now or miss out forever. We've been dating for two years and really only kissed. Why would that change now?

Voices carry on the humid breeze from the front of the church

Wednesday night is bible study and youth group. That hasn't changed my entire life.

Timothy has been part of the church as long as I have, and since we started dating, we sometimes sneak out early and hide in the shadows behind the sanctuary to make out or just hold hands and talk. It's the only time we get a few minutes alone.

"We don't have time for you to get ready. I don't want to go to college a virgin," Tim hisses at me, crowding me against the wall.

My stomach twists, and I fight back the tears threatening to fill my eyes. Who the hell is this Tim?

"I promise it'll feel good." He smiles at me and dips his head to press his lips to mine. It doesn't feel the same, though. It's tainted now, dirty, like he's just trying to distract me long enough to say yes.

If only I wasn't so desperate to be held.

I give in a little, wrapping my arms around his waist so he'll pretend to care about me for just a minute. He groans into my mouth and runs his hand up my neck and into my hair. A spark of arousal shoots through me when he pulls on the strands, changing the angle of the kiss, and taking control.

Tim's free hand slides under my shirt, and I shiver. A part of me wants to be touched, wants to know pleasure, craves the physical affection, but I don't want my first time to be a rushed groping while he hurries not to get caught. Both of our parents are inside and will kill us if they find out.

"My parents are here. We can't."

"I'll come over tonight. They've let me stay before. They won't know. They think we are friends." Tim grabs my belt, and I try to shove his hand away, but he kisses me again.

I give over to the kiss, whining softly. "Tim . . ."

"They won't know." He shoves me back, putting his arm

between what feels good and what I know is wrong. I've pushed it too far. Let this thing with Tim go on too long. I know it's wrong and what my father will do if he finds out.

"We can't." I try again as Tim lowers my zipper.

Tim pulls my belt from the loops with a triumphant smile. His lips part, and he's about to say something—

"Isaac Mathew Becker!" My father's voice booms in a terrifying snarl.

I startle and shove Tim away from me while fear and shame leave my body quaking. *Oh god, what's he going to do?*

I don't dare look at Tim. Maybe he can back away into the shadows and make a break for it. Maybe he can tell his family it's all a misunderstanding when my father calls his, because I know he will, and they can laugh it off.

"Mr. Becker." Tim takes a step forward, all cowering shoulders and trembling hands. "He told me to meet him back here, that he wanted to show me something. I think he has the devil inside of him."

The blood drains from my face, hearing the lies falling from my boyfriend's mouth. What little pitiful hope I have falls to ashes at my feet. Quickly, I scan the crowd, looking for my little brother, Noah. I find him peeking around our mother, the horror I feel reflected on his face, but he doesn't condone it. He's the only other person who knows. The only person I've trusted with my deepest, darkest secret.

I can barely breathe through the panic. Can hardly think past my instincts that have me frozen in place as my father storms over and lifts his bible in the air. I can't move my arms or turn my back to protect myself as he hits me with the holy doctrine that tells of love and acceptance from a forgiving God.

But that's not what they preach here.

Over and over, he hits me while my heart breaks and my world crashes down around me. I don't notice the tears running down my cheeks or the body-wracking sobs as my parents scream scriptures. My skin burns. The sting of every impact taking all my focus.

I deserve this punishment for the sins I've committed.

The other members of the church hear the commotion and come to investigate, witnessing the worst moment of my life. Timothy's parents rush him off, out of the spotlight, while my mother pours holy water over my head and prays for my eternal soul.

I'm humiliated.

Ashamed.

Terrified.

I've known since I started high school I'm not interested in girls like the boys I'm friends with and that I have to hide it from everyone around me. For years, I've played the part they forced me into. I didn't choose any of this, yet they will punish me like I did. The mold they expected me to fit never did, but I've tried every single day to make it work. Finally, that perfect impression they thought I would become has shattered, and there's no faking it anymore.

No one chooses to live a harder life.

No one chooses to live in fear of being hated by everyone around them.

No one chooses to look over their shoulder constantly, waiting for someone to attack them for simply existing.

My knees give out, and the rough, pebble-strewn asphalt digs into my hands and scrapes my shins. The fall makes my body ache, but no worse than the emotional pain my father is causing with his damnation.

At some point, it ends, and Father grabs my arm in a bruising grip, yanking me from the ground, and drags me across the parking lot. He throws me into the car and slams the door behind me with a rage so hot on his face it may leave blisters. I cover my face in my hands and bend in half, but all I want in this moment is to disappear or to stop breathing. Noah gets in next to me but doesn't say anything, doesn't reach for me.

He has to protect himself, too. I understand.

"You are not going to college this year," my father shouts. "You've managed to stray too far from the path we raised you to follow! You've let the devil corrupt you and tempt the Roberts boy to follow you to hell!"

Mother sniffles in the front seat. "I thought we raised a good boy," she cries. "What have we done to deserve a homosexual as a son?"

"And to force your perversion onto a good, God fearing boy is unacceptable!" Father roars, taking a turn too sharply, and my head slams into the door. The pain barely registers.

My father continues to berate me, telling me what a horrible person I am, how I'm going to hell unless I beg God for forgiveness and promise to never even look at another boy. My stomach twists into a knot, and my head swims. I feel like I'm going to pass out or throw up, maybe both. Maybe then he'll leave me be. Just for a minute.

We squeal into the driveway of the home I grew up in, and before the car has come to a complete stop, the doors open, and Father grabs a fist full of my hair to yank me out. Mother is quietly sobbing as she unlocks the door and steps aside to let us pass. Using the hold like a handle, he throws me to the floor in the living room and stands over me. I curl into a ball to try to protect myself, but it doesn't work. It never does.

"Get up!" he demands, but the fear coursing through me makes me stumble. When I fall back to my knees, he kicks me over and yells again at me to stand up. With trembling knees, I make it to my feet this time, and he smacks my cheek with his bible before shoving it at me. "You're going to stand here and read Leviticus out loud until you can recite it from memory."

One

Isaac

"Why are you crying, kitten?" A soothing male voice comes from a stranger who's walked past. Again.

"It doesn't matter." I wipe my eyes with my palms and try to shove everything back down into a box.

Like he cares. No one in the finance office does nor my boss. Ex-boss I guess.

"It's been at least an hour since I walked by and you were here then and it looked like you've been here a while." He slides his hands into the pockets of his perfectly tailored slacks as he comes to a stop in front of me with his Saint Laurent boots that probably cost more than the payment I need to make.

I can't bring myself to look him in the eye. Someone like him won't care about my problems. I doubt he's ever had money issues. He was probably born with a silver spoon in his mouth.

"It's just life." I shrug when he doesn't walk away.

"You're a student here. A freshman, if I'm assessing the situation right." He pauses, and I can feel his gaze scanning over me. "So what could it be . . ." His words aren't unkind, but they are probing. "Family issues or money issues."

Ding ding ding.

How did he know? Is it written on my face? A stamp on my forehead?

"I must be easy to read." I suck in a shaky breath to collect myself and keep my voice steady. "Both."

"Ah, yes, I can see how one would easily follow the other." He takes a seat on the bench next to me. "Want to talk about it?"

"Not really." I laugh without humor. "It's not going to help."

"You never know. Sometimes discussing things with a stranger can give you a perspective you might not have seen yourself. What do you have to lose? I don't know you, and you don't know me. Even if you told me the innermost details in your heart, I don't know your name."

"You know where I live, and we go to the same school." I assume anyway.

"You live in a building with hundreds of other kids, and we go to a school that's attendance is in the tens of thousands. It's nearly the same as being anonymous. You don't seem like you have anyone else to talk to. I'm a good listener, I promise."

I exhale a weary breath I feel in my bones, knowing he's right. I don't have anyone else. "My parents cut me off because they think I slept with my high school boyfriend." I sneak a half glance at him to gauge how he'll react to my statement.

Stone face. Not even a single twitch of his mouth.

"And I thought I had it all figured out," I continue, just to fill the awkward silence. "I had my loans lined up and a job. I knew it wouldn't be easy to juggle all the work and studying, but I really thought I could do it." I swallow back a sob, refusing to let anymore weakness show. But my chest is tight, and my stupid lip trembles.

"What happened?"

"I got fired, and my first loan payment hasn't processed yet, and while the school will wait, nothing else will." I pull my knees into my chest and drop my head to hide the fresh wave of tears threatening to fall down my face.

"The school will wait. Is there a textbook you need or a computer? Usually you can sit in the library and use theirs. They don't let anyone check them out for this exact circumstance."

Well, that solved one problem. "I didn't know that. Thank you, but textbooks were the lowest on my list of emergencies."

"What am I missing? What is higher?" He gives me another once-over, finally settling on my face with his deep probing blue eyes.

"I had to skip a meal plan because I couldn't afford it. I only got so much aid and scholarships, and because they take into account my parents' income, they wouldn't loan me anymore, and my parents won't help, so I had to remove something. I thought if I worked I could at least buy textbooks and food if I'm really careful, but then I got fired, and I've put in dozens and dozens of applications, but no one has called me back, and my phone will be shut off if I don't pay in a few days, so they won't even be able to call me. I have six dollars to my name, and I've been over and over it, and I can't make it work. I'm down to my last ramen." I'm barely breathing at the end of my rant. My face flushes with frustration and embarrassment. I should be able to figure this out, to take care of myself, but I can't. I can't get a break, and I'm tired of trying.

He doesn't say anything for a long time. I'm pretty sure he's attempting to come up with an exit strategy.

"You don't have to stay and keep listening to me. I know it's a lot of word vomit from a stranger. No need to say anything. I know you want to find a nice way to leave," I mumble as I pick at a string on my pants.

"You're quite wrong on the direction you think my mind went."

I meet his eyes for the first time. He's younger than his style suggests, or maybe he has a young face, but where at first I'd thought he was a doctoral or master's student, he's probably not more than a few years older than me. "What were you thinking?"

His expression strains between amusement and a deeper ruefulness, but that doesn't give me any clues to what he's thinking. "I shouldn't say. My mind goes a lot of places better left off public consumption."

"Can it be worse than the direction my life is already going?"

"That entirely depends on your definition of bad and proclivity to solve your problems with out-of-the-box thinking." He shrugs, smile not wavering.

"I'm willing to try almost anything at this point." My voice has a breathy quality I've never heard from myself before.

"Have you tried the food pantries?"

I scoff. "Don't tell me that's what you had in mind? And yes, one. I'm only allowed to get one box a month, and the other is run by my parents and their church. I know the second I show my face in there, they'd know about it." I realize after I said it how easily I can be found with that information, but what did it really matter?

"Zealots for relatives. Delightful."

"Hardly." I let out another shuttering breath. "Thanks for listening. I should pull myself together and go hand out resumes."

"But of course, I won't keep you." He stands but lingers. "Would you like a different way to earn a few thousand dollars?"

I cough as my eyes bug out of my head. "A few thousand dollars? I'm not selling drugs."

"It's not selling drugs, and I can assure you it's legal." He's almost amused by my response.

I narrow my eyes, not believing him. "If there was a way to

make thousands in a night without selling drugs, wouldn't everyone be doing it?"

"No, because I wouldn't pay just anyone." He's not amused now but watching me with a heat in his gaze that I've never felt before.

My heart skips a beat or two, and my breath catches in my throat. "Wh-what do you mean?"

"Give me twenty-four hours of your time, and I'll give you, say, a thousand dollars." There's no hesitation. He offered the amount like it's pocket change. That much money might get me through the whole semester if I'm careful.

"Twenty-four hours of my time to do what?" My voice cracks. Deep down in my gut, I know.

"Anything I want." The seductive lilt to his voice has my stomach fluttering.

I gasp, despite knowing what he'd meant. "I couldn't." *But I want to.*

"No? Not even to not starve?"

I shake my head. "Thanks for the offer, but I really can't. I've- I've never slept with anyone."

He cocks his head to the side. "But you said . . ."

"I said my parents *thought.* I didn't say it was true." My voice quivers, betraying me even more.

He blinks, but his smile returns with vigor. "You're kidding."

"No," I whisper.

"Why didn't you tell the zealots as much? Surely, they would have accepted you back into the fold."

"Because they wouldn't believe me, and they wanted me to put off going to college until I'm more mature." I jut out my chin out, not ashamed I've chosen myself.

"A bit of spirit then. I like it." He lingers for another moment before reaching into his inner jacket pocket and pulling out a metal case. He takes a card from it and holds it out. "Three thou-

19

sand dollars for twenty-four hours. You don't have to answer now. Think it over."

I take the heavy black card from him expecting to find a name, but there is only a number, and when I look up, he's gone.

I know I can't do it, but three thousand dollars . . .

I lift myself from the bench and make it up to my dorm room. It is for now, anyway. If I don't make my payment, I'll be kicked out with nowhere to go.

The building is buzzing with students moving in and emotional parents. A pang of jealousy and sadness hits me in the gut. I didn't get that. Mine didn't help carry boxes up or take embarrassing selfies.

Dropping onto my back on the bed, I stare up at the ceiling. What am I going to do? The thick black card flashes in my mind. Closing my eyes, I can feel his presence standing over me. It's terrifying. Enticing.

What would a guy like that want with me? He's hot, well dressed, rich, and his tone clearly said he wanted sex, but I don't have any experience. I don't know how to *please* him.

He could have anyone.

A shiver runs through me, and goosebumps pop up along my skin. I cover my face with my hands and groan.

I shouldn't want this. I shouldn't even be considering this. It's wrong on so many levels.

Am I really desperate enough to sell my virginity for three thousand dollars?

Yes.

Ugh!

The door opens, and I sit up to find my new roommate with a big brown box in his arms and an overstuffed backpack.

"Oh, hello. I'm Colin." He puts the box on his bed and drops down next to it, groaning when the backpack slides from his shoulders.

He reaches a hand out to me, and I shake it, telling him my name.

A man in dark slacks and a button-up blue shirt comes in with a hand truck carrying more boxes.

"Just drop them there," Colin points to the end of his bed.

I can't help but watch the interaction with interest. Is that guy Colin's dad? A brother? An employee? They don't look anything alike. Colin has bleached blond, wavy hair long enough to pull back into a small ponytail and golden-brown eyes that dance with mischief. Despite the tattered look of his clothes, they scream expensive.

The man who doesn't look old enough to be Colin's father puts the boxes where indicated, then leaves without a word.

"You a local or from out of state?" he asks as there's a knock on the door. Colin rolls his eyes and yells that it's open before I'm given a chance to answer. A well-dressed couple comes in and closes the door. This man is older, wearing pressed khakis and a white polo. She has on heels and a pencil skirt with a silk blouse and a designer purse hanging from her elbow. The audacity in the air says they are worth a lot of money and expect to be treated as such. Everyone here has the same air about them while I'm trying to find a way not to starve.

They look around, drag their eyes down my body, find me wanting, and turn to Colin.

"Do you have everything you need?" the woman asks rather coldly. More like she is required to ask, not because she cares.

"Yes, Mother. You and Father don't need to babysit me."

Mother? Yikes.

I guess I'm not one to judge since my parents turned their backs on me for something that didn't even happen, but this is so . . . formal.

"Don't be an idiot. Go to class, and don't get anyone knocked up," the man says with a huff.

"If anyone is getting pregnant, it'll be me." Colin smirks and winks at me. What the hell does that mean?

The older man pinches the bridge of his nose and sighs.

"No sex tapes. Our family name has enough to recover from with proof of you being fucked like a bitch going viral," he barks.

Colin cackles, but the anger on his dad's face is enough to make my heart race.

"Oh Daddy." The condescension dripping from Colin's tone is thick. "Did you look up *breeding* on Urban Dictionary?" He puts his hand on his chest. "I'm so proud."

Breeding?

Remember to look that up later.

The man's face flushes a deep red, and the woman's face contorts into disgust.

"If you're going to be crass, we're leaving." She lifts her nose to look down at Colin. Are these people really his parents? I hate it for him if they are. I know what it's like to be hated by the people who are supposed to love you unconditionally. It's a bone deep ache that makes you question everything about yourself. What did I do to deserve this?

"Oh, Mother, I can be a lot more crass." Colin pops a hip and looks directly at her, not hiding or cowering.

How does he do that? Doesn't he want their approval? Doesn't he want them to accept him? This isn't the way to do it.

"Don't start," his father spits out. "We're going. Behave."

Colin smiles, and it's a look that promises trouble. "Don't worry, Daddy, I'll be a good boy." He winks, and the older man huffs before leaving the room with his wife in tow.

My cheeks heat at the words *good boy,* and I'm not entirely comfortable with it. Why did it make my stomach tingle?

The slam of the door shakes me from my dangerous thoughts. I blink and focus on my roommate, who is now facing me with his head cocked.

"So that is Mr. and Mrs. Covington. They are homophobic assholes."

"I got that impression." I nod and run my hands down my jeans. "I doubt you'll ever see my parents. If you do, watch out for my father's bible."

"Ah, yes. The zealots are a sturdy bunch." Colin starts unpacking the boxes, and I lie back down since it feels weird to watch him. I'm definitely curious about him, though. I've never been allowed to be around an out gay man. Father ran off anyone who gave even the slightest hint of homosexuality.

What's it like to be out? Is it freeing, or is he constantly looking over his shoulder for an attack? I want to be free. To be me. But I don't know who that is. Not really.

My stomach growls, and I curl up on my side, wrapping myself around my pillow. I don't know if I'm strong enough to do this. I can't go home, but I don't know what to do from here. Pulling out my phone, I open up my bank app, and my gut sinks when I see the negative balance.

Great.

Something I wasn't expecting came out, and now I owe the bank $24.53. Tears fill my eyes again, and I do everything I can not to make a sound or move. The last thing I want is for Colin to notice how much of a baby I am.

No job, negative bank balance, about to get kicked out of housing, and hungry. I'm killing this adult thing.

TWO

Isaac

After crying myself to sleep, I wake up with my eyes aching and swollen. My stomach is empty and grumbling, but there's nothing I can do about it right now. I have to save my last packet of ramen as long as I can.

Colin is asleep, and the room is darkish, so I quietly grab some clothes and head to shower. Maybe some magic answer will hit me while I stand in the steam.

At the sink, I stare at myself. The messy, big curls that point in every direction, the sharp angle of my jaw and chin, the big dark brown eyes. I'm thin and wiry. I look toned because of my lack of calories over the last few weeks. I've lost probably ten pounds that I didn't have to lose. My hipbones stick out, but my little six pack is visible.

Meeting my eyes in the reflection, I say the words I've never uttered before.

"I'm gay." The words are quiet, barely audible, but I said

them. I don't want to be ashamed of who I am or who I fall in love with or who I have sex with.

The stranger from yesterday flashes in my mind, and my dick perks. He called me kitten.

I smile a little and duck my head. I like that too. Men shouldn't want to be called *cute* pet names. Right? It's emasculating. Men should want to be tough and protective.

The smile on my face drops. That's not me. I'm not big or intimidating or tough unless I'm on the piste with a foil in my hand. I clench my hands, missing the bruised knuckles and bloody fingertips that come with the sport I love.

Climbing in the shower, I'm disappointed to find the water pressure still sucks, and it's barely spitting water. After putting in a request to have it fixed, I was hoping it would be. Apparently, that was wishful thinking.

The hot water cuts out halfway through, and I scream as the cold hits my warm skin.

What the crap!

I bend over to rinse the conditioner from my hair without getting the rest of my body in the cold water, then shut it off. Today can already go to hell.

After getting dressed, raking my hands through my hair, and grabbing my backpack, I head to class. I have to do this. I'll find a way.

Since I don't have a laptop, I get settled with a notebook and pen. The professor comes in, and the class quickly fills. Someone sits next to me and smacks my arm with the back of a hand.

"Dude," he says as I turn to see it's Colin. "You could have woken me up before you left."

"How was I supposed to know you were in this class?"

He sighs dramatically and leans back in his chair. It takes me a second to realize he has a short baby blue shirt on that says "Yes, Daddy" across the chest.

"Are you trying to get hate crimed?" I ask, pointing to his shirt with my pen.

He laughs and waggles his eyebrows. "This is advertising for the deeply closeted jocks who just want a quick fuck in the locker room."

I was not expecting that and just sit there blinking at him for a minute with my cheeks on fire.

He laughs again, and this time I'm pretty sure it's at my expression.

"Oh sweet summer child." He pats my cheek. "So, so innocent. I can't wait to corrupt you this year."

If I'm being honest, I can't wait either. Maybe I can learn how to find myself. Over the last few years, I realized Christianity probably wasn't for me. So many people in the church I grew up in condemned and outright hated anyone who wasn't like them. Anyone who was part of the alphabet mafia, anyone who didn't believe the same interpretation of the bible, they were all going to hell and didn't deserve kindness. But I still lived in my parents' house and had to be what they expected or lose everything. Even my major was picked by my father, religious studies. If it had been up to me, I would be in art school. I want to draw and paint. I love to draw eyes and hands but paint trees with watercolor.

Facial expressions are so tricky to get right, but I love the challenge. All my notebooks have eyes or fingers sketched in the margins, a random branch thrown in every once in a while. Fencing will pay for me to get through college with the addition of grants and some loans, but nothing pays fast enough. I'm going to starve before the money hits my account.

We manage to get through class, Colin eyeing my doodles more than paying attention to the lecture, and I have a break, so I head to the library. Colin drops into step with me, chatting about some time he was in an underage gay club.

My face is on fire as he tells me about sucking off someone in the bathroom. The idea of anonymity is enticing. The person doesn't know who you are, so they can't tell anyone and ruin your life. For a few moments you could be anyone you wanted. My father will never find out about my exploits if it's anonymous . . .

"How did you lose your virginity?" I blurt out while he's talking.

"Virginity? You mean the concept of purity the church forced on society in order to institute a sense of entitlement, making a natural bodily function shameful, while also using it as a construct to give young girls a value system?" He takes a breath while I digest what he said and blink at him. "I don't believe in virginity or in giving it power. It is merely the first time you have sex. Find someone you're comfortable getting naked with that won't just treat you like a hole—unless you're into that kind of thing—and will take the time needed to prep properly." He flicks his gaze over, narrows his eyes, then adds, "unless you're into girls, in which case find someone who lets you put it in her and not laugh when you come in ten seconds."

This entire conversation is so uncomfortable. Everything I've been taught about sex talk is only to be between the couple. Never a public discussion, and you don't talk to others about it unless it's a doctor or a pastor if you have some kind of addiction.

"Wait, what do you mean, if I'm into girls?" I stop in the middle of the walkway and turn to him.

Colin rolls his lips between his teeth and cocks an eyebrow before stepping closer while dropping his voice so no one over-hears. "Boys who are into girls don't look at me like you do."

The heat rushes up my neck, engulfs my ears, and lifts to my hairline. Crap. How have I been looking at him? I don't want to have sex with him.

Have I?

No, he doesn't do it for me.

"How do I look at you?"

He hooks his arm through mine and leads me toward an empty table. "Like I interest you. Like you wish you could be more like me."

I snap my mouth shut. I don't know what I expected him to say, but that wasn't it. Pulling the chair back, I sit and look across the wood top at him as I contemplate what he said. He isn't wrong. I do find him interesting, and I am kind of jealous that he has the inner strength to be unapologetically himself.

I've spent my entire life trying to be what my parents wanted me to be. The good kid who was seen but not heard. Never getting into fights, only making friends with kids they approved of, and shutting myself down to make them happy.

Until Tim.

And one night at a church summer camp when I was sixteen, when he kissed me in the shadows of our cabin. That night changed everything. I found who I was supposed to be that night, and it rattled my bones.

Now I have the opportunity to explore myself with a stranger. Someone I won't ever have to see again. This campus is huge, so the odds of running into him are slim. He doesn't know my name, and I don't know his. It's anonymous.

Am I really considering whoring myself out for three thousand dollars, though?

"Don't look so sad-panda." Colin puts his hand on top of mine on the table. "You'll get there."

"If you were inexperienced, and the opportunity came up for you to *explore* with a stranger, would you take it?" I need the money, but for a rich kid, I don't think the money would be a big motivator. Plus, if I go through with it, I don't want him to know I prostituted myself.

Colin sits back in his chair and looks at me, clearly contemplating his answer. His gaze is so intense I want to squirm. It's like he can see through me and read my secrets on my skin.

"Is that idea exciting?" He leans on the table to keep his voice low. "That it's a stranger, so if you're terrible at something or dislike something, you don't have to worry about embarrassment?"

"Who-who said anything about me?" I stumble over my words, and he smirks.

"It's written all over your face."

Ugh.

Embarrassment heats my skin, and I cover my face with my hands.

"If I were in your position, with very limited experience, and the opportunity came up, I probably would do it." Colin waits until I meet his eyes. "Then I would date every person who caught my interest. Kiss, fool around, and fuck anyone I could because the pleasure of it is addictive. Those early days especially. Once you get a taste of it, you won't want to quit, and there's no shame in it."

My stomach picks that moment to grumble loudly in the quiet space.

Colin snickers. "Let's grab lunch. We can study in our room."

Not only can I not afford to buy lunch, but I need to borrow the textbook that can't leave the library. I really don't want to explain to my extremely rich roommate that I can't afford lunch or textbooks.

"That's okay." I drop my head to my lap. "I'll eat in a bit. I need to check out a book."

Colin eyes me with suspicion, but eventually walks away.

Once he's gone, I borrow the textbook and settle back at the table. My stomach starting to cramp from the lack of food. It's so hard to think about anything besides hunger. My mouth salivates at the thought of a sandwich. I could probably eat four of them right now.

I want to sleep and pretend this isn't my life. How long can I really go without eating? Isn't it something like three days without water and seven days without calories?

My knee is bouncing under the table, and I can't make it stop. It takes too much brain power. Too much energy.

I spend the next forty-five minutes trying to focus on the homework from this morning's class, but I only make it through two questions.

By the time I get back to my room, I'm dizzy and shaky and feel like I'm going to puke. I've been drinking a lot of water to try to make the cramping stop, but it's not helping. Not really.

Colin isn't here when I open the door, and I thank my lucky stars. Saliva fills my mouth, and I rush for the bathroom as my stomach turns with a vengeance. There's nothing but water in it, but apparently that's enough to throw up.

Clutching the sides of the toilet, I expel everything I've had today. Acid burning my throat and nose and making my eyes water at the force of the contractions on my body. Once the dry heaves stop, I'm breathing hard and wipe my nose on the back of my hand as I sit back against the wall.

I can't live like this, even for just a few days.

Once my stomach calms, I stand, and my head swims, forcing me to lean against the wall or end up on the floor again. I rinse out my mouth and head to my bed. Pulling the thick black card from my pocket, I stare at the number for a few minutes.

Can I really do this? Sell my virginity?

Tears spring to my eyes, and I curl into a ball on my bed as I type the phone number into my phone.

Three

Oliver

I wanted him the moment I laid eyes on him.

An experience I've never encountered.

I'd be lying if I said I hadn't spent my entire life getting everything I wanted the moment it occurred to me to want it, and my parents indulged those whims with my siblings and me. It makes things less exciting.

No one tells a Godfrey no.

I enjoy sex, and have it often, but this is different.

Lust at first sight.

I want to own him.

I don't want anyone else to have him.

Long after the encounter, I sat with it.

He invaded every part of my mind.

His perfect pink lips and rosy cheeks. Eyes red from crying. Those dark curls falling into his face. He needs a haircut and a new wardrobe, but there is something under it all. A diamond in the rough. But that isn't why I want him.

The simple conversation breathed into my lungs like an addiction, and now he's all I think about.

"Why do you keep staring into space?" Owen, my twin, asks.

"Thinking?"

"About?" he pours a drink and holds up the bottle.

I shake my head. The last thing I need is alcohol clouding my judgment when I'm already on edge.

My phone buzzes with an unfamiliar number.

"Hello," I answer, turning away from my brother.

"Er . . . hello?" comes the sweet voice of the guy. I realize I don't know his name.

No matter. I won't be seeing him a second time. I want him. I'll have him. Get him out of my system so I can stop thinking about him.

Godfreys aren't allowed to date. It would draw too much media attention. My father would murder me if I got smeared all over the gossip rags like other American heirs and heiresses. We fuck around discreetly until the appropriate time to settle down, and then my mother will find me the right breed of woman to carry on the family name.

It is all very clinical, and I will be putting it off as long as possible.

"Yes?" I excuse myself to my expansive balcony so my brother doesn't overhear. "Is this the sad kitten from campus?"

A strangled sound comes out of him, which is more of a confirmation than anything he'd say. "Yes."

"Are you coming?" I ask, laughing at the play on words. Not yet, but he would be. I'm generous like that.

"Yes." His word quivers.

Heat flashes through my blood. How beautiful he'll be spread

ON GUARD

out on my bed. How can he turn me on with one word? He already has me imagining all the ways I'll have him.

He has more effect on me than I'll ever admit.

"Tonight." I check my watch, knowing I would have to make my apologies for my absence at my parents' anniversary dinner, but I won't give him another day to change his mind. "Eight sharp. Not a minute late. I'll text you the address. Tell the doorman the penthouse is expecting you, and he'll let you up."

He swallows audibly. "Okay."

"And kitten?"

"Yes?"

"Not a single minute late, or I will make you pay for every second of my time you wasted."

Another half-strangled groan comes over the line. I feel it all the way to my dick.

I wait half a second before I speak again. "Confirm you understand."

"I understand."

"Good little kitten." I hang up and text the address.

Now to make excuses to my mother. My father will hardly notice my absence, but my mother will bitch for a year if I don't play this exactly right.

I'll have to bribe Owen to make it work. But with what?

He is the favorite but also the one they expect the least from, in a weird twist. Maybe it's because he's the baby.

I slip back inside, but my brother isn't in the living room. I find him in his room, tipped back in his gaming chair, staring at the ceiling. "Owen, I need a huge favor."

"Can it wait until tomorrow?"

"What is it this time, existential dread or the weight of your immorality?"

"Can it be all of the above?" Owen asks, sitting up to look at me.

35

We might look exactly the same, but we couldn't be more different. He knows the weight of what we are and has too much empathy for his own good. I understand his arguments, but why worry about something we have no control over? Hating our parents' money won't change that they have it or that they left us trust funds. He can worry about it when it's his turn to inherit. Until then, we aren't the rich to be eaten, and if the public wants to overthrow the billionaire class, they can have at them. I won't be standing in the way.

"If you want." I cross the room to stand over him. "You do remember we have the anniversary dinner tonight, yes?"

"Fuck my life. Do you think I could throw myself off the balcony and not have to deal with mother haunting me in death for not showing up?"

"I'm going to need you to battle those inner demons, at least for tonight, so I can skip."

Owen tilts his head to give me an intrigued look. He is on to me. "And what keeps you from the Godfrey's soirée?"

"I have a date. So if you could be so kind as to over-exaggerate my near-death status with some sort of back-to-school flu so I won't hear about it until Christmas, I will make it worth your while."

"What are we talking?" The way in which my brother flips from contemplating the meaning of existence to a shrewd businessman can only be described as impressive.

"I will do like for like. A get out of jail free card so to speak. I will cover for anything you want me to." It's a big ask and a big return. Getting out of family obligations would be easier with the president.

"Deal, but I have one addendum."

I wave for him to proceed.

"A date? You've never gone on a date." Owen seems concerned. Overly so.

"Not in the way you're taking it. An engagement would be a better descriptor."

"One worth missing their anniversary? Who is she?" Owen crosses his arms.

I laugh. "He. And I haven't a clue. Some guy I met yesterday."

"And you're missing their *anniversary* for it?" He emphasizes the word like it will make my answer any different.

"I am." I won't give into his probing.

"Why? You know what this means to them," he asks me like I'm a moron, which amuses me and makes me not want to tell him.

"I'm aware. It comes around every year, right on time." I grin, considering my words. "Why not?"

"Why risk it? You know how Mom will react. What about this guy is worth pissing her off?" Owen stands, narrowing his eyes to suss out my motive.

"I'll tell you after?" I don't know why I'm holding back, but something about him makes me want to keep it to myself.

I don't want to share him just yet—or ever.

I need this one indulgence before I give my life over to what my parents want.

He won't understand. I already know as much. Sex isn't a thing to covet. People come and go. None of them understand us or our world, so we don't expect them to stay. Friends are hard to acquire with parents like ours. We are elite by even our exclusive New York private school standard. Our parents have too many enemies to trust anyone, and they don't believe in trivial human needs like human connection, so my brother and I were often each other's only playmates. The only emotional stability we had our whole childhood.

We've shared everything from birth. He isn't used to me holding back.

He's my best friend, and I feel bad for not telling him, but I can't.

"I don't like this."

"Don't spend too much time worrying about it. Just an itch I need to scratch." I clap a hand on his shoulder. "I'll always love you first. Don't worry."

He sticks his tongue out with disgust. "We aren't the Princes. We don't keep it in the family."

"Who'd want to be a prince in this day and age? Public work and far less money." I smile, hoping to put him at ease.

"Do I get to meet him?" Owen asks.

"No. It's a one-night thing." I hold out my hand.

He grips my hand, pulling me in chest to chest, arms crossed between us. "Promise?"

"I promise."

Four

Isaac

Hanging up the phone, I look around and find my last ramen. Without any kind of preparation, I open the bag and crunch on the dry noodles. It tastes like nothing, but I don't care. It's physical food going into my body. Wet cardboard would probably taste like a T-bone steak right now.

Too quickly, the noodles are gone and I'm tipping the bag up to get the last little crumbs. That will have to hold me over for now. I grab a bottle of water, chug half of it, then get in the shower.

I don't have a lot of time before I have to show up, and I have to figure out how I'm even going to get there since I don't have money for the subway. I'll have to walk and hopefully not get sweaty.

In my pathetic excuse for a shower, I scrub myself until my skin is red. Once again, the hot water runs out with no warning, and I scream when the freezing water hits my heated flesh.

I hate this stupid shower. How on earth does this school have showers this bad? The most elite families come here. How is this acceptable? Is this the poor kid dorm? That doesn't make sense because Colin's family is clearly loaded.

Doesn't matter.

I finish up as quickly as I can and dry off, making sure to put on cologne and deodorant before getting dressed.

With the towel around my waist, I open the door to find Colin on his bed in short pink shorts with white trim and nothing else. He drags his eyes down my bare torso and lifts a brow.

"Hot date?"

My face heats, and I force myself to swallow before answering. "Kind of. I'll be home tomorrow night."

He sits up, clearly interested in what I'm doing.

"Oh really? And what is going to keep my innocent roommate busy for that long?" The tone of his voice drips sexual innuendo.

"I'm not going to a brothel or anything, relax." I turn and clench my eyes closed for a second. Idiot. Why would you say that? Brothel? Is that even a thing anymore?

I pull open my dresser looking for my best clothes when Colin steps up behind me. Our eyes meet for a second while he's crossing his arms and waiting for an explanation.

"What are you up to, baby bird?"

"Baby bird?" I pull on my underwear under the towel, then turn to look at him. "What does that mean?"

"It means you're new to the world and don't yet know all the nuances. But don't worry, I'll push you from the nest and make you learn to fly before you know it."

"That doesn't sound like much fun."

"Growth rarely is."

I think my roommate is crazy.

Anyway, I don't have time for this.

Pulling on my nice pair of jeans, a button-up shirt that could

40

use an iron, and my sneakers, I try to get my hair to do something but give up.

"I have to go."

"Where is it you're going, exactly?"

He's watching me like a helicopter mom, ready to pounce.

"None of your business." I shove my phone in my pocket.

"How are you getting there?" He leans on our door so I would have to shove him out of the way to leave.

"I'm walking."

"Must be close by then . . ."

My cheeks heat again. "A few miles."

Colin widens his eyes in surprise. "A few miles in New York City? No. Take the subway."

"I can't afford it."

Colin rolls his eyes and points a finger at me. "Wait."

He grabs his phone and swipes at the screen before handing it to me. "Put in the address and a car will come pick you up. Uber is amazing."

I refuse to take the device from him. "I can't let you do that."

"Isaac, put in the damn address. I promise not to follow you unless it's an emergency." He rolls his eyes, and I concede. Fine. It's probably not the worst idea to have someone know where I'm going.

I enter the address from the text and hand the phone back. Colin lifts a brow but doesn't say anything as he taps a few more things on his phone.

"Someone will be here in ten minutes." He looks at my outfit critically. "That's what you're wearing?"

I look down at my clothes, then back up at him. "Yeah, so what?"

He sighs and shakes his head. "Come on, let's wait for your ride."

Standing in front of the high-rise building, butterflies tickle my stomach and flutter through my veins. What the hell am I doing? He could be a murderer. Am I really selling my virginity for three grand?

I let out an aggravated groan and force my feet to the glass door. A young man in a suit is waiting and opens it when I step forward. Pretty sure the rent in this building is more than my tuition. The floors are that kind of polished stone that looks like glass. Everything about the space says "I'm rich ,"and I'm afraid I'll leave a dirt stain if I touch something.

An old man in a suit and tie lifts his head when I enter. "Good evening, sir. How can I help you?"

He looks like a sweet old man but was probably alive during the turn of the century, and I don't mean the twenty-first. I think his wrinkles have wrinkles.

His back is hunched, and his fingers don't straighten anymore. Why is he still working?

"The penthouse is expecting me." My words barely tremble when I say them. I'm not sure how I managed that.

"Of course." He stands from behind the desk and heads toward an elevator. He lifts a key card to a screen next to it, and it dings before the doors open. "Have a good night."

He steps back and waves me inside.

"Wait, how will I know where the penthouse is?"

"The elevator goes directly to it."

So what the movies show is accurate? How is that safe? And who wants people just randomly showing up in their house?

Before I can ask any more questions, the doors close, and I'm lifted. It's the smoothest ride I've ever had in an elevator. Of course it is.

I sigh and crack my neck, then pull on my fingers. I wish I had a sketch pad and my pencils. Not that I expect to have much time to draw.

What if I get there and he laughs at me? Is this all a joke? Or what if he tries to kiss me and I'm so bad at it that he kicks me out and doesn't pay me?

I ate the last of my food, I have literally nothing left.

The lift comes to a stop, and I hold my breath. *Please let me make it through this.*

Six

Oliver

G eoffrey, the doorman, called as soon as he arrived. I check my watch.

Early.

Good.

The elevator doors slide open with three minutes to spare.

"Cutting it a little close."

He stammers before he manages to form a sentence. "I didn't think you'd want me to be early . . ."

I didn't want him to be early. My brother only left about thirty minutes ago. Them crossing paths wouldn't have gone well. I don't need more questions on this little indulgence.

"Since you're early, let's go over the rules again. Twenty-four hours. The cash is there." I nod at the antique writing desk that sits in the foyer. "If you leave before the twenty-four hours is up, you forfeit the cash. Understand?"

He swallows hard, then nods. "What are we going to do?"

"Anything I want." I revel in the spike of fear pulsing through him. I don't plan on hurting him—too much—but he hasn't an idea of what I'll do. He's trusting me. More than I deserve.

"Any other questions before we get started?"

"Why does the elevator open right into your living room?" He shakes his head, glancing around the place.

"Why wouldn't it?"

"Someone could just come into your penthouse and kill you."

"They'd need the keycard and to get past the doorman. I trust Geoffrey. He's been working here at least eighty-seven years."

"You trust the old man to save you from a murderer?" he asks skeptically.

"Obviously."

"Why not have a hallway and a door? It's another layer of security."

"Hallways are for peasants," I say in my dry humor, holding back a laugh.

His mouth drops open, and I step forward to push it closed with one finger. He doesn't seem to get my humor. Poor little sheltered kitten.

"Are you a student?" he asks.

"Why do you ask?"

"I want to know how you live like this as a student." He barely gets through his words. "This can't be a dorm."

"So nosy." I laugh. "I wouldn't live in a dorm. They keep all of you packed in those buildings like animals. Absolutely not."

"I thought freshman and sophomores had to live in dorms?" His lips quiver.

I stroke my knuckle down his throat. "I had a dorm room freshman and sophomore year. I never stayed in it. The rule says we have to have a dorm, not that we have to live in them. Nuances of contracts."

"So you are a student. Or you were." He studies my face like he can find answers there. But I've been trained since birth to disguise my feelings. "How can you afford that?"

"The same way I can pay you three thousand dollars for twenty-four hours. Do you want to question it anymore?" I draw my fingertip down his sternum. "Times up. Take these off." I tug at his jeans. "No clothes."

"For the whole twenty-four hours?" he asks, pupils dilating. His fear so thick between us, I could drink it from the air.

"Yes. I bet no one except your parents has seen you naked. Am I right?"

He nods, his gaze flickering to the elevator. "Why do I have to be naked the *whole* time? You can't possibly—there is no way—" He shakes his head, dropping his gaze to his feet while his cheeks heat. "You can't want to—do it—for the whole time—" He finally lifts his eyes.

I laugh. Deep and refreshing. I haven't laughed that way since I was a child playing in the schoolyard. I love the innocence. "It would be impressive, but I don't think anyone has such stamina."

"Then—" He cuts himself off.

"Go on," I prompt, wanting his words. Strangely, I want everything he's thinking. It is part of the appeal. I like the little bit of a stammer. I like the hesitation. I like how innocent he is. I love the way his cheeks pink when he gets embarrassed. I can't wait to see how far down his throat the color extends.

"Then why would I need to be naked the *whole* time?"

"Because I want to look at the art I've rented." I hook him by the belt loop, stepping into his space so he can't escape. "I want to be able to touch you any time I please. Not just for sex."

He glances between us. His breathing hitching. "Not just for sex? What else are you going to do to me?"

I capture his jaw with my free hand and whisper over his lips. "I'm not going to harm you."

47

His eyes slide close, and his lips part. "No?" The single word begs for reassurance.

"Other than some bites and maybe smacking that perfect round ass, no. I only like to hurt people who enjoy it." I tighten my grip, hard enough to leave little bruises. "If the other party isn't turned on, it loses the appeal," I say, but don't let our lips touch.

"Then why pay me to be here?" He doesn't pull back. He doesn't shy away from my lips. So much more willing than I expected.

"Are you attracted to me?" I flick my tongue out enough to taste his breath without kissing him. I have to keep my rules.

He hesitates.

"Be honest."

"Yes," he says like he risked opening the floodgates.

"I could tell from the moment we met, and I've never fucked a virgin."

"And that turns you on?" The hesitation returns.

"Before I met you, no." It's the truth.

"Then why me?"

I lift a shoulder. "Why is anyone attracted to anyone else?"

"Then why did you offer to pay me and not ask me out?" His eyes are open again, and hurt wavers there.

"Because you needed something I have a lot of and doesn't matter to me. Who knows how long you'd still be here if you didn't get it? And with all that religious trauma and baggage, who knows how long it will take you to decide to give that to someone? Who has that kind of time? I have a full course load, an internship, sports, and other demands on my time. So instead of letting you give it up to some other horny underclassmen who will take the time to make you trust him to get it, then leave you when he's bored, it's more beneficial to both of us this way." It's cold, but it's the truth. I'm not allowed to have those things. So I'll immerse myself for one night in the fantasy.

"So you are in school."

"Yes." I don't see what difference it makes.

He side-eyes the door again.

"Remember why you're doing this? Three thousand dollars. Freedom from your parents. Does it matter why I'm doing it?" I'm not fully sure why I'm doing it. The money doesn't matter, sure, but I have some concept of the enormity of it to him. Even if it is peanuts for me.

He moves his hands to roughly unbutton his shirt.

I throw them off. "I want to undress you."

"Oh . . . okay." His chest heaves with his labored breathing.

I release my hold on both his jaw and jeans, mostly sure he's no longer a flight risk. "It's like unwrapping a pretty package. Don't you savor pretty presents on holidays or your birthday?"

"We don't celebrate birthdays."

"What? Seriously?" I've heard of such things done, but I've never met anyone who was that kind of religious before.

"Seriously." He keeps his eyes lowered while I open his buttons.

I push the shirt off his shoulders, getting my first contact with the soft, cream-white skin littered with freckles. He truly is a work of art, like Michelangelo hand-carved him himself. "You're lovely."

His brows pull in a frown.

"Has no one ever told you that before?"

"No." The word is barely audible.

I lift his chin with a knuckle so he'll look at me. "Captivating." I thumb his lower lip and look into his dark eyes. "Are you hungry?"

"A little." He'd said he didn't have enough money for food.

I open his belt, then his button, before slowly lowering the zipper. The backs of my knuckles brushing his bulge. He's hard. Not fully, but enough to tell me he wants this. I'm elated and even more turned on.

"I had the cook prepare a meal, thinking you might be." I shove off his jeans. "And I like to play with my food before I eat it." I hook a finger into his briefs. "Take these off and your shoes, fold them and set them on the writing desk next to your money. You won't need them until you go. Then join me in the dining room." I step back, smoothing a hand over my tie while I give him another once-over. "Delicious."

I leave, not waiting for him to finish. Dinner will be getting cold, and I don't want to waste anymore of our time.

Six

Isaac

H e makes me nervous.
I'm sure he can tell.

The confident way he moves is impossible not to watch. He is in complete control of himself and his surroundings, like he's a gift to the world. Everything about him is put together, like he's never had a bad hair day or let life stress him out.

His dark hair is perfectly styled to look like he doesn't care but is still somehow elegant. Maybe it's the way he's dressed with slacks and a tie. Who wears a tie in their own house?

Why did the anxiousness in my stomach also turn me on? I was with Tim for two years, and I was never as interested in what he could do to me as I am right this moment.

With trembling fingers, I do what he told me and put my clothes on the antique desk he pointed to. A stack of cash is sitting there, and I can't stop myself from running my fingertips over the bills. I've never seen that much money at once before.

"Kitten."

I jump at the sudden sound and spin around. My cheeks flush, and I cover my nakedness on instinct.

"I don't like to repeat myself." His eyes drag over my exposed body, and I shiver. Between not knowing when he'll touch me, being naked, and the coolness of the room, I have goosebumps and a flush creeping up my neck.

Why can't he just do something and put me out of my misery? The never knowing when he'll do it or what he'll do is going to drive me insane.

"Dinner. It's getting cold." He turns his back and walks away. "And stop covering yourself. I'm paying good money to see it."

I have to force my hands to move and ball them into fists to keep them at my sides as I follow him into what I hope is a dining room.

This place is huge with dark walls but tons of natural light and high ceilings. It doesn't feel closed in, but comfortable and moody.

He's sitting at a dining room table with two chairs and one plate. He's watching, both interest and appraisal in his brilliant blue eyes. Something about the way he holds himself and his impossibly perfect jaw line screams attention. There's no way he can be in a room and no one notice him.

My stomach grumbles loud enough for him to hear it if the lift of his eyebrow is anything to go by. But the savory smell of the roasted vegetables, baked potato, and grilled chicken is making my mouth water.

I'm so hungry, but I don't know what he expects of me. Do I just sit down? Do I wait for him to tell me to?

I don't even know his name.

"What's your name?"

"Does it matter?" he replies indignantly. "You won't see me again after this, so it's pointless to make it personal."

Does he have a response question for everything I ask? Why can't he just answer a simple question?

"It's weird to not know what to call you in my head."

He looks at me like he's trying to decide what to tell me.

"My name is—"

"Kitten. You are kitten to me. Nothing more."

I roll my wrists and fight not to cross my arms over to my chest. Do I like being exposed like this? Not really. It's weird. Who just wanders around na–

"Sit."

My feet move before I've really thought about it. Following orders is easier than having to think.

I sit in the empty chair that's facing him, hissing at the cold against my skin, and wait for him to do . . . something. Is he going to touch me now? What does touching without sex mean? Is he really going to have sex with me while I'm here, or is this just a big power trip?

"Are you really not going to tell me your name?"

He turns his whole body toward me, reaches for the back of my knees, and jerks me forward. I grip the seat of my chair on reflex, barely keeping my butt on it when he puts my knees over his so my thighs are spread. Our eyes lock together for a long moment as my pulse pounds in my ears.

He leans in until his mouth is barely a whisper from mine, but his eyes are still holding me captive. "The only time you need to refer to me is when you come."

Heat floods my body, making my dick twitch against my leg. "And what should I call you?"

"Do you need ideas? Sir—Mister—my Lord, if you must." His gaze flicks down to my half hard-on, and with a knowing smile, meets mine again. This is so embarrassing. There's no hiding my reaction to him. It's not fair that he can hide behind clothes and whatever mask he's perfected while I'm bared to him. I have no experience in this area, while it's clear he has plenty.

Then why is it turning me on to feel the fabric of his clothes against me?

One finger trails up my torso from my belly button, up to the center of my chest, where he stops to pinch one of my nipples.

I gasp at the unexpected touch. It isn't hard enough to hurt, more just pressure, but oh god it feels good.

He smirks and moves his hand to the other nipple, pinching that one harder. I can't help the groan that rumbles from my throat or the whimper when he lets go. I feel like I'm vibrating and on fire. I'm hot but want so much more. Blood is starting to fill my dick, and despite knowing he wants to turn me on, it's embarrassing to have it literally out there for him to see.

"So responsive."

The tip of his tongue runs along the edge of my jaw, and I shudder. I desperately want him to kiss me. I ache for it, or at least some part of me does. He's barely touched me, and I can already tell I'm going to be addicted. Is this what sex is always like? If it is, I no longer wonder why people sleep around. Pleasure is world changing.

My stomach grumbles, and he chuckles softly. I expect him to turn away from me, to make me sit on display in this chair next to him like he's above me, but he doesn't.

All of me is on display. There are no secrets about my body between us. It's terrifying and arousing and humiliating.

I hate admitting even to myself, I like it.

He stabs a bite of roasted carrot and brings it to my mouth. I lean forward to take it, but he pulls back.

"Open your mouth."

I swallow down my nerves and sit with my lips parted, waiting. He drags the bite over my bottom lip before slipping the fork inside my mouth. His eyes track the movement of the metal, and I wish I had paper and a pencil. I want to capture this expression on paper, to look back at it and remember exactly how I felt at this moment.

"Take the bite." He watches as I close my lips around the carrot, and he slides the metal utensil out. I chew slowly, and as I get ready to swallow, he drags his knuckle against my throat.

I don't know why I like the simple touch so much, but I do. That small pressure on such a vulnerable place is exciting. He could hurt me if he wanted to, but he doesn't.

We continue eating this way, with him taking a bite every once in a while. We don't speak much, but I guess we don't need to. Everything in the world revolves around him and what he'll do next. There is nothing else. My head is quiet as he commands my attention.

"I'm full."

"Good." He puts the cutlery down and slides both hands up the outside of my thighs, but doesn't touch me where I want him to. "Do you want dessert?"

From the way he asks, I'm not sure if he means actual food or something else.

"My stomach is full."

The smile that lifts his mouth promises sex and debauchery. "Good, you're learning."

Quickly, he slides his hand into the hair at the nape of my neck, jerking me forward onto his lap. He grips my ass cheek, and I rub myself against his body. His lips drag along my skin, making tingles zing across me. The soft cotton of his shirt rubs against my dick, and I'm afraid there's going to be a pre-cum stain on it.

That thought takes me out of my head enough to push on his chest to look.

"Hands behind your back," he orders. The hand in my hair

pulls, and I drop my head back while he bites and sucks on my neck. The roughness of his five o'clock shadow sends shivers across my skin.

Both of my hands are captured in his, leaving me helpless to do anything but feel. It's too much and not enough. I want to come, but don't want this to stop. What does he look like when he comes? Does he finally lose that control? I need to know.

I whimper when he sinks his teeth into the soft flesh of my neck, my hips bucking against him as tingles spread along my inner thighs into my groin.

He pulls my mouth to his, not in a kiss but so close, and I moan "please" against his lips. This position isn't giving me enough contact.

"No," he says and nips my lip hard enough to sting. This infuriating man sucks softly on the abused skin to lower the raging fire in my blood to embers.

"Up." He pats my ass, and I stand, still hard and breathing just a little faster than is normal. He stands too, lifting my chin with a finger. "You are delicious." The pad of his thumb drags along my swollen mouth.

Seven

Oliver

"Thank you," he stammers, reddening down his neck.

"Adorable. You really haven't done anything, have you?" I'd believed him the other day on the street, but it's still shocking to think he'd made it through high school looking like he does without anyone taking advantage of him.

Better for me.

He shakes his head and drops his gaze. "I really haven't."

I trail my knuckles down his sternum, debating how I want him first.

Face down, ass up.

Riding my cock.

Over the table.

Against a wall.

Slow or fast.

I swirl my finger around his bellybutton, making a shiver run down his spine.

Slow. Definitely slow.

I'll take my time and devour every inch of him.

A smile tugs up my lips, warmth flooding through me.

"What are you thinking?" he asks, searching my face.

"How I want you." I press a finger into his chest, forcing him backward one step at a time.

He glances over his shoulder, shaky on his feet at first, but he gains more confidence in his gait, lifting his eyes to meet mine. Thatta boy. I find the little streaks of certainty sexy. He'll grow into it too. Once he gets the awkward virgin mentality out of the way. I almost envy who finds him later, knowing the man he'll turn into. The boyfriend he'll turn into.

But I can't follow that line of thinking. I can't let my mind even daydream of a universe where I'd be allowed to choose my partner. My world doesn't work that way, and it never will. Plenty of my peers believe they can defy their parents' wishes and call their bluff of disinheritance. It always ends poorly.

I don't relish a life unlike the one I live, so I'll play by my parents' rules.

It's only one night.

I can have one and let it sate this stupid urge.

It would have to.

I exhale when his back hits the door to the guest room. I made the decision before he came over not to have him in my room. It would only give me a taste for a boyfriend. Bad idea. So the guest room it is.

I step into his space, trapping him against the solid oak. Off balance. Just the way I want him. He arches his back, trying to grind into me. I grab his hip, digging my fingers into his flesh, preventing the rock.

"So desperate. Embarrassing."

The shade of red on his cheeks deepens. Almost scarlet now. I suppress a groan. I don't know who waiting is harder for, him or me.

"I wasn't—"

"Weren't you?" My touch softens, stroking my thumb over his hip. "What were you doing if you weren't trying to grind against me, kitten?"

He swallows—hard. "I want to—"

"Speak up."

"Please you," he whispers.

"Me? Or yourself?" With every word he speaks, my touch lowers, thumb circling over his skin, getting closer to his straining cock. A little Pavlov's dog encouragement.

"Both of us?" His voice pitches up.

"Are you asking me?" I pause, nearly touching his dick.

"No. Both of us."

I skim around his base, ever so softly. "How close are you to coming?"

"Not very," he says, only sounding slightly unsure of himself.

"We'll see how true that is." I turn the handle and pull back, letting him stumble into the room.

The room has never been used. We did it in earthy, natural colors and modern furniture. I prepped it just after my brother left in the helicopter. Restraints on the bed, lube, clothes, water, and everything else we could need. I click a button on my phone, igniting a thousand tiny candles I'd had the butler put up this afternoon.

He regains his footing, then glances around the space. "Did you do all this for me?"

I tilt my head, trying to decipher what he means. "I did."

His brows pull together, a mix of his lip lifting in confusion and a tiny frown like he's trying to do complex math in his mind.

"Spit it out, kitten. What has you perplexed?"

"You went to all this *effort* for me?"

"Yes." I narrow my eyes, unsure where his issue lies. "And that is?"

"I'm surprised. No one has ever done something like this for me." His words come in barely a whisper, like he's ashamed of them.

I laugh. Deep and full, approaching him again. "I put in effort for all things I want. Just because I'm paying you doesn't mean I don't want you. Don't accept anything less, kitten." I slide my thumb between his lips while I lecture him. "You deserve more than that, even when you're being a whore."

He lowers his eyes at the word.

"Don't do that."

"What?" he mouths around my thumb.

"Retreat into yourself. I obviously like you being a whore."

"You do?" He lifts his gaze, searching my face.

"Do you really believe I'd be paying you this much to fuck you and putting this much energy into it if it didn't turn me on?"

"I guess—I guess that makes sense."

"You guess? Do you doubt I'm aroused by you?" I hook my thumb behind his teeth, forcing him to look at me.

"I don't know you. You might get off on making me do this or the control."

"I get off on those things, sure. I won't deny it. But I could have a dozen submissives at my feet if I so wished. They are a dime a dozen in this city. I've never paid anyone for the plea-sure." I walk him into the wall, pinning him there with my hips, pressing my hard-on into his hip. "Do you feel how hard I am for you? Try again."

"Because I'm a virgin, then?" He tries to lower his chin, but my hold won't allow it.

"Also easy to come by." Purity culture runs rampant thanks to people like his family.

"I don't know why."

"Because you're beautiful. Like art. I've never wanted anything more in my life." I shouldn't admit any of this to him, but the anonymity makes me bold. I fuck my thumb in and out of his mouth, letting him hang on my words. "I've thought about fucking every hole you have since I laid eyes on you."

"*What?*" The gasp that comes out of him only makes me harder.

I rock into him, unable to stop myself, needing a bit of friction to not take him right here, right now. If I let myself lose control— I won't let my mind go there. I want to fuck him more than once over the next twenty-two hours, so I have to follow my rules.

"What do you need me to clarify?" I grab the back of his thigh, lifting his leg to wrap around me. "Which holes? The fantasy?"

He hesitates before he speaks. "I never thought I would be a fantasy to someone like you."

With his leg securely around me, I brush my fingers over his hole. "You don't see yourself as I see you."

He moans with his whole body, and it's like watching the slow bloom of a flower. I need more. His lips come dangerously close to mine, and I pull back.

"I don't kiss." I grab his wrists, twisting him around to shove him over the chest at the foot of the bed.

He hits the unforgiving wood with a grunt, ass in the air. I knock his ankles farther apart, taking my place between them.

"I'm going to open you up for me." I pour lube into my palm and warm it between my hands before spreading it over his cheeks, spreading them and playing as I do.

He lifts on his toes, pressing into the massage with soft groans.

"So easy, my little whore."

He makes a face but doesn't fight the name. It brings a smile to my lips. I circle my thumb around his opening, spreading the lubrication there. His body relaxes, and he melts against the chest, eyes closing. I keep up the prep, waiting until every bit of tension bleeds out of him before I push two fingers inside him.

He jumps with the intrusion, gasping, eyes shooting open, pain written in the harsh line of his mouth.

"Shhhh, push out and lean into the burn. It will get better. I promise."

He does as I ask, the strain in his forehead quickly turning to relaxed pleasure again.

I work my fingers deeper, lightly brushing over his prostate, earning a moan before I add a third finger.

His breathing hitches, and his body stiffens. "Oww . . ." He chews his lip, nearly breaking skin.

"Wait until my cock has you stretched so wide you can't breathe, and you don't know where pain ends and ecstasy begins." I unzip my slacks. I won't be fully undressing. I won't give him the satisfaction. Or at least I tell myself that is the reason. I can't give too much of myself. I have to have lines. "You're going to come so hard you'll think about it for the rest of your life and wish all the fucks you'll date could come close to the orgasms you had with me, kitten."

Eight

Isaac

I *can't believe I'm doing this.*

My heart hammers in my ears, and I can't get my balance. Thank God, he has me bent over some kind of wooden furniture piece, or I'd have fallen over. I catch my lip between my teeth as his fingers enter me. Blinding burn, and I barely catch his words. My chest gets tighter, but I try to follow his directions, opening myself to him.

My cheeks heat as he stretches me. I've never been so laid bare to anyone.

He is *inside* me.

I block out the implications of what it means. What it would be to my father, my God, my religion. What it means about me.

What liking it means.

"Breathe, kitten." His words are softer than before. His touch, too.

I squeeze my eyes shut, knowing I don't deserve the kindness from him or anyone else.

What the fuck am I doing?

"You're holding your breath."

I nod. He's right, but I don't know how to force myself to inhale. I try, half sucking in a shuddering gasp.

His fingers withdraw, but that's worse. It leaves me empty, so empty. As empty as I felt when my father kicked me out.

"Kitten?"

I can't answer. I don't have enough oxygen. My vision narrows, and I wobble.

A loud crack reaches my ears before the sting hits my ass. I draw in a breath sharply against the pain. One becomes two. Two becomes three.

I'm breathing.

"Good boy."

I thaw a little under the praise.

"Do you want me to stop?" he asks with an edge to his voice.

"Would you?"

"Of course. What would have you doubt as much?" He isn't touching me at all.

I don't dare to look behind to see where he's gone. I've repulsed him. He doesn't want to touch me again. "Because—um —the money." It feels like the wrong thing to say.

"You can leave any time. I'm sure I'd enjoy a little force play, but not when my—" He hesitates. He's never hesitated before. After a long pause, he continues. "Not when my toy isn't into it."

"Oh . . ."

What had he almost said?

"Do you wish to leave?"

"No," I say firmly, already calming down. "Please touch me." As soon as the words leave my lips, his hands are on me again. No hesitation.

He massages over my stinging ass. "If at any point you want me to stop, say so."

I couldn't. He's already been inside me. I've gone too far.

Another crack, this one with an immediate burn, and I yelp.

"Stay with me. Wherever you keep going—stop."

I nod, focusing on his touch, letting my brain empty.

I relax, and he enters me again. It's weird but so good when he hits some magical pleasure spot I didn't know existed. If gay sex is a sin, why is this breathtaking?

I moan, arching into his touch. I barely bite back a plea for more.

More of what I don't know, but I need it.

"Such a good little whore."

I risk a glance over my shoulder. He's obscenely hard in his slacks. Huge. I bet I could see the outlines of veins if it were any lighter in the room.

My mouth waters, and my hole clenches.

Another needy whimper parts my lips. His fingers aren't enough. I'm dying for more, but I can't ask. The words won't form on my tongue.

I arch into him. Needy, my entire body on fire.

"How badly do you want my cock?"

My brows pull. How did he know?

"I see it in your eyes, kitten. But more than that, it's in every movement. Every whimper. You're begging with your body. You can't hide from me." His smile is filthy, and he strokes over himself.

"I'm—" Sorry? But I'm not, and that isn't what he wants to hear.

"Tell me the truth." His fingers pull out, and I clench around the empty space. I want to be full again. "Your hole is aching for me."

The voice behind me sends a shiver up my spine. He's not wrong. How does he read me so well?

There's a rustling of clothes and the sound of a zipper before a warm, hard cock is laid against my crack. I tense at the unfamiliar feeling but lean into it. I want him to own me, to take me out of my head until all that's left is pleasure and sensation. But I want to feel connected too. Like I matter. All of this is so overwhelming, and I've gotten used to the bare minimum, so I don't know what to do anymore.

"I'm not giving you what you want until you say it." His voice is taunting.

I hate him. I close my eyes and take in the wood's feel warming under my face. "Please."

His hand grips my hip, but he doesn't move. "Please what?"

I chew on my lip for just a second before I let the words tumble out. "I want to see your face when you take my virginity."

Wet lips press against my spine, and his hum is like electricity in my veins. I'm not used to physical touch, especially from other men, but I want it. Need it. Since I walked in here, he's had his hands on me, and I don't know how I'll cope once I leave.

A sharp slap stings my butt cheek, and I yelp at the unexpected pain.

"What was that for?" I demand.

"Get out of your head. Nothing matters but me."

He has no idea how true that is.

Will I be able to go back to my normal life after this?

His hand slides down my side, around my hip, to my thigh where he digs in his nails and reverses the path. All the hair on my body stands up, and I gasp at the rapid change in sensation.

"Turn around on your knees." The man who is the source of my pleasure and humiliation steps back, and I move to do what I'm told. "Wider, open your knees."

He taps the inside of my leg with his foot, and I spread my

thighs. My dick is hard and confused. Why is being embarrassed making my dick ache?

Slowly, I lift my gaze up his long form. The perfectly tailored clothes that hang beautifully from his graceful body. His hard cock standing proudly in front of him, pointing at my face above his round balls. He's thick and veined, slightly curved upward, with a perfectly shaped red head peeking out from the cover of his foreskin. My eyes snap from the dick in front of me to his eyes. He's watching me carefully, taking in every line on my face, every movement, like he's studying me.

"I want your mouth on me."

Leaning forward, I bury my face against his base and balls to breathe him in. I've always wanted to do this. To smell the musk of my lover and know I'm the reason for his lust. I can't see all of him, just what he's pulled through the zipper, but the hair is trimmed and dark.

He smells like the best temptation. Warm man and sex. I lick along his base and am rewarded with a small gasp.

"Such an enthusiastic whore, aren't you?"

I moan with him against my lips and smile when he shivers. I don't know what I'm doing and feel awkward, but his reaction is a good sign, right?

"I love it." He grabs a handful of my hair and holds his dick to my mouth. "Open."

My lips part, and he drags the skin-covered tip of his cock along my mouth. My eyes lock on his face while he watches his dick slip between my lips.

He groans, head tipping back. I try to take more of his cock into my mouth, but he holds me off with the grip of my hair. He's careful, not forcing himself down my throat like I expect. Riding the edge of his brutality, he's holding back, I can tell.

There's something about him that's almost starting to unravel, like he's losing some of his control.

I like that too.

Suddenly, he pulls my hair back and spits into my mouth.

"Get on the bed."

I'm so shocked I don't say anything or react except to scramble onto the mattress. It's soft and cradles my body as I lie down on my back. Knees open, head lifted, so I can watch what he's doing. It feels like morbid curiosity watching him, giving him my virginity.

I know I shouldn't be turned on, but I am. My cock aches, and he's right, I want him inside of me.

With a bottle of what I assume is lube in his hand, he climbs on the bed and settles between my legs. It's a vulnerable position. I want to clamp my knees together and cover myself, but something about being bared to him is making my whole body throb. I feel my face heat and creep down my neck and chest as I watch him pour clear liquid in his palm and slide it between my cheeks once again.

"Condoms?" The question is out of my mouth before I've had time to dwell on it but safe sex is important right? That's what sex ed tells us.

"If you insist, but if I'm paying for it I'd rather feel you. All of you. Inside and out."

My body is trembling with anticipation and anxiety as I wait for what he's going to do next. Pre-cum drips slowly down my dick, and he smirks when he sees it.

One of his slick hands wraps around my cock and strokes in torturously slow movements, while the other hand shoves what feels like three fingers back inside my hole.

It burns, and I hiss, tensing against the intrusion I'm so unfamiliar with.

"Deep breath, push into it."

It doesn't take long for the burning to fade around his thrusting digits. I dig my hands into the blankets for something to hold on to as I watch him pump me. It's so erotic. So much more arousing than I thought it could be.

I'm panting. My lungs forcing the air through my throat so hard it's like I'm running.

"Ha ung oh faa…" Meaningless sounds leave my lips, and I'm helpless to stop it as he works me over. "Name…" I close my eyes and try to focus. I need his name. "Wh—what's your name?"

"It doesn't matter." He drops my cock, and it falls to my stomach with a *thunk*. I throw my arm over my eyes and try not to cry at the denial of my orgasm. I'm shaky and sweaty and almost desperate.

He shifts, and I feel the bed dip next to my ribs as the blunt head of his dick pushes against my stretched hole. "Look at me," he demands.

Dropping my arm back to the bed, I meet his gaze and hold it as he pushes inside of me. He's leaning over me as he thrusts in. It's slow, but there's still a sharp pinch of pain that makes me tense up.

"Breathe, push against me. You can take it, kitten. I know you can."

The compliment makes me preen, and I do my best to relax. He slides his knuckle up my sternum again, and my back arches. He growls and pushes farther into me, farther than his fingers were able to reach.

"Oh God," I whimper and cling to his forearms.

"There's no God here." He chuckles. "Just me, and I promise I'll make you cum better than any god ever could." He pulls back and pushes forward again, going farther this time.

"How much more can there be?" My whine is almost a yell, but he's going to split me in half.

A dark smirk twists his lips, and it's possibly the sexiest look I've seen him wear so far. I shiver at that expression, and my nipples harden. He backs out again, then thrusts forward until his hips meet my skin. I cry out and arch against him as my fingers dig into him. He's dropping kisses along my flesh with nips and sucks and the scratch of his five o'clock shadow while he waits for me to adjust.

He thumbs over my nipple, around and around until it's sensitive, then sucks it deep into his mouth. I moan and rock against him, but I can't get much movement with his hips pinned against mine. I'm so full, but it's not enough. The discomfort has faded, and now I want the pleasure.

I want to be fucked.

I've gone this far and I need the rest.

"Please move."

Nine

Oliver

Sinking into him washes over me like a religious experience. Like I'm baptized and made new in the all-encompassing tightness of his hole. I don't want to move. I want to stay buried inside his body for the rest of the time we have.

I know now how dangerous he is.

More than I ever imagined. I knew I wanted him when I first laid eyes upon him, but this, this is something entirely new.

One taste and I'm addicted.

"Please move," he gasps the words into my ear.

"What a perfect, needy little slut. How bad do you need to be fucked?" I whisper against his ear, pulling back a half inch, giving him only a taste of what he wants, fighting every instinct I have to fuck him into the mattress.

"Please . . . please." It's all he can manage, and I am drunk off the need.

"Please what?" I want him to say it.

He arches his back, reclaiming the little I pulled back, forcing me fully inside of him again. He meets my gaze, a little pout forming on his lips.

"Tell me what you want." Twenty-four hours might be a mistake. Every look, every movement, every fucking pout and arch gets me. He's had me riding the edge of release since he put his mouth around me. I'm already bordering on obsessed, and I haven't even come.

What is wrong with me?

"You."

"Me how?"

He whimpers and wraps his legs around me, trying to get friction, rubbing his cock against my abs. He feels entirely too good, and I can't handle it. "Move. Please move. I want to feel it."

"You want me to fuck you?"

He nods vigorously, biting down on his full lower lip.

"Maybe I enjoy making you wait." I pull back, slamming into him.

His eyes roll back in his head while he gasps another needy moan. "Why?" The word is painful.

"Because you keep rewarding me with this." I slide my thumb along the curve of his mouth and slip it inside, past the pouty lips. But it's more than that. I need to calm down or I'm going to lose it.

He sucks my thumb, and my cock throbs inside of him.

"You—" How he is a virgin, I have no idea. He is entirely sex. A siren of my self-destruction.

"What?" he says around my thumb, letting his tongue etch each word into my skin.

"You know what." I've never had anyone bring out such a strong response in me. I've slept with countless men and women in NYC and never looked at anyone twice.

What spell does he have me under?

"Like that?" He is coy. He has to know what he's doing.

"I like everything about you." A slip. Words I shouldn't have uttered. "Which is why I'm inside you." I give him another rock to distract from what I said.

I force down thoughts of keeping him tied up in my room for a year. Having him whenever I'd like. Keeping him to my fucking self so the world can't spoil him. Or more so, so I don't have to share him. I'm a selfish prick, but few things brought out such a strong response in me.

"How badly do you want it?" I pull out, slowly, as I speak until just my tip rests in his tightness.

He tightens like he could prevent me from fully withdrawing. "I don't think I've ever wanted anything more in my life."

A smile curls over my mouth, despite myself. "I'm going to wreck you tonight."

"Promise?" His word surprises me.

"I promise." I drive into him, sinking until I'm fully sheathed.

He bucks, eyes rolling with pleasure while his entire body contorts with it. I don't stop. I can't. I pull back to immediately slam into him again, filling and stretching his hole. The way his body reacts to mine is ungodly, or maybe heavenly. I'd experienced a lot of faking, and people acting like they enjoyed sex more than they did. Usually to impress me. This is entirely the opposite. Unbridled and unabashed pleasure.

I need more.

He comes alive under my touch.

He presses his face into my chest, grasping at the back of my neck. "Harder. Please, please, don't stop." He grabs at me, digging fingers into my shoulders and neck, begging.

"You're so easy," I whisper against his ear.

"I can't help it." His words tremble out of him in the most endearing way. I don't even like people. What is wrong with me?

"Should I slow down, so you don't come?" I won't. But I have to tease him.

"No!" Every touch is desperate.

The evil laugh that parts my lips should give him a clue as to who I am, but he's too far gone in his lust to see clearly.

I slow my hips, fixed on his every reaction. He starts to crumble, clutching at any part of me he can reach, moans mixed with a chorus of pleading. His vulnerability offered on a silver platter. And maybe I'm not worthy, but that doesn't stop me from wanting it.

He buries his face in my neck, and I use the moment to torture him further by grabbing his cock. He doesn't stand a chance. He's coming almost the instant I close my fingers around him. His body stiffens, coiling to come without a stroke, clenching around me as he pulses with his release. His eyes roll back, and I ram myself deeper, fucking him through his orgasm.

Writhing and whimpering.

Moaning and drawing me closer.

He collapses back against the sheets, breathing hard, legs spread wide open, hair wild, eyes fixed on mine while he recovers.

I pick up my pace, splitting him open. He wraps his legs around my hips, forcing me fully inside of him, making me come undone.

My thrusts falter as I erupt in pleasure. I ride out the high, taking full pleasure in him.

Both spent, we lie for a minute breathing hard.

"You lost control." His voice is filled with wonderment.

"You know, not many guys can get off by only penetration," I reply with amusement.

His cheeks pink. "I guess I am easy."

I can tell he's overthinking again. "I like it." More than like it.

His eyes flicker up. "Why?"

"Do you know how sexy it is to make you come with only my cock?"

He fights looking down, but loses the battle. "Tell me."

"First, it's like an accomplishment. I love a good ego stroke, and second, I enjoy my partner getting off. Some guys only care about their pleasure, but how shortsighted is that? I'd rather leave people thinking about me for the rest of their lives."

"You really are an arrogant jerk."

"Thank you."

"That wasn't a compliment." He rolls his eyes.

I sit back on my heels, pulling out of him, admiring the aftermath of our fuck. He's slick with sweat and cum. Fucked and beautiful.

He pushes his fingers into his hair, eyeing my body.

The way he looks at me.

I grab his hips, flipping him to his stomach, to lie over his back and pin him to the bed. My knees slot between his, spreading open his thighs, giving me free access to his hole. I slide my cock along his ass, dropping my lips next to his ear. "It is to me, and my opinion is the only one that matters when it comes to myself."

He squirms but doesn't fight my hold. "You like that people think you're a jerk?"

"I simply don't care what others think. You should try it."

He arches, pressing his ass into my tip, instantly making me hard again. I find his opening, sliding inside easily because he's still slick with my cum. His used hole still so tight. I could stay inside him all night.

We spend another hour lost in a slow fuck. Bodies pressed. Breath heated. I bite his neck and leave marks.

We dozed after that.

But he kept touching me. I wake to his hands or arms around me. Limbs tangled. Entirely too intimate for my comfort. If I were a smarter man, I'd have left him there and gone to my bed. But I stay, waking in the early hours of the morning with his head on my chest.

My chest tightens, and I slip out from under him, to kneel next to him, pressing the tip of my dick to his lips. I rub the tip there until his eyes slowly blink open. Without a word, he opens his mouth, presenting his tongue.

"Such an easy whore. Barely awake and already ready to be filled." I don't give him a chance to reply, claiming his mouth.

His lips tug into a smile around me while I use his mouth in a shallow fuck. His hand strokes my thigh and ass. Caressing. So willing and eager.

I feed off it, quickly losing it.

"What does that feel like?" he asks, resting his head on his hand while I grab a towel to wipe myself off.

"A blow job?" I ask, not sure what he's getting at.

"Yeah."

"You've never had your dick in someone's mouth?"

He shakes his head, teeth digging into his lower lip. "Nope."

"Lay back."

"*What?* Why?"

"So I can suck your cock." A hint of amusement crests my mouth.

"But—why? This is about you . . ."

"Do you believe there is no pleasure in giving oral?" I shove him back, putting my knee on his chest to pin him to the bed.

He gets more aroused by the second, cock pulsing. "It seems so personal, and you said you don't want to be kissed."

"It is, but I have an affinity for taking your firsts." I wrap my fingers around his base. "Relax."

He does, partly, lying back, but there is still tension coiled in his body.

"Why?"

I ignore his question. "After I was buried inside you, you are objecting to my mouth? I would think as wide as I had you stretched open would make you more nervous."

"I . . . expected that."

My nerve endings erupt in flames. How easily he does this to me with words alone. "Good. I want you guessing." I lick the head of his erection, and a heavy moment passes between us. I took more than his virginity tonight, but I'm not ready to acknowledge it yet.

His entire body shudders in pleasure before I even suck. I'm walking a tightrope, poised on his reactions as I wrap my lips around him. His abs flex, fighting the invisible ending. He stammers and gasps, finally sitting and grasping the back of my head. He's gentle, stroking his fingers through my hair, meeting my eyes as he struggles to breathe.

I moan around him. A sharp knife of emotions stabs into my chest. This fucking beautiful boy. I take him deeper into my mouth, more into this blow job than I've ever been.

His grip tightens on my head, like he'd have the audacity to face fuck me.

"*Bring it,*" I say with my eyes, knowing he wouldn't dare.

His whole body coils, and his nails dig into my scalp, but our eye contact wields an intense band of emotion. It digs between my ribs and burns in my lungs.

His hips come off the bed, losing himself in a wild fury of lust. One leg wraps around my shoulders, to give him more leverage to fuck my face.

I let him come in my mouth as an added treat. He tastes as sweet as he looks. Is there a downside to this boy? He's temptation wrapped in the most beautiful package. I can't handle it.

I wipe my mouth with the back of my hand and smirk at him, lying back. "Now back to sleep with you."

"Sleep?"

"The sun is barely up, and we fucked half the night." I yawn and pull the sheet over us.

He ducks his head under the sheet, sinking lower in the bed.

"What are you doing?" I ask lifting the sheet to look at him.

"I want to give you something back." He hovers on a high note of venerability.

"I know you're eighteen, but I've already fucked you twice last night and once this morning, some of us need some time to recover." I laugh, waving a hand at my cock. "I'm going to need at least twenty minutes."

He frowns. Is no really such a big blow to his ego?

"You want me inside you when you've just come?"

He half shrugs. "I can't help it."

"I've broken the dam, have I?"

He lowers his gaze. "I like feeling like someone cares about me."

"I do care. I wouldn't take such care with you if I didn't care."

He nods, but still doesn't look at me.

"Do you think I'd be so convincing if I didn't? I'm not that good an actor."

"I like feeling like you can't keep your hands off me. Like I'm important," he murmurs, and I realize I'm filling a hole in his life he's had for some time.

"Is that how you felt with my lips around your cock?"

His whole body flushes. "Yes."

"You taste good." I thumb his lip. "I will be doing that again before you leave."

He throws off the sheet and palms his cock, already hardening.

Christ.

78

He is insatiable.

He strokes himself. I tuck a hand under my head, watching. He takes it as encouragement, getting up on his knees to fuck his hand over my chest. I let it slide, happy to watch the free show. His back arches, and my blood flows south. His lips curve up when he notices. He's good.

He reaches for me, and I catch his wrist.

"I told you, twenty minutes." Now it's the principle.

"Fine, but you didn't say where I had to wait." He climbs over me as he speaks, sitting his perfect ass just shy of my tip.

I release his wrist and tuck my other hand under my head, stretched out to watch what he'll do, shocked by the confidence he's found. He works over his length, lifting up on his knees, making me harder by the second.

The way he handles himself. How his long fingers glide over his girth, slick and sticky with pre-cum. I don't know when he does it, but he scooted back, inch by inch, until his ass rocks over my tip with each thrust of his hips. I flex, barely staving off lifting my hips to rub over him.

"I feel you," he says breathless, flushed from head to toe, and glistening in the candlelight. His body a masterpiece.

"And?" I ask, wanting to know what he'll do.

"I want you inside me again."

"Let me see." I slip two fingers into my mouth and bring them to his hole.

He squirms, pressing into the intrusion. So willing and wanton. He fucks himself on my fingers, pinned between his hand and me.

He reaches for the bottle of lube, watching for my reaction. He lifts farther, upending the bottle over my cock. I hiss as the cool liquid meets my dick. I glance at the clock, eighteen minutes I've made him wait. I'll have to fill another two.

One-hundred and twenty agonizing seconds.

He lowers to rub himself all over my cock. Ours sliding together, then up his split. He begs with his eyes. They say, "*I need you.*"

With a minute to go I withdraw my fingers, letting the full length of me ride between his cheeks. He arches, rubbing my tip over his needy hole. I grab my cock, not allowing myself to enter.

He whines on all fours over me, our lips a breath apart. He redoubles his effort to get me inside him, rocking, and rutting. My back lifts and chest heaves. He forces me to the edge, barely in control.

"Please." He breathes over my lips.

Our mouths crash, and for a moment I'm stunned, too stunned to do anything but kiss him back.

I never kiss anyone I hook up with.

Kissing is too personal.

I try to pull back, but he chases, locking his knees around my hips, kissing me harder.

Both his hands find my face—possessive, needy, demanding—a side of him I hadn't expected to come out.

I'm lit up. Lightning in my veins. Lost to his assault. Almost.

I grab his throat, reclaiming control of the situation.

A smile plays on his lips, and I finally allow him to sink onto my cock. The moan he gasps into my mouth is pure ecstasy.

I expect him to feverishly fuck himself on my cock, instead he slows the pace, taking me inch by inch. Agonizingly slow.

I squeeze his ass, forcing him down on to my cock. "Tease," I manage through my teeth.

"Payback." He's so confident in his word. In his riding of my cock. He's like a prince ready to be crowned on his mount.

It fucking turns me on. "I love your twisted idea of payback."

He presses his hands into my pecs, fighting against my grip on his ass. "And if I slow down like you did when you're close."

"Be my guest. Unlike your near virgin ass, I enjoy the art of edging."

"Then why are your knuckles white?" he asks playfully.

"Because I want you to sit on me and kiss me again." I've already crossed the line. What's one more time?

He does. Passionately. Rough and needy. All while he rides me, bucking his hips while circling them, keeping me so fucking deep.

"You're lucky you have people who would miss you, if I kept you locked in my room."

He smiles, taking the compliment for what it is. "I don't."

"Don't tempt me, kitten. You must have a roommate."

He laughs, grabbing my wrist, keeping it on his throat. "I doubt he would care much if I didn't return."

"It's not good for me to want you." My life is entirely too complicated.

Twenty-four hours will have to suffice.

Ten

Isaac

I 'm sitting in the back of an Uber staring out the window with three thousand dollars cash in a bag smelling like a man I don't know the name of.

"You okay, kid?" The older man turns and looks at me with care on his face.

"Yeah, fine." I climb out slowly and walk toward the building I'll call home for the next year, maybe longer. Numb. I think I'm numb. No thoughts running through my head. Like I'm in a vacuum or a bubble, there's nothing around me.

The door opens before I can scan my keycard, and I think I mumble thanks as I brush past whoever is leaving.

"Hey," someone says and grabs my arm. I turn and look up into my roommate's face.

"You okay?" He looks worried, I think, his eyes taking me in before meeting mine.

"Yeah, just tired." The words tumble from my mouth with no

thought. How many times have I said that same thing when it wasn't what I meant? Just so someone would leave me alone.

"Come on." Colin leads me to the elevator, and when we get inside, I lean against the wall and close my eyes. I am tired. Drained. Sore.

Not in a bad way though. The last twenty-four hours were amazing. I feel . . . different. Like maybe coming out and being myself will be okay. While he controlled every aspect of what happened, I never felt like I couldn't make requests. Everyone has fantasies, things they think they want to try but are too embarrassed to ask for but knowing I would never see him again gave me a sense of freedom to take what I want. I'm free to be the version of me I've always wanted.

Things make a lot more sense now. Why my father was so dead set against sexual contact? Do girls feel like this after being with a man or another woman?

It's almost like I'm high. I've never been high, so I'm not a hundred percent on it, but my limbs are loose but heavy, my body humming almost. Not numb like I thought, just busy.

My skin is sensitive, and my clothes feel like little electric shocks when I move. Almost overstimulating after spending so much time without them.

"Hey," Colin says, snapping his fingers.

I jerk open my eyes to see him watching me. His eyebrows are pulled together and low over his warm eyes.

The doors to the elevator are open, and I stand up. He moves out of the way and unlocks our door. I don't say anything, just kick my shoes off, drop my jeans on the floor and face plant onto my bed.

Sleep.

I need glorious sleep.

"What the hell have you been doing for exactly twenty-four hours?" Colin's voice holds a sternness that stiffens my spine. I roll over onto my back and look at him. My nosy roommate has his arms crossed, leaning against my bed. There's no way I'm copping to what I've been up to though.

"Why do you care?" How would I even explain to this virtual stranger that I sold my virginity for three grand, and I don't even know the guy's first name? I really am a whore.

"Listen, while I'm proud of you stepping out on your own, you have to be careful. This city is easy to get lost in if you don't know where you're going or who you're with."

Interested now, I sit up and cock my head.

"How do you know?"

Colin purses his lips, watching me closely for a minute before he answers.

"I have rich daddy issues, remember? I'm a slut and use sex to feel loved."

I blink at him, not expecting his explanation. Who says things like that?

"Listen." Colin looks at me with the most serious expression I've seen on him so far. "If you want to get your rocks off, good for you. But seriously, you have to watch yourself. There are people that will see your innocent face, your naivety, and take full advantage. I was on my way out to go find you when you popped up."

Guilt settles into my gut. I worried him and didn't realize it. I didn't think he would care or notice that I was gone.

"I'm sorry, and thank you for caring enough to worry."

"Hey, I know what it's like to be a young gay man in this city." He winks with a smirk. "I would be happy to help you find a good time, any time, with people who won't rape you and leave you for dead in an alley."

Cold fear shoots up my spine. That didn't occur to me, and it probably should have. I went to some stranger's house, didn't tell anyone where I was going, and I don't know who he is. He could have lured me there to kill me.

He grips my shoulder for a second until I look at him.

"Did you have a good time, though?"

My face heats, and he tosses his head back with a laugh.

"Good. That's my boy." His phone pings, and he pulls it from his perfectly ripped up jeans to check the screen. "I guess I'm leaving." He shrugs and shoves the phone back in his pocket. "I hope you see this boy again."

I don't expect to see him again. Ever. That idea makes my heart race though. I can't imagine anyone else making my body feel the way he did. The control he has over me, the way he is able to get me out of my head, and the pleasure. That pleasure is more than I could have thought possible. I know I'll be jonesing for it once my mind rests. Once the bruises fade, I'll ache for them again.

I already miss his energy. Just being in the same room with him forces my attention to him. There's nothing else.

"I—I" My voice cracks, and I swallow down the lump forming in my throat. "I doubt I'll ever see him again."

Something crosses Colin's face, but it's gone so fast I can't figure out what it was. He grips my shoulder for a second, offering comfort I didn't realize I needed.

"If the dick was good, don't lose that number." He winks at me, and the serious moment is broken. "If you want or need to talk, I'm here. I'm really good with dicks and assholes."

He smiles a self-satisfied smirk, and I chuckle.

"Thanks, I appreciate it. But right now, I just want to sleep."

Colin taps under my chin with his knuckle and turns to leave.

"Don't wait up, but do wake me up in the morning for class," he tosses over his shoulder before the door closes.

I shake my head with a smile and lie back down, the bite marks on my skin a tender reminder of what I've done, and the smile drops from my face. My father's words infiltrate my head, turning the experience sour and dirty.

Any man who sleeps with another man or has the urge to is an abomination. They have more sin than the Holy Spirit can forgive. Jesus didn't die on the cross to save homosexuals. Even if they could be saved, they wouldn't be worth it.

Turning onto my side, I hug my pillow as tears fill my eyes, and my throat tightens. I've lived my entire life for my parents. Tried to be what they wanted. Even in my relationship with Tim, I never let things get further than making out. We never got each other off or got off in front of each other. He begged, but I always said no.

I wanted to do the best I could to follow what my father wanted. I wanted to wait for marriage.

Now, I'm sullied. Dirty. Used.

But how can something that felt so good be so wrong?

The way my body accepted him is world changing.

Virginity is a misogynistic construct to give value to young girls.

I wish I had someone to call. A friend to talk it out with. All the jumbled thoughts running through my mind that they could pick apart and help me find the truth. I know my father's words are based in bias and hate, but I was raised to believe it too.

When you hear something over and over, you start to believe it. My father is wrong, logically I know that. But knowing he thinks I'm an abomination, disgusting, and going to hell hurts. To know he thinks I'm gay as a choice, like I consciously made the decision to make my life harder, hurts. If anything, I tried to be straight. I tried to find girls that I could be interested in but from that first kiss from Tim, I knew it was over for me. No girl could ever feel as right as that did.

Now, after the last twenty-four hours, it's even more ingrained into my soul. I need a man.

Quiet sobs wrack my body as I hide my face in my pillow. I have nothing to show for my life. The clothes I have I got second-hand since Mom and Dad kicked me out, and the same goes for my bedding. I don't have any of my things. No pictures, none of my art supplies or old sketchbooks. Not the teddy bear my grandmother gave me when I was born. Not what I needed for school, like my computer. Nothing. They kept my entire life.

The memory of reading Leviticus in my living room while my mom wailed prayers on her knees and my father chanted scripture with his bible and a wooden cross plays through my mind. The bible preaches forgiveness, tells Christians not to judge, to help others, yet here I am. Alone.

I'm not sure how long I lie there, crying into the scratchy fabric of my cheap sheets, but eventually the tears slow and I'm able to fall asleep.

Eleven

Oliver

I have a strange twinge as he walks out of the door and out of my life.

It isn't my usual post-fuck euphoria. Not regret. I don't ever experience regret. I cannot put a finger on what it is.

Maybe I feel a little bad as I stand on the balcony watching him climb into the Uber. I did my best to mitigate the drop he'll have after the experience, with lots of aftercare, but I still expect it to happen. Especially with as little support as I can only guess he has. Will his roommate take care of him?

I root my feet in place, not allowing myself to follow the cab so I'd know where he lives. I know the dorm, but not the floor or number. It would be so easy to pay some computer science major to hack into the database.

Stop.

This line of eventuality won't work, and I won't allow myself to go down that road. The biggest poison to the mind is hope. I know what I am allowed.

The helicopter passes overhead, and I force myself to regain my composure. If anyone will see through me, it will be Owen. We are too much alike for him not to use his magic twin powers to suss out every thought in my head.

"How was it?" Owen asks as if on command, taking his place in one of the chairs around the fire pit.

"Fantastic." I offer him a smile as I refill my drink. "Want one?"

"Yes. I need one. You owe me." He tips his head back, acting over dramatic.

"I've already offered the same in return for your effort." I hold the glass over his turned-up face.

He snatches it out of my hands and downs it. "My mental health is not good enough to ever do that alone again. I will run myself on a knife and die in the most sensational act ever right on the dinner table if you ever force me to."

"You weren't alone." I lift a brow, not giving him an inch. "Don't tell me Olivia ditched out as well."

"She didn't, but you know she's useless at managing mother and that boyfriend of hers. He's a stuffed shirt." Owen shoves out of the seat, returning to the bar to refill his drink. He rarely drinks like this, which has me slightly concerned.

"And what made it different from every other dinner that made this one so bad?" Our mother is a lot, but we're used to living with her. We are all used to it.

"She asked me when I'm going to settle down!" He waves his arms theatrically, spilling half his drink.

"Why? What did you do?" I cross my ankle over my knee, studying my brother.

"Nothing. All the focus was on me because you weren't there. You know you're her favorite."

"You're the favorite. You're her sweet baby boy. She's not asking me about marriage." Thankfully. I'm not ready to deal with her antics. Olivia has been the focus of them since she got engaged.

"No, because she expects you to be a fuck boy until you take over for dad." He crosses his arms and then his legs, but then uncrosses them to adjust his seat, ending up looking like a pretzel. "She knows I'm too" — he waves at himself — "fucked up to do any of that nonsense, so I think she's got it in her head to marry me for political gain."

"Isn't she already using Olivia for that?" I set my drink aside and rub my temples. The last thing I need is my brother to have a meltdown. Not when I am so on edge.

"Why not have two instead of one?" Owen hasn't resigned himself to our fates like Olivia and I have. He has some strange resistance to our station in life and the rules that come with it.

"What are you going to do?"

"I don't know yet." Which means he's planning a coup d'état.

"Owen, she won't. Let it blow over. I'll be at dinner next month, and if she's still plotting, we'll figure out what to do."

"If she tries to force me to marry someone, I don't know what I'll do."

I cock my head, appraising him again. "Don't do something drastic." As far as I knew, Owen liked women, and mother finding someone to be obsessed with him wouldn't be the end of the world. He isn't dating anyone and hasn't in a while.

"I see that look." He points a finger at me. "It's not a good idea, and if I'm backed into a corner, I'm going to make it everyone's problem."

"Please calm down."

"I'm not kidding."

I sigh. At least this presents a new distraction to keep my

mind off finding kitten. "We do not need another incident like freshman year."

"If you think that was bad, do not test me."

I scrub a hand over my face and get to my feet. "I am not doing anything. You know I'm not on her side."

Owen narrows his eyes. "I saw the look on your face."

"Nonsense. You saw no such thing. I was processing the situation while trying to come up with a distraction for mother."

"So you'll help me then?" He stands, bringing us eye to eye.

"Of course. You know you come first." I hold out my hand. "Let me get you another drink and put you to bed."

He reluctantly hands over his crystal tumbler. "What's in your mind?"

"I don't know. I'll have to turn her attention to me if she's serious, but I don't know how. It doesn't matter. I told you if she's still out of her mind next month, we will plot."

He searches my face, lower lip trembling. Anyone else would miss it, but I know him too well. I see through him. He is really worked up over this. "Promise me."

"I promise you. I will always take care of you."

He nods and lets me take him to bed.

I sit in his chaise lounge while he flops on to the mattress, still in his dress clothes. "Don't you want to change?"

"Why does our entire apartment smell like sex?"

"Because you're having a stroke? Does it smell like toast?" I refuse to engage with his line of questioning.

"Don't patronize me. I know you had someone here, even if you turned off all the cameras."

"I told you I'd be entertaining. Why does it matter?" I sip my drink, keeping my mask in place.

"Because it feels different."

I lift a shoulder and shrug it off. "Perhaps it's because you're all worked up."

"Who was he?"

"I don't have a clue. I didn't catch his name." My lips curve up when that seems to relax him.

"You needed a whole twenty-four hours?"

"I had things to work out, and what better way?" We grew up verbally sparring in our house. If one wasn't quick on their feet, we ate them alive. I don't regret it. It gave me the skills to lie when I need to and hold my ground against any opponent.

"Hurry up. Our car is waiting." I stand in loose sweats, with my mask under one arm in the doorway of Owen's room.

"We pay them to wait. What's gotten into you?" Owen isn't even dressed. He's lying draped over his bed with his head hanging off the end.

"I need a release," I reply, coldly. "And since you've said you won't spar with me anymore this week, I want to get to our first practice."

"It's been over a month. Still?"

"I don't have a clue what you're referring to."

He sits up, narrowing his eyes. "The guy. The one you had here."

"What of him?"

"It's been like six weeks. Why are you still bothered?" Owen slowly gets to his feet.

I don't like where this is going at all. "I'm not. I'm trying to get to our fencing practice."

He checks his watch. "Over an hour early. I know you like to be punctual, but this is excessive."

"I told you. I need a release, and since you won't let me run you through with my blade, I'll go take out my mood on the new victims." I tap my foot, knowing it will drive him mad.

He looks at my foot, then returns his gaze to mine. "I know you think you're being evasive, but really, this is only more evidence to my point."

"What ever are you talking about?"

"You have been in a *mood*. You insist on being at the gym hours a day when your course load is demanding and . . ." He marks off his fingers as he speaks. "Now you're refusing to talk about it. I've known you your whole life. If you think I can't read you, you're being naïve."

"Have you considered I may need this because my course load is overwhelming, in subject areas I despise because our parents insisted on me double majoring in fucking business?" I throw back at him.

"You could have taken those classes earlier. You put them all off to the end." He shuffles over to his dresser and just stands there.

"Because they are unpleasant." I stare at him, hoping the pressure will give him some motivation to get moving.

"It still doesn't explain why you are like this. Don't act like you struggle. You love outdoing everyone, even in classes you hate."

"Irrelevant. I still have to go to them, and then work with Father after we graduate." I'm not in the mood for this. "Will you get dressed so we can go?"

"Not until you answer." Owen crosses his arms over his chest.

"I'll take the car and you can call another." I turn on my heel and walk out of the room.

He slips into the elevator as the doors close. He hasn't changed, but he has a duffle over his shoulder. "Will you get laid or hire a prostitute to beat or something?"

"For what?" I ask, feigning innocence.

"So you don't kill all of the freshmen?"

Silence engulfs the ride, but I'm not about to let it bother me when sweet release is only a few blocks away.

The crisp October air promises winter as I step from our car service in front of the Goldstein building, which houses our practice facility. Our campus is tucked just above lower Manhattan, nestled into Greenwich Village. One of the most beautiful in the world. Making my penthouse in the West Village the perfect commute.

I can already taste the quieting of my mind. It will be the only way I'll get through until someone else catches my fancy.

But relief is short-lived when my worst nightmare emerges into waking life in the form of a beautiful boy.

Twelve

Isaac

F or weeks I've been anticipating today. Our first fencing practice. I didn't sleep well last night, spent more of my time drawing the eyes that haunt me than closing my own. My notebooks are full of him. Every inch of blank space is covered in his eyes, fingers, lips.

In the emptiness of darkness, he invades my mind when I have nothing left to distract me. My blood heats, and my skin becomes over sensitive. I can only hope that Colin is fast asleep when my breathing picks up and the little whimpers I can't keep inside escape. Most nights I force myself to ignore the lust licking at me, but a few times I've been weak.

"Come on!" Colin's excitement pulls me from my memories. "It's time to hit our teammates with weapons!" He wraps his arm around my neck, forcing me to lean over since he's shorter. His shoulder-length blond hair is pulled back into a ponytail today instead of flying around his face in the wind.

It took us a week of living together to realize we were both on the fencing team. He's not on a scholarship, though. I'm not sure how I managed to get one since I'm barely a B-rated fencer, but here we are. I'm hoping to be able to squeeze in some art classes as electives while I'm here. I want to be an art major, but my parents refused to help me with the scholarship paperwork if I didn't do biblical studies.

Colin is talking about the history of the Goldstein building where the fencing space is. All I get from it is blah, blah, blah, some rich guy donated a lot of money to the school and his kid was a foilist.

I open the tall wood door with glass panels, and Colin walks through first.

"Have you ever been here for a tournament?" Colin leads me down the hallway to the impressive armory. My last club had a closet that was always a disaster, but this is an entire room. There's space for everyone on the team to store their stuff so it doesn't get mixed up or damaged. There are benches with room for our backpacks or jackets.

The practice equipment of those around me is better than my *good* stuff. My face heats as I take it all in. What am I doing here? I don't fit in or belong. I'm a peon. A peasant compared to these guys.

"Let's go boys!" Coach Kennedy hollers from the doorway of the armory. "You can grab equipment after introductions."

I trail my fingers over my foil grips. I appear to be the only one who doesn't use a pistol grip on foil.

My foils are old, and I had to work hard to afford them. They're also cheap because price matters when you don't have enough money. This sport is expensive, and my parents didn't like to pay for things.

I guess I stall too long in front of the gear because Colin grabs my shirt and pulls me toward the door.

"Sorry," I mumble and follow him out. He's so excited he's almost vibrating with energy. It's infectious, and I find myself smiling and getting excited too.

While we messed around with sparing a few times in the last few weeks, Colin is a sabreist while I'm a foilist. The swords and rules are different. I have the bruises on my arms to prove how much I suck with a sabre.

In the main room of the building there are three stripes set up, perpendicular from each other, with room for an audience against the long wall. The space is huge, with high ceilings and beautiful windows to let in natural light. The wood floors are polished to within an inch of their lives, too. Everything about this place reminds me of how I don't fit in.

Our coach introduces himself, tells us about his journey to the Olympics, and his passion for helping others perfect their sport. All while making it abundantly clear that he will not accept any slacking off. We get our practice and workout schedules along with our competitions. It's going to be a busy semester.

He separates us into our specialties so we can get to know the guys we will be practicing against when the doors open behind us. Everyone turns and watches as two guys stride in like they own the place.

There's something familiar in the way they move and flashes of the night I spent in the penthouse tickle my brain. They're tall and hold this air of sophistication I will never have. They command the room, have everyone's attention, and the closer they get the further my stomach sinks.

Oh God.

No.

Please.

The air in my lungs evaporates as one of them meets my gaze. For a split second, faster than a blink, surprise is there, but it's gone in an instant.

"Ah, boys, nice of you to join us." Coach Kennedy's tone tells everyone how unhappy he is with their tardiness. But his voice is an echo in my head. I swear I can hear this man's heartbeat over my own.

He knows parts of me that I don't know about myself, and now I'll have to see him every day at practice.

He blinks and looks away from me, both of them coming to a stop next to our coach.

"Apologies Coach, we had to take a call from our father."

They shake hands with him and turn to face the group when Coach calls another guy forward.

"Now that we're all here, let's meet your captains." Coach claps. "Owen Godfrey is the sabre captain, Oliver Godfrey for foils, and Ryan Abbott is for epees."

The abrupt sound of clapping jolts my hands to clap on instinct so as to not stand out.

Oliver Godfrey.

That's the name of the man I sold my virginity to and my new team captain.

My body doesn't know how to react. I want to cry and vomit and punch him all at the same time. Why do I feel betrayed? He didn't know I'm on the fencing team any more than I could have known he is, yet some part of me says he tricked me. That he's messing with me on purpose.

And he has a twin? What the hell is that?

I flick my eyes over to the man who looks just like the one I spent time with. Sold myself to.

He meets my gaze that says he's trying to figure me out. Like he noticed that swift shift in Oliver when he saw me, but how is that possible?

My face is hot, and my mouth is dry, and I just want to leave. I want to pretend this isn't happening and go back to my life.

I thought I was doing okay after this man turned my world upside down, but this tells me exactly how wrong I was.

"How long have you been fencing?" His voice sends an electric pulse up my spine and snaps my attention back to him. Oliver is staring at me like he expects an answer.

"Wh—what?" My dry throat has my voice breaking.

"How long have you been fencing?" He looks bored or maybe irritated. I didn't hear him the first time. Why is he asking me first? There are other guys around me.

"Oh, um, a couple years."

Everyone in the group is silent and looks between themselves like what I've said is wrong. My cheeks burn with embarrassment, and I straighten my spine as I face off with Oliver.

"I've worked really hard to be here. I've earned my spot on this team just like everybody else." I'm proud of myself when my voice is strong and doesn't waiver.

"I've been fencing for over a decade, and you think you're as good as me?" He steps closer, into my personal space so all I can see is him. All I can smell is his expensive cologne. That woody, warm spice, leather, and musk that I've never smelled on anyone else is permanently embedded into my brain.

My pulse spikes at the memory the scent invokes, and I almost gasp. I want that smell wrapped around me like a pleasure-filled blanket.

"I didn't say I was as good as you." My voice isn't as strong now, and I hate myself for the weakness. "Nothing about me is, but I'm here anyway."

What the hell did I just say?

I close my eyes for a second in a useless attempt to pull back the emotions threatening to choke me, but I can't breathe. Not with him so close.

Knowing I shouldn't show this man weakness, I do it anyway and all but run into the first room I find.

I'm a coward.

How am I going to make it through the season with him in my face all the time? As much as it would hurt, it would be so much better if he just pretended I didn't exist.

I throw myself in a corner and slide down the wall until I can bury my face against my knees. I try to breathe, but I can't get his scent out of my nose or my lungs. It's a whisper in my mind, and I hate how badly I crave it.

"Hey." Colin's voice is soft, but it still makes me jump. "What's going on?"

I sniffle and wipe at my face, hating myself for the weakness. Why does everything have to be so hard?

"It's Oliver." I manage to force his name from my trembling lips.

"What is? Besides the world's most arrogant dick?" Colin sits next to me, shoulder to shoulder, on the floor.

"That's who I was with." My broken words hang in the air between us for a minute before understanding transforms Colin's face.

"Oh, for fuck's sake." Colin laughs, and once again embarrassment heats my cheeks. "I bet it was good, though. He's just cocky enough to know what he's doing. Is he gay? I don't think I've ever seen him with a guy. Maybe he's bi or pan . . ."

Colin is talking like he knows Oliver. I know his family is rich, but Oliver's penthouse was a whole other level of wealthy.

"Wait, do you know him?"

"Of course, I do." Colin shrugs. "Our parents mingle in . . . similar circles, and my sister was obsessed with Owen for a minute a few years ago."

I open my mouth to ask another question, but Oliver appears in the doorway.

"This is not a book club meeting. Stop gossiping and get back to work." That demanding, posh tone is like a slap in the face. I loved it when we were locked away, but here, in this space that should be safe, it forces me to acknowledge that I can't have him. I don't mean anything to him.

He said he cared while I was there, but if he did, wouldn't he have called me? Something. Anything. But it's been radio silence. I'm just as guilty of not reaching out, but I couldn't make myself any more vulnerable to him.

"Oh fuck off, pretty boy," Colin huffs.

"Don't you have a senator's son to de-virgin while daddy is away on an important vote?" Oliver sneers down his nose at Colin like he was somehow beneath him.

Excuse me?

I glance at Colin, who has a devious smile on his face as he stands and saunters up to Oliver.

"Aww, you don't have to be jealous. I'm not going to steal your toy." Colin reaches to pat Oliver's cheek, but Oliver catches his wrist. "This time."

Steal his toy?

Does he mean me?

That idea has me warring with myself. Part of me is very turned on by the idea of being Oliver's toy, but the other part of me is offended. And confused.

This time?

Oliver's mouth twists in a sneer. "I don't sleep with the pretend rich, so you're not stealing from me."

"What does that even mean?" Colin asks, and it surprises me he's indulging Oliver.

"They have to work so hard to pretend to be one of us. So much scamming. It's a little desperate. Don't you think?" Oliver grimaces.

"Semantics. Don't pretend like you don't remember," Colin shoots back.

"I don't have a clue what you're referring to." Oliver plays stupid well, but Colin isn't a liar.

Colin glances back and winks. "I guess I know why you were such a prick to that poor guy after I found him in the pool house." Colin shrugs while Oliver returns a look I could only describe as "Already hiring a hitman in his head."

That expression scares me, yet I want him to touch me. I want to know what he'll do, how he'll make my body pay for his anger.

This reaction isn't normal. I scrub my hands over my face and take a deep breath. I have to fight my connection to him. He's nothing but my captain.

Colin pulls his wrist from Oliver's grasp and shoves past him, leaving me with the one man I don't think I can stay away from.

Our gazes are locked as I stand and square my shoulders, prepared to spar with him in more ways than one.

"Oliver." His name feels strange on my tongue. I swear I see him hide a flinch, but he's so good at hiding behind this mask. This side of him isn't the same one I was with.

"Don't expect acknowledgement or special treatment." That cold mask is firmly in place.

I cross the room, and he watches me like a hunter stalking prey. I do my best not to let him see weakness, keeping my spine straight, my shoulders squared, and my head high.

"I don't want special treatment." I stop a foot from him. "Just pretend I don't exist and we'll be fine."

It's interesting to know his mind is spinning, but his face is set in stone. He's so much smarter than me, quicker on his feet, always ready with a comeback.

"You don't exist. Not even on this team until you've proven yourself."

Thirteen

Oliver

Was it mean? Undoubtably, but am I turned on? Absolutely.

Isaac's pretty little face shifts through the full range of emotions. First confusion, then it falls, filled with hurt, and finally anger. I can almost taste the look he gives me.

Not the time to get hard.

Not in these restrictive sweats. Nor would I give him the satisfaction. He opens his mouth to speak, but I hold up a finger.

"We don't know each other. We aren't friends, and you are new to this team and yet to prove yourself. Go find a partner so we can warm up." My words are curt. I don't trust myself around him, that much I'm sure of.

My sanctuary morphs into hell, and I can't escape fast enough when practice is through. I need a gallon of alcohol. I take my spare button-down from my locker and don't bother with a shower. The last thing I need is to see Isaac naked. Lord help us all. How easy it would be to find him naked in the showers and pin him to the wall and take the last month of pent up need out on his ass.

I close my eyes, swallowing hard.

"You can't lie to me anymore." Owen points the tip of his sabre at my bare chest. "I saw it."

"Your eyes deceive you. You saw nothing."

He scoffs. "I may spend most of my time in a void, but I was paying attention today."

"I don't have time for this. I have a date."

"*What?*" Owen asks, and I see Colin's head pop up behind him.

Nosy fucking bastards.

"With the best bottle of Bourbon I can find." And this is how I find myself and a group of the seniors at the Walker Hotel in Tribeca of all places.

I love the Golden Age aesthetic of the place and the bar was similarly modeled. Cozy and modern, but with all the refinement that went out of style after the 1920s. It has an old-world fleeting feel to it, and it almost takes my mind off Isaac.

Alcohol soaks into my blood as I throw back glass after glass, talking myself down from the situation. Who is this little prick after all, and why did he bring out such a reaction in me?

It was good I don't know his last name. A first name could make him anyone. I don't know his family or his connections. There have to be hundreds of Isaacs going to school here. This means ignoring the tiny detail that his full name would be on our roster, but I digress, I would take the hits as they come.

"Isn't that the new kid?" Archer Walton nods at the door.

There stand Colin and Isaac, glancing around.

I look at my brother, who conveniently avoids my eyes, chatting with Dean Byron. A prodigy in the sabre. Had he not been in his sophomore year, he would have been captain over

Owen. This feels like a trap, and I don't react well to being caged.

I grab the bottle of bourbon off the bar and refill my glass.

Alcohol will either fix this night or make it worse.

And at the moment I don't care which. My buzz sets in and rational thought quickly takes a backseat.

I like alcohol because it makes things easier. It strips away all our inhibitions, leaving who people truly are on full display. If you ever want to know a true character of a man, get him blackout drunk and watch closely. If they put themselves in the position they will. Alcohol is only the vehicle and excuse.

I try to follow the conversation the other guys are having, but it's boring, and I don't care about teams and who's improved and who's favored for the national team trials. My parents would never dream of letting Owen and me draw attention to ourselves on an international stage like that. This little flight of fancy ends the minute we graduate, and if we continue, it would be in the way men play pickle ball at the Y on their weekends to escape their wives, not in any professional capacity.

My gaze drifts across the bar to see what Isaac is doing. He lingers on the edge of the group, laughing. Isn't he too young to be in a bar? I have half a mind to call Colin's father and tell him what his son is up to. But as doing that would involve my father and make his social life unpleasant, I resist the urge.

A much older man approaches Isaac. He wears a pullover on top of a button-down, and too tight, off-the-rack slacks. Brown loafers without socks, and his hair styled in a slick-back cut. A finance bro.

I barely hold back a gag.

Isaac blushes, falling all over himself and flattered by the man's attention.

Red engulfs my vision, and I'm on my feet, shoving through people.

"What do you think you're doing?" I drop my voice, making it silky sweet while my eyes could kill.

"What's it look like I'm doing?" Isaac's words come with a slight hitch, telling me he knew exactly what he was doing. His half-ass denial makes me more irate than if he'd just owned it.

"Why are you here? There are thirteen thousand bars in Manhattan alone and you're in this one."

"Because this is where the team is hanging out, and Colin invited me." The boy grew bolder.

"You're not even old enough to be here," I snap.

"Colin said it doesn't matter. They don't check IDs."

I shoot Colin a snarl. He is going to be a problem. "And you thought coming to the bar I was at was the best idea? To what end?"

He half shrugs. "I wanted to get to know the team."

"And you were getting to know the team, sitting on the fringe, flirting with guys ten years older than you?"

"They were nice." Isaac avoids my eyes.

"You wanted me to see."

He still won't look at me.

"Go home." I can feel my resolve slipping. I don't need this this year.

"Is there some sort of issue?" Finance bro number one asks.

"Yes, you're my current issue."

"Whoa, whoa, no need to overreact. He was flirting with us."

I give Isaac a scathing glare. "Yes, the barely eighteen-year-old with daddy issues is responding to your advances. Please grow up and find someone your age."

Finance bro number two holds up his hands. "He's legal. You can't fault us for that."

"He's not for you." I step up to him. "And if you know what's good for you, you'll leave."

"What claim do you have to him?" the first guy asks.

"He's mine." I ignore the look Isaac gives me when I say it, keeping my focus on the guys.

"He doesn't look like he's yours. Maybe it's your problem he wants to talk to other guys." Guy number two has a mouth on him.

"It's about to be your problem if you don't leave."

"My problem?" one of the finance bros asks. "How you gonna do that?"

"I don't know who you think runs this city, and maybe you're new to money and think flaunting it makes you appear to be some hotshot. Maybe you think you're something because you're earning a six-figure paycheck. But if you don't step off, I will make sure you're not allowed in any bar in lower Manhattan again. That's how it will be your problem. You'll find yourself working at some bank in Iowa when I'm done with you, wishing you had walked out of the bar tonight."

The guys exchange a look and laugh.

"Like you could do that," the second guy hedges.

I pull my card out of my pocket. "Not only could I do that, but your job prospects are vanishing with every word you say."

"Fuck," the first says, before passing it to the other. "We don't want any trouble with your father, man."

"Crap. I'm sorry. I thought you were some college kid speaking out of turn. We don't mean anything."

"Maybe you should consider what you're starting before you speak to strangers." I turn on Isaac, done with the two guys. "I'm going to ask you one more time. What do you think you're doing here? Trying to elicit a reaction? You got one. Now leave before you make your punishment worse."

Isaac crosses his arms over his chest in the cutest, pissiest way. "My punishment? I'm not a child."

"You heard me."

"I could just go to another bar and meet someone else."

"You could, but you didn't. You came to a place you knew I'd be. You asked for this." I step closer, looking down my nose. "If you want me to be a prick, I'll be a prick."

"You can't just stop everyone from speaking to me." Isaac half glances at Colin, like: can he do that?

"Would you care to make that a wager? Because I am absolutely petty enough to put a moratorium on speaking to you."

"That's not even enforceable."

"Watch me."

Fourteen

Oliver

The next day I begin practice as usual, and Isaac falls into the team's routine, except no one speaks to him. I've put a moratorium on it. I despise games, but if Isaac wants to play, we'll play. He wanted to taste my jealousy, so I deliver the full effect of it. Colin was over with Owen and the sabre group, so Isaac has no one to rescue him. It's the perfect team building exercise to start off the year, combined with a little light hazing.

By the third day rage flickers in Isaac's eyes, and I won't ever admit it out loud, but it turns me on.

"Take a water break, and then we are going to be sparring," Coach Kennedy says softly. He is in a mood today. He's the type of guy who has never raised his voice in his life. A three-time gold medalist and many time national champion, his discipline was world renowned. I'm a little envious of Kennedy. Must be nice to be let out of all his family obligations to fight for the rest of his life.

I don't know what has gotten into him, but I'm not going to deal with it. If he wants us sparring half of practice instead of running drills, I won't complain.

When we come back to the piste, he tosses us color arm bands, dividing us into teams.

"We are having a team relay." Which means we all have to face all three opponents of the other team, and since he put Isaac on the other side, I have to face him for at least one round. "Three times three and then rotate. Upperclassmen rotate in as refs when you're not on the piste."

Isaac is on the opposite end of the piste from Charlie. I nod him off. "Let me take this one first."

Charlie glances between us. "Going to school the new kid?"

I shrug.

He laughs. "Enjoy it."

Isaac fumes, but there is nothing he can do about my ambush. He has to spar me, and no one will offer to switch with him when I'd made a point to come fight him first. We connect our body lines and take our places behind our en-garde line and wait for Coach Kennedy to tell us to go.

Isaac doesn't say a word, not even when the ref tells us to go.

He jumps forward, but I deflect easily, sending him scampering backward.

"So much rage." I advance slowly, playing with him.

I see a flash of his curled lip before he lunges.

Another deflection, and I riposte in to touch on his shoulder, barely inside his chest to have the board flash green for my point. "You're not protecting your shoulder when you lunge. You need to lift your foil another two inches, or a good fighter will exploit the weakness every time."

He ignores my correction, and we back off to reset on the en-garde lines.

Our ref tells us to go again.

I don't move.

He takes a step forward, testing my defenses.

I tap his foil, holding my ground.

He shoves forward, and I parry his attack. Lazily.

Isaac grunts, springing forward in an aggressive attack.

I give, stepping backward, deflecting.

"Get it out."

He blows out a breath and sprints in a wild plunge.

Our foils meet, crossing, bringing us face to face with locked blades, a rare occurrence with a foil, but I'm having too much fun to stick to form. "Give me all your rage."

He hisses in frustration. "Stop talking to me."

"Can you not converse and spar? Shame. It can be so erotic when done right."

"This is not some twisted foreplay." He shoves out of the lock and retreats.

"Isn't it?" I ask, chasing him.

Isaac attempts to parry and riposte, but I touch.

Our time is called, and we reposition to start our second match. Isaac pulls off his mask to wipe his forehead, his hair damp with sweat.

I adjust myself, my cup getting uncomfortable. Worst time to get a hard-on. "Still not speaking to me?"

His dark eyes lock with mine, but he doesn't answer. He puts his mask back on and takes his line.

"Come get me, kitten," I say after our ref calls it.

He doesn't move, so I go after him. He parries and strikes, getting in a touch.

"Kitten's getting the first touch. Well done." I clap as I return to my line to reset.

"Stop."

"I know you've been thinking about it." I blatantly adjust myself while he watches.

"You're insufferable," he says, but his eyes drop to my hand.

"Thank you." I allow him come at me, slowing the match down as much as possible to build his rage.

"It wasn't a compliment." He feints, but not well.

I deflect, and counterattack, diving him back to score another touch. "Maybe not to you."

We return to our lines.

I lunge, catching him off guard, getting in a touch, but I don't back off, dropping my voice. "But I don't need to see your face to know the thought of my cock hard for you has your mouth watering. Don't worry, I'm thinking about it down your throat too."

"That's not what I'm thinking about." The rage in his tone tells me he's lying.

"If you say so."

He loses all form, coming at me with an aggression I haven't seen in him, forcing me to retreat. I beat his blade and shove forward in a remise. He stumbles back, losing his footwork, and I get a touch.

"Excellent. I want to see more of that."

"What?" he asks, confusion coloring his tone.

I don't bother to fight the last ten seconds of the match. "The rage. If you can bottle it and stick to your form and footwork with it, you'll be a much better fencer. Might even get that A rating."

He must not like my assessment because he pulls off his mask and stalks off the piste.

"We have one more match," I call after him.

"You've already won two."

I take off my mask, coming up behind him. "And? This isn't a tournament. Get back to the line."

Isaac turns like he would spit something vile my way. He sets his teeth, anger flickering in his gaze.

"If we weren't in a room full of people, I'd take you right here. I'd force you to the floor with one knee on your chest and force those beautiful lips open to shove my cock down your throat."

He wasn't expecting that. He blinks and bites back a groan.

"You'd like that, wouldn't you? Me on top of you fucking your face." I don't need confirmation. His big, expressive eyes tell me all I need.

"No, I wouldn't." His voice quivers just a little, but it's enough.

"Liar."

He stiffens. "I hate you."

"I know, but that doesn't mean you want me any less." I tell myself to walk away. To stop playing with him, but I can't.

His chest heaves as he tries to contain himself.

"How badly do you want me to fuck you after destroying you in this last match?"

Isaac shakes with rage.

I drink it from him, and it only makes me want him more. This is quickly becoming a dangerous game. One I can't win. Even if we keep fucking, there is no happy ending. Telling myself as much worked in the past, but it doesn't now. I want to keep playing, and I don't want anyone else to touch him.

Isaac is becoming a real problem for me.

"Come back to the line," I whisper.

"Fine."

I walk backward, keeping my eyes on him. The things I would do if he were mine.

I have to find a reprieve before I break and go against all my rules.

Fifteen

Isaac

I don't know how he did it, but no one will talk to me except Colin. For the last week, all the guys on the team basically pretend I don't exist unless I'm sparing with them. People in my classes too. I'm tired of playing his stupid game.

After another infuriating class, I storm back to my room and throw my backpack onto my bed, where it bounces and smacks into the wall with a thud.

Colin lifts his eyes from his laptop screen and smirks. "Trouble in paradise?"

"Shut up." I pace the length of our room, furious he played me so easily. "If you aren't going to help, then zip it."

"Oh sweet summer child, I am helping you." Colin closes the laptop with a click and stretches out on his bed.

"How? How are you helping me? You're the only person on campus who will speak to me." I throw my hands in the air, eyes perated that this is even possible. How did he get to literally everyone I come into contact with?

"Have you talked to him?"

I whirl around. "Talked to him? Why on earth would I do that? He's the reason behind all of this!"

Colin sighs and stands up, then grabs my shoulders.

"You really need to learn how to deal with spoiled rich boys. Lesson one: everything is a game. Lesson two: You will not win. Ever. It's not a fair fight. These boys have been playing mind games since they were old enough to think." I huff and open my mouth to respond, but he puts his hand over my mouth, so I glare. "Where was I? Lesson...something. I don't know. The Godfrey twins are a league of their own. I get no higher pleasure than by getting under their skin. I do so by being a brat and shoving my sexuality in their faces. You, my sweet innocent friend, are already under Oliver's skin. It's clear as day to anyone who knows him."

"Is there a point to your monologue?" I cross my arms when what I really want to do is beg Oliver to take me. *Stop it!*

"Yes, there is." Colin pats me on the head like I'm a child. "Ask him what it will take to make this cone of silence stop. If I know him at all, it'll be some kind of dominance display. He's like a rooster, all puffed up. He has to prove how in charge he is. Let him get his cock out and he'll be fine." He waves his hand like it's silly, but Oliver having command over me is one of the best feelings I've ever experienced. I want it so bad it hurts. It haunts my dreams.

"Roosters? His—really? No, never mind. Don't distract me. Why won't you tell me how he did it?" I demand like I have multiple times, every day, for the last week.

"I know about all kinds of cocks." Colin winks at me. "And it's not my business to spoil how he does things. Just trust me.

I sigh and finally break, leaning my forehead onto my only friend's shoulder. "At the bar, he said something about punishment. Do you think that's what this is? The silent treatment on steroids?"

Colin pats my head again and laughs. "Oh, absolutely not. He has something planned. I guarantee it."

"Ugh!" That thought shouldn't entice me. He's a jerk. Sure, I lost my virginity to him, but I should experience other people too, right? "I don't want to give in. That just tells him he can play me."

"Oh honey, he *can* play you, and he will. He's basically a master at playing people at this point."

"Should I even be playing his game? Is it worth trying to get to know him and letting him control my life? I just left my dad, who was controlling me with the threat of damnation. How is this better?" The fear of being ripped apart by Oliver is already there in my chest. He will destroy what little of myself I have left. I wasn't even able to figure out who I really am in my parents' house, but I have a feeling allowing Oliver to have access to me will mold me so no one else will be able to fit. I will be left broken and unusable to anyone but him.

"I will help you navigate the waters of spoiled rich boys. Will it be a painless process? Of course not. Will it be worth it? Solid maybe." Colin shrugs like it doesn't matter, like this isn't a big deal. To him, I guess it isn't since he grew up in it and knows the score.

"I'm scared," I whisper.

It's quiet for a moment as my words sink into the walls of our room.

"You're . . . different," Colin finally says.

I stand and look at him, confused. "What does that mean? Different how? From what?"

"I've grown up around—the Godfrey twins. While we definitely aren't friends, I know how Oliver and Owen operate, which is how I get under their skin to annoy them." Colin sits on his bed, and I sit on mine across from him. "But I've never seen Oliver react to anyone like he does you. Ever. Owen sees it too. He's watching Oliver as well, and that's telling. Owen doesn't know what to expect from his *twin* brother."

"Why is that important?" I really don't understand these people.

"Because Oliver is always in control, always has a comeback, an answer, never lets his emotions control him. He's never left floundering. You unbalance him. Make him act rashly. It means you've gotten to him. You have power over him too, you just have to figure out how to wield it."

"I don't know how to do that."

"I told you, I'll help." Colin grabs his laptop and backpack, leaving me alone to digest what he's said.

How do I have any power over Oliver?

He's untouchable.

Colin said to talk to him, but I don't know what to say besides "stop being a jerk", and I don't think that will get me anywhere.

With a sigh, I pick up my phone and open my messages.

> ISAAC: Make the silent treatment stop.

> OLIVER: Demands will get you nowhere.

> ISAAC: So you're talking to me? That makes 2 people.

> OLIVER: After you admit you were wrong. We can discuss punishments, kitten.

> ISAAC: How was the silent treatment not punishment?

Crap. Colin was right. Oliver has something up his sleeve, and I'm either going to love it or hate it.

> OLIVER: It's a consequence of your actions.
> Much different than a punishment.

> ISAAC: What am I being punished for? Having a social life?

> OLIVER: I won't be taking questions until after you've accepted your punishment.

> ISAAC: What is the punishment?

> OLIVER: You're either willing to accept the punishment or not. You don't get to decide after hearing what it is.

An erotic kind of fear tickles my stomach. I'm sure he'll find a way to use my body against me, use me for his pleasure, but why does that idea turn me on?

I'm broken.

I deserve to be punished for the sins I've committed and will continue to commit without repentance. I'm not sorry for doing them, only sorry that they're wrong.

> ISAAC: What's the punishment?

> OLIVER: Agree to the punishment and find out.

I need to know more. If I really do have some kind of power over Oliver, I have to be around him to figure out what it is.

Taking a deep breath, I type out the next message.

> ISAAC: Fine. I agree.

Sixteen

Oliver

> OLIVER: You're exquisite when you're angry.

> ISAAC: What?

I laugh, tossing my phone on the table to make him wait for his answers. He made me wait a week, so I'll drag this out. I have a paper to write, and this is the first time I've felt calm since I'd met Isaac. I need to utilize it while I can. My phone keeps buzzing, but I don't return to it until after midnight to a barrage of texts from Isaac.

> ISAAC: You don't know what I look like.

> ISAAC: Hello?

> ISAAC: I agreed to your terms. What is my punishment?

ISAAC: Is my punishment you ignoring me, too? Pretty sure that's a reward.

ISAAC: Ugh! Just tell me.

ISAAC: YOU ARE INFURIATING!

"Baby, you're playing right into my hands." But I wouldn't tell him that.

"What are you laughing about?" Owen asks.

I hadn't heard him come in. "Are you going to be judgmental?"

"Like you need to ask. Is this about that" — he waves his hand — "new kid on the team?"

"Isaac, and yes." I fix him in a stare and wait for him to comment.

"Is he the guy you had here?"

"Yes." My word is curt.

"What's your deal with him?" Owen sits on the arm of the chair across from me.

"What exactly are you inquiring about?"

"You know what I mean. You like him or something, and I hesitate to say like because I'm not really sure you like anyone. So maybe infatuated is a better choice. Why are you infatuated with him?"

I stifle a visible reaction. I won't give even my brother the satisfaction. "I like fucking him. Is that a problem?"

"It is when you're lying," Owen says smugly.

I set my phone aside and sit back, crossing my ankle over my knee. "Why do you assume I'm lying?"

"Do you not think I know you? You like fucking, but it's never been centered around a person. I've watched you fuck people since we were fourteen. You will fuck the same person as long as it's convenient and they don't get too attached, but never was it more than convenience. You get bored easily and despise attachment." Owen does know me better than anyone else. We've spent our entire lives side by side, but it still annoys me that I'm this transparent, even to him.

"And? Isaac is convenient. I'll see him daily."

"You've gone about him differently since you met him. You bribed me to miss dinner. You kept him here for twenty-four hours, to do God knows what. You wouldn't speak about him for almost two months, and now you're texting him." He counts the reasons off on his fingers. "It's suss."

"No one says suss anymore."

"Let me act like an elder millennial if I want to. I feel like one."

"Christ." I tip my head back to look at the ceiling. "Just because you act like a thirty-seven year old man doesn't mean you are one."

"I identify as one! And you can't take that away from me. I refuse to feel bad for enjoying cozy nights at home in my Snuggie with my cat."

"What the fuck? Are you claiming to be trans-millennial now? Is this what it's like in your brain all the time? No wonder you want to throw yourself off a building."

"Yeet. I want to yeet myself off a building."

"Now I think you're fucking with me." I scrub a hand over my face. "Are we through? I have plans."

"Plans? It's nearly one in the morning."

"I have to dole out a punishment, and no better time than now since I'm horny and would rather not be subject to anymore of the contents of your mind."

"I don't want to be in my mind either!" Owen calls after me as I leave.

I successfully avoid answering my brother's questions, which is a win for the time being. If I knew what my fucking issue is, I'd have dealt with it myself.

I'd looked up Isaac's last name to make sure the right Isaac was cold shouldered, and with it his dorm. The doors are keycard only, but I merely wait until a student walks up. I hold up a hundred-dollar bill, and she opens the door wide.

"Thank you." I slip into the elevator beside her.

"You're not going to rape or kill anyone, are you?"

"Do you think I'd tell you if those were my intentions?"

"Fair. But you're not, right?" She narrows her eyes at me.

"While I can make neither of those particular promises, I can assure you he wants it."

"Is this one of those voluntary cannibal situations I've read about?" She wrinkles her nose.

"No. I'm not in to that."

"Would you tell me if you were?" she asks.

"Probably not," I admit. How long is this elevator ride?

"So you're not doing anything against anyone's will?"

"Don't you think it's a little late to be posing these questions?"

"Maybe. I'm broke, but I have a conscience."

"I'm not doing anything against anyone's will. Do you imagine I have a key for someone's room if I'm not welcome?"

"That's true. Promise?"

"I faithfully swear."

She nods and gets out on the next floor.

I ride up another couple of floors to get off on Isaac's, fishing out the key I'd procured on my way. I find the right door and checked the handle, finding it locked. At least they aren't total morons. I unlock it and slip inside.

Their beds are opposite each other. But which is which? I'd never forgive myself for getting in the wrong bed. Thankfully,

126

one of them has a motion sensor nightlight that triggers as I walk deeper into the tiny dorm.

Isaac's mop of wavy hair is easy to spot, draped over a pillow. I sit on the edge of his bed and fist a hand into his hair. "Wake up, kitten. Time for your punishment."

Isaac startles with a whimper, curling into the fetal position, and covers the parts of his head he can around my hand.

"I didn't do anything." His arms and the blanket muffle his words. Words he's probably said before. "Please leave me alone."

"Isaac." Colin's sleep rough voice sounds like he's familiar with the situation. "You're okay."

My hand relaxes in his hair, and his arms slide down enough for him to peek up at me. Then he bolts upright.

"Oliver? What the hell! You've been ignoring me for hours."

"I had a prior engagement," I say, wanting Isaac to wonder where I am.

"For fuck's sake," Colin grumbles. "Isaac, get your fuck toy to shut up or get out. Some of us need our beauty sleep."

"It's the middle of the night. What the hell are you doing here?"

"It's barely one thirty. Hardly the middle of the night."

"That's not the point. What are you doing here?" Isaac asks again, pulling farther away from me.

"I told you, I'm here for your punishment." I slip into the bed next to him, not letting him get away from me.

"Is this like Door Dash for kinky people? You just bring it to the door?" Colin mutters pulling his pillow over his head.

"Only on very special occasions." I look at Isaac sternly. I don't want him to sink into the headspace he'd woken up in, which is clearly some sort of trauma response. "Have you changed your mind?"

"You could have given me some warning!" Isaac hugs his arms around himself.

"I did. It's not my fault you weren't waiting."

"It could have been weeks, knowing you. Do you expect me not to sleep?" Rage flickers in Isaac's eyes.

I push to my knees in front of him and grasp my cock through my thin pinstriped slacks. "Your anger turns me on."

Isaac's eyes widen, and his mouth waters.

"Do you want this?"

He nods.

"Then you better get up and earn it."

Once free from Colin, I escort Isaac to my waiting car.

"Are you going to tell me where we're going at least?"

"No, I won't be doing that either."

"Will you tell me anything?"

"I plan on fucking your throat so raw you won't be able to speak tomorrow."

Isaac swallows hard.

"Still willing to accept your punishment?" I ask.

"Are you letting me out?"

"I won't force you to do anything against your will."

"That's not a yes." Isaac adjusts his seat, clearly hard. Why did I love it so much?

"It's not a no either. Make your decision. I won't ask again." I check my watch to drive my point home.

"I'm not backing out." He juts his chin out.

"Good." As if the universe is on my side, we pull up at the Goldstein building, and I throw open the door, turning to offer my hand to Isaac.

"What are we doing here?" He takes my hand, letting me help him climb out onto the sidewalk.

"Are you going to keep asking questions or figure out I won't be answering?"

"How do you even have a key to this place?" he asks as I unlock the door.

"I bribed a janitor."

"That is less exciting than I expected . . ."

I hold the door, and he slips inside. "Are you going to strip me naked and beat me with a sword or something?"

"No, but I could be persuaded for a third date."

He scowls at me.

"Come on. Up to the second floor."

He follows without question. I bring him to the second floor and flip the light on. The harsh fluorescent light blinding after the dark drive over here.

"Strip."

"When are you telling me what my punishment is?"

"When you're undressed," I reply coldly.

"You're not going to make me streak, are you? That could get me kicked out of school . . ."

I don't answer, waiting for him to finish undressing.

"Oliver?" he asks hugging his arms around himself again.

I put a finger on his chest and walk him back until his ass is pressed against the massive wall of windows overlooking Washington Square. "On your knees."

He drops, looking up expectantly.

"I'm going to fuck your throat in this window so all of lower Manhattan knows who you belong to."

Isaac's cock throbs, standing straight out from his body as he glances out the window. I see it all register. The lights. The wall of glass. He trembles.

"Open your mouth."

Seventeen

Isaac

T he window and the lights bring a fantasy into harsh reality.
Is he serious?

But I know the answer.

Dread colors the moment. I've already been caught once. The fear of it happening again licks my skin, but when my knees hit the floor and I'm looking up at him, arousal takes over. I can't fight him. I want Oliver to take me. I want him in my mouth again. I don't want him to stop. I want a taste of how I felt at his apartment.

Owned. Wanted. Safe.

My mouth falls open, and I stick out my tongue, presenting it to him. If he is going to play this game, dragging me out of bed in the middle of the night, I'm going to at least tease him back.

The frigid November night chills the glass at my back and seeps into my skin as two fingers slide between my lips. I suck on them on instinct, wanting to be good for him while knowing it's going to be the end of me.

This dominating part of him calls to a part of me I didn't know existed. A part of me is free when I give him control.

I need him, but I don't know how to protect myself from him. Does he need me too? Knowing him makes it seem so, but his reputation and Colin's opinion contradicted everything I felt when I'm with him.

His free hand strokes over his cock, swiping his fingers through the pre-cum pooling there. He rubs the fluid over my lips, giving me just a taste of him. I moan at the flavor, mouth watering for his dick.

"My eager little slut," Oliver murmurs, thumbing my lip.

My.

The word burns into my chest.

Did he mean it?

I look up, pleading with my eyes.

"Do you want this?" He brushes his tip over my lips, but stops me with his fingers when I try to lick it. "Answer first."

I nod.

"Do you know how much I like watching your lips around me?"

My brows pull, and I give a slight shake of my head.

"You're exquisite." He withdraws his fingers, letting me taste him.

Something comes over me. I am eager and greedy.

I want more.

He smiles, letting me have him inch by inch. His fingers slip into my hair. Gentle. Caressing and giving me false hope. I try not to cling to the softness. But I want it.

How is he so nice when we're alone?

I hate him.

I want to hate him.

But I also want this so badly.

My eyes close, sucking him deeper into my mouth.

"Your tongue."

I lift a brow without opening my eyes.

"You know what you're doing." He cups my face, thumbs rubbing over my cheek bones, making me feel cherished.

For the first time ever, I realize.

He goes too far, and I gag, jerking back on reflex. Oliver grips my face to keep me still and, with his eyes on mine, he pushes between my lips again. My hands come up to push on his thighs, hoping to keep him from choking me again.

"If you use your hands, I'll take them away from you. Touching is a privilege."

When he gets to the back of my mouth and I start to gag, he speaks again.

"Open your mouth wider, relax. You're so lovely when you gag. Do you feel how hard it makes me?"

His head is so thick it brings tears to my eyes and drool pools in my mouth when I choke again. My stomach muscles clench so hard my body bows.

"Breathe through your nose," he instructs, and I try to do what he's says, but I don't think I can do it. "Tears and gagging will not stop this. Be a good boy and take your punishment."

It takes several slow tries, but I finally manage to get some of him into my throat. Tears and saliva drip down my body, tickling my skin as he uses my hair to pull me onto his dick.

"I'm throbbing in the back of your throat. Can you feel what you do?" His voice is sweet, and mesmerizing. "I'm so hard for you, kitten."

My dick aches, and I want so badly to touch it, but I doubt he'll let me.

Oliver's thrusts are smooth between my lips, harsh, while the rest of his touch is soft and attentive. The contrast is confusing, and some twisted part of me likes being used. Like my only purpose is this, to make him feel good. It's heady and makes me feel like I'm floating.

"This is what your mouth is good for."

I gasp for breath every time he pulls from my throat, making more noise than he is in the empty space. I want to hear him, taste him, smell him.

"No one gets to touch you but me. Do you understand?" His words are harsh, almost angry in their intensity.

I try to answer, but it's more of a strangled sound until he pulls back enough to allow me to say "yes," then he's thrusting back in, faster now, chasing his orgasm.

I tremble on the floor, sloppy and used and waiting for his cum, for his next command where anyone can walk past and see. Someone could take a picture or a video, and I would be condemned to hell by everyone I've ever known. There would be no going back.

I want it anyway.

There's no way I can go back to that life, so take it away and don't give me the option.

Oliver's breathing turns harsh and finally he groans as his cock throbs on my tongue. He stops in the back of my throat, filling it, making me gag again, but I find the will to swallow, wanting his taste. I chase it when he finally pulls back. Cum fills my mouth and dribbles down my chest as I try to swallow but am overwhelmed with the volume.

I squirm, wanting my own release, wanting him to take me hard right here in this room where we can be found while I'm messy and used. I want him to show me how I belong to him and only him.

Oliver's hands relax, and he pulls himself free. Strings of

saliva follow, and he wipes the tip of his cock again and feeds me the last drip of cum.

Oxygen deprivation leaves me lightheaded, and I sit back on my heels, but he doesn't let me stay there. He drags me to my feet. My legs shake, but his arms wind around me, keeping me upright. He licks my swollen and sensitive lips, kissing me again. I freeze, not at all expecting it after he said he doesn't kiss.

My heart stops, and now I can't breathe for an entirely different reason.

"Good boy." His words and smile are smug, another contrast to the delicateness of the kiss.

I'm dizzy when he releases me, and I'm not sure if it's from the kiss, the compliment, or all of my blood flow going to my cock.

"Get dressed."

My body convulses in a shudder, and I whimper, a pathetic sound. I knew he isn't going to let me get off, but it hurts. My skin is tight with the need for the release.

"Please, Oliver," I whisper, my head dropped toward the floor.

"This is a punishment. You aren't rewarded during a punishment."

I dig my fingers into my bare thighs as I tremble. With my eyes closed, I force my breathing to slow and focus on the pain from my nails biting into my flesh. It takes me a few minutes, but once I've calmed, I lift my head and Oliver tucks my hair behind my ear.

"Get dressed. You're coming with me tonight." It's not a question, and I don't ask why since I know he won't answer it.

When we get back to the car, I'm exhausted, but edgy. Getting so close to an orgasm and being denied it is going to hurt soon, make me more irritable, and I'm sure Oliver is going to torture me more before I'm allowed a release.

Maybe I can sneak into the bathroom after he's asleep . . .

Glancing sideways, I sigh and lean against the window. He would know and make me pay for it.

"Are you done messing with my life now?" I ask before I can think better of it.

"Messing with you? Kitten, you've gotten off easy tonight."

"What's the point? Is it fun? It's apparently easy for you to do." I cross my arms and stare out the window. Part of me hopes he doesn't answer. I don't want to hear that he just likes to cause me pain, physical and emotional.

Going to college is supposed to be a time for me to figure out who I am, experience new things, live a life I was forbidden from.

I just needed to eat. To pay for my dorm room. How did I end up here, second-guessing everything this guy does?

"Act like you haven't enjoyed every minute of it," Oliver says with a smug satisfaction.

"And what's your point? That I'm easy? That all you have to do is snap your fingers and I'll come running because I'm so desperate to matter that I'll accept whatever messed up situation this is for a moment of your attention?" The words pour from my mouth, angry and hurt and so damn pathetic.

"I've never thought you were easy. If you were easy, you'd be boring. I could have a hundred easy fucks at my feet tonight if I wanted them." Oliver grabs my jaw, forcing me to look at him. "Don't sell yourself short, Isaac. It's unbecoming."

We pull up in front of the Casa Cipriani, and I gawk at it. Is he serious? The building is beyond gorgeous, with its early twentieth century architecture and old-world charm. Getting a room here on the waterfront in lower Manhattan isn't cheap or easy, especially at a place like this. The historical maritime building is almost iconic. I've always wanted to see it but never gotten a chance to.

Getting out of the car in my secondhand pajamas, I feel completely out of place. Oliver leads me inside with a hand on my elbow while the driver does whatever they do. He strides

through the place like he owns it. Like he's completely comfortable. I guess he would be. This is the kind of luxury he's used to,
that he grew up with. I grew up staying in a Motel 6 that had a
sign on the inside of the door saying to lock it for your own
protection.

What could he possibly see in me?

Don't sell yourself short, Isaac. It's unbecoming.

Is it selling myself short or being realistic? I'm the complete
opposite of him in every way. Is that what he finds interesting?
I'm not chasing him, not after his money, don't care who his
family is. I wonder how hard that is to find in his world.

Maybe he needs a real friend, and he doesn't know how to ask
for it . . .

Eighteen

Oliver

I pick an out-of-the-way hotel on the lower tip of the financial district. Far enough where Owen won't easily find me, while not being inconvenient to return to school tomorrow. I had my black card concierge arrange it before I got to Isaac's dorm. I'd had him mask the charges too, in case my brother got nosy. At least until I had to explain myself to Owen. I'm not in the mood to deal with him. As a member of their club, I've been meaning to find a reason to stay at the Casa Cipriani. I love their other properties, so hiding away with Isaac is the perfect excuse.

We pull up to the historic battery maritime building, which is over the still operating ferry terminal on the tip of lower Manhattan. I love old architecture, and the site doesn't disappoint. The hotel has been modernized without losing its early twentieth century feel. I knew it was the right place to bring Isaac when I laid eyes on the large terraces and can already see myself fucking him against the railing.

I wait for his reaction, finding embarrassment coloring Isaac's cheeks. He pulls into himself as we cross the lobby, clearly feeling out of place, but I find his attire becoming. The mix between the sweats and his messy hair from our encounter giving him an innocent appearance.

This infatuation for him is baffling, but tonight I'm leaning into it.

The hotel concierge waits with our keys, escorting us to the room.

I tip him and send him on his way, closing the door before turning on Isaac. He hasn't moved from the entryway, arms wrapped around himself with tired eyes.

"Stop it." My words make him snap out of it a little.

"Stop what?"

"This pulling into yourself. You're hiding."

"And? Why do you care?" His grip tightens on his arms, turning his fingers white.

"Because you close off. I don't want you closed off."

"How else do you expect me to be after giving me the silent treatment for a week?"

"I wasn't giving you the silent treatment. You didn't try to speak to me."

Isaac frowns, but he can't refute the claim. "How would I know you'd speak to me?" he says at length.

"Did I give you any indication I wouldn't?"

"No one else would."

"Then why would you assume?"

"You said you would make everyone stop talking to me!" His voice carries a hitch I delight in.

"No, I believe you said I *can't* keep everyone from speaking to you. I never said that."

I watch him work back through our conversation in real time, laughing to myself. "I see I need to watch what I say to you a lot closer."

"I asked you to leave the bar I was at and stop flirting with douche bags who are too old for you. You could have gone to any other bar, but you chose the one I was at to elicit a reaction. Then you told me I couldn't prevent everyone from speaking to you. I did what you asked." I wait for him to come to his own conclusion.

"Asked? You didn't ask. You demanded. And so, what if I had spoken to guys too old for me at any other bar?" he asks with a bratty defiance.

"Asked, demanded, same thing. But I wouldn't have known, now would I?" I say, and Isaac glares as I exploit the flaw in his logic. "You wanted a reaction. You got one, and you made it worse for yourself by challenging me." I step into his space, towering over him. "And you liked the punishment." I draw a finger down his chest, stopping at the hem of his pajama pants. "You're still hard. Even now." I trace the outline of his cock through the thin material. "Now, come to bed. Please." I don't have to add the request, but I want it to be his choice.

"I never know what you expect from me, but I'm not a mindless idiot who just follows what he's told. Not anymore."

"Have I not given you a choice in your own fate every step along the way? I don't tell you to follow. I let you decide, and I act or react accordingly. I've never tricked you or made you blindly follow. Except, of course, your punishment, but that's an act of penance and requires trust."

"You push until I'm backed into a corner, and I have no reason to trust you." Isaac's energy shifts from horny to angry. Still hard, but fuming.

"You started in a corner, kitten. I didn't put you there. I offered you freedom from the corner and from your parents." I step back, letting him have his space. "Have I ever broken my word to you? Or ever done anything different than exactly how I told you it would be?"

"You make me feel like I'm losing my mind. I don't know where I stand with you. One minute you say I'm yours, then turn around and say I mean nothing. You can't have it both ways."

"I've told you what I expect from the start." Maybe it's a bit of a white lie. I hadn't expected to be bombarded with him at my place of relief. "I'm not particularly fond of anyone else touching you. I fail to see how that isn't clear, and I gave you an opportunity to leave. You declined."

"You said twenty-four hours for three grand—"

I put a finger to his lips to cut him off right there. "And then you followed me to a bar."

"After you told me I meant nothing! And I didn't know you would be there. It was Colin's idea." His deflecting pulls a snarl.

"Don't try to tell me when Colin said with the team you didn't believe I'd be there. You knew. So you did it to either push my buttons or try to prove me wrong? It would have been easy to leave, but you didn't. You wanted a reaction, and you got one. I won't apologize. Take ownership of your actions."

"I didn't know you would be there. I figured you would be too superior to hang out with the team, and I wanted a chance to get to know them. When I saw you . . . maybe I wanted to feel powerful for once."

There it is. The last, the most important part of his statement. "First, I don't believe you didn't know I'd be there. I'm the captain. A team isn't a team without bonding outside of practice, even in solo sports like fencing. Second, at least you're admitting it. That might get you the orgasm you want tonight."

"Believe what you want. I'm tired, and I'm done arguing with you."

"Then you don't want the orgasm? All right." I brush past him, venturing farther into the suite, taking in the view from our room. It's breathtaking. Perched on the tip of lower Manhattan overlooking the Hudson River, with views of the Brooklyn Bridge and the Statue of Liberty, it gives me a stark reminder of the city I live in. Those features blend into the background after years of seeing them, but presented as a backdrop to our stolen night makes them feel different.

"From you? No. I'm fine taking care of it myself tomorrow."

I open the door to the terrace, letting in the cool air. "Shame. I imagined fucking you on this balcony so many times on the ride over here."

"Find someone else to fulfill your fantasy. I'm going to sleep. Will I have a ride back to campus in the morning, or are you going to leave me stranded? I'd rather be prepared."

"Very well, do you want to watch or . . .?" I undo the buttons one by one on my shirt, turning to face him as I strip it off. Fingers finding the fasten on my slacks next, undoing it and lowering my zipper while I wait expectantly. "You going to sleep next to me after that display? You can ride back in my car in the morning, but that would require more time with me." I take my phone out of my pocket before draping the slacks over the back of a chair. "I can get someone over here right now for the balcony if that's the direction you want to go . . ."

"Go ahead, but I hope you like the way they feel sleeping next to you because it won't be me if you do." Isaac takes a defiant posture, standing up to me. His gaze hardening. Why do I love it when he stands up to me? "But if you're that dead set on screwing someone over that balcony, how much is it worth?"

I can say a dozen things about wanting to fuck him, or this being about him having his release, not me, but it's not what struck me. "So you want to sleep next to me?" A smile edges at the corners of my mouth.

"I didn't say that. I said if you call someone to have sex with, you won't be sleeping next to me. You obviously want me here, or you would have left me on campus."

"I *do* want you here. I want you in bed with *me*. I want you to get off, which is why I suggested the terrace. I didn't demand it." I lose my briefs, turning down the duvet. "I sleep naked. Hope that's not an issue."

Isaac's chin trembles as he tries to contain the emotions that are getting the best of him. "You've turned me into a whore once, don't be shy about it now. If you want my orgasm, what's it worth?"

I pause mid knee on the bed, tilting my head. "Does it turn you on to be paid?"

"It turns me on to feel like I have a choice."

"You always have a choice. It doesn't have to be about money for you to have a choice. If you don't want to get off, don't. If you want me to buy you something, then ask . . . unless it's not money you're after . . . what do you want, Isaac?" I want to spoil him I realize in that instant. I want to see his smile. What is wrong with me?

"I want to be able to take a shower in my dorm without the hot water running out." He takes a deep breath and seems to ponder something before he says, "And take me out somewhere nice, like you're not embarrassed by liking me."

"Done. Now come here." I crook a finger at him. When Isaac gets close enough, I pull him into my arms and tilt his face up with a finger. "Jokes on you. I don't feel embarrassment."

I lift him into bed, forgoing the balcony to shut him up for the night, sure he needs aftercare and to be held more than anything else tonight.

He curls into my arms, and my chest gets warm.

I slide a finger under his chin lifting his face. "Isaac."

He looks up at me with sleepy eyes. "You never call me by my name."

"Do you like it?"

He thinks for a second, then nods.

I brush my lips over his. "I'm not embarrassed to be seen with you." I'm confused and obsessed, and utterly not myself, but I'm not embarrassed.

"Are you sure?" he says into my mouth.

I flick my tongue deeper into his mouth. "I just fucked your throat in the window where anyone could happen by. I have no trouble with putting my ownership on display."

He rocks into me lightly, grinding his hardness against my hip. "Why? It doesn't even feel like you like me."

"I like you a lot."

And therein lies the problem.

Nineteen

Isaac

The sound of boat engines and lapping of water is confusing while I'm in the half-asleep state. There's sun and a breeze, I'm so warm and comfortable with weight against me.

My brain starts to turn on when I smell him, that cologne that's only him.

Oliver.

Turning my head toward the scent, his soft hair tickles my nose, and I nuzzle into it. One of his legs is between mine, his arm is wrapped around my waist, and his face on my chest. It's such a vulnerable position for him it takes me by surprise.

Opening my eyes, I let my gaze wander down the skin I can see peeking out from the luxurious blankets. He's . . . frustrating. So used to getting his way that he will find a way to make your life miserable until you agree to his terms. It's not a fair fight. ike bringing a pencil to a knife fight.

What does it mean when he says he wants me? Temporarily? When the mood strikes? Only for sex, but nothing else?

I scoot down until we're more level and slide my leg over his hip and butt. Both of us naked and half hard from the testosterone boost the morning leaves us with. But I'm sensitive from my denied orgasm last night. It only takes a few rolls of my hips, the brush of my dick against him, for me to groan in his ear.

Last night, after our fight or argument or whatever, he pulled me into the bed and just held me until I fell asleep. It's odd and felt good last night, but I'm still not fully sure how I feel about what he said. I need time to process, but not now. Now I want what he offered me last night. A release at his hands.

"I don't remember consenting to somnophilia, kitten." Oliver's sleep roughened voice makes me jump. It awakens a part of me I didn't know existed.

"I don't know what that means," I moan as he brushes his thigh against my balls, and I dig my fingers into his skin. "Please, I want to come." My face heats at the words that tumble from my mouth. I'm not use to talking like this.

"You could have last night, but you chose not to." Oliver shifts between my legs, gripping mine under the knee to press into the mattress. Stretching me wide open. The position is vulgar. It makes me blush. His cock rubs against mine, and I don't care about anything else.

I arch as we slide together. His cock against mine almost better than him inside me.

"I'm going to fuck you like this. Open and exposed. Nowhere for you to go to escape my cock."

I shudder at the idea and groan. "Yes, please."

I reach for our dicks, wrapping my hand around both of us to jack us off together. Oliver stops and reaches for the bedside table drawer and returns with a packet of lube.

"Presumptuous of you." I huff out with a laugh that ends with a moan when he slides against my most sensitive flesh.

"Hold your legs back," he tells me and gets to work opening me for him. In this position, he can see everything on my face. I can't hide from him, from the way he makes me feel. It's humiliating to not be able to shield myself.

Why does it make me hard?

With both of my hands occupied, I can't touch myself either. Can't find any relief as Oliver slicks up my hole and presses one, then two fingers in.

"I should take all morning to make you come. Edge you until you can't stand it anymore and make you beg for it. Make you show me you deserve it after denying me last night. I'll be nice since we both have class," Oliver says as he leans over me and lifts my dick to his mouth. "But rest assured, you'll come on my cock, kitten."

My muscles tremble in anticipation, and I stop breathing as I watch Oliver's mouth envelop the head of my dick.

"Oh, God!" I yell as he bobs. "Stop. Stop. STOP." I tighten every muscle I have control over to stave off the orgasm that's racing toward oblivion.

But he doesn't stop. A third finger is added to my hole, and he takes me the rest of the way into his mouth, swallowing, and I can't hold back. My orgasm rips through me on a scream. I'm overloaded with sensation, stretched and sucked and warm heat. It's blinding light and a buzz in my ears as my brain shorts out on everything that isn't pleasure until I'm gasping for breath and limp.

"If you think just because you came you're released from coming while I'm inside you, you're wrong." Oliver's smug voice has me opening my eyes and blinking through the blurriness. "I want to feel it, even if it's excruciating."

"Okay," is all I can mumble. My arms are lying limply on the bed, my legs splayed indecently because I don't have the energy to hold them up anymore.

"I want to make you come over and over until you can't anymore." Oliver grabs a pillow and makes me lift my hips, then spreads me wide again and pushes into me.

I groan, but welcome him into my body.

"Good boy." Oliver puts his hand high on my thigh to use for leverage and leans over me, taking my lips as he sets a hard, deep pace.

I can taste myself on his tongue. I didn't think I would be okay with that or like it, but I haven't found anything that he's done to me that I didn't enjoy. "You're kissing me."

"I've already broken that rule." His cock finds the spot inside me, and I almost can't form words.

"But you keep breaking it?" I finally manage.

"You have a way of making me break all my rules."

Oliver rests his forehead against mine, his rhythm never faltering.

"I'm going to fill you so full of my cum you'll be thinking about me all day as it drips down your thighs, reminding you who you belong to."

I reach for him then, desperately wanting his lips on mine. I want this to be true, but I'm scared. He's so far out of my league, it's not funny. We don't make sense, but I want it anyway. I want him. I have a feeling no one gets to see the side of him that he shows me when we're alone. It's intoxicating to think it. That I'm the only one who gets this softer side.

I arch into him, hooking my feet around his legs to keep him close and am rewarded when he groans into our kiss.

"Take me," I whimper against his lips. "Make me yours."

Oliver growls and picks up his pace while wrapping his hand around my half hard dick.

"Show me how much you want to be mine."

The deep pools of his eyes are endless as he makes his demands, and my body follows suit. It only takes a few strokes for me to be hard again, and he smirks, knowing he's won. Or that he's about to.

I don't understand why I want to give him what he demands. It's so hard to fight against the need to offer myself up to whatever he wants, but it's dangerous to my heart.

Oliver presses me harder into the mattress and sits up some, leaning onto my chest. The angle changes, and suddenly he's deeper, stretching a part of me that isn't ready, and the burn mixes with the pleasure to confuse my nerve endings.

"Please, harder," I beg. So close, almost there, just a little bit more.

Soon I'm going to be so exposed there will be nothing left. I'll be all his.

Oliver snaps his hips and I'm done. Lost to my release, cum spills onto my stomach as my dick pulses in his hand. Victory shines in his eyes before he lets himself go. That tight control he keeps wrapped around himself slides away, and he shudders, cock throbbing inside of me as he fills me.

A low moan comes from deep in his throat, and he collapses forward, spreading my mess onto himself. I smile to myself at the thought of marking him. I doubt he would ever allow me to leave an actual mark, but this is enough. He smells like sex and me. There's a basic urge that enjoys that. Like others can smell me on him and know to stay away.

Oliver lifts onto his elbow and brushes a soft kiss against my lips. It takes me by surprise. I don't expect softness from him.

"You're going to sit in every class today and remember how good I feel." He drops his face to bite the curve of my shoulder. I hiss in pain, and it's over before I can beg him to do it again.

"When you touch yourself later, stand in front of the mirror and know I leave marks to remind you of who you belong to."

"I thought you were going to make me come until it hurts?" I ask.

He lifts a brow. "I thought you had class."

I grumble.

"Another time. It's getting late. Time to shower." He slips out of me, and when I move to sit up, he stops me with a hand on my chest and stares at my hole. I can feel a dribble of cum slide from me, and he uses his finger to catch it and push it back inside. His gaze finds mine, and I blush. Part of me wants more of this, wants to stay wrapped in this bubble he's created for us, but I know the longer I stay here, the more it'll hurt when he walks away. Because it's inevitable that he will.

"I need to pee," I blurt to get out of this moment that already aches in my chest and sprint for the bathroom. My body has been used in the best sense of the word, but now I'm empty.

Flipping on the water for the shower, I don't look at myself in the mirror. I know what I'll find. A boy falling for a guy he can't keep. Maybe Colin is right, and I need to go on dates to get more experience.

Once the steam fills the space, I step inside and groan at the heat and water pressure. I haven't had a decent shower in weeks. For a minute, I just stand in the blazing heat and let it pound onto my shoulders and back.

The door opens, and Oliver's scent carries on the steam. My poor dick tries to thicken, but it's worn out.

"Breakfast will be here shortly." Oliver steps into the stall and presses himself against my back to enjoy the rain shower with me. His lips find the spot he bit, and my entire body shudders.

"I still have your cum on me from yesterday. I think you should clean it off." I bite my lip and wait for his response. Why did I even say anything? Him taking care of me will only embed him further under my skin.

His hand slides up my stomach, and I lean into his touch. Why can't I stay away from him? How does he get through all the walls I've put up to protect myself?

Finding the complimentary body wash, I squirt some in Oliver's hand. He washes my body, making sure not to miss even a centimeter of skin. Up my torso to my neck, between my thighs, in between my toes. I don't think I've ever been so clean. He's gentle, soft even. Caretaking, and I crave it. How can someone who's so hard on the outside be like this with me in private? He presses kisses to my lips as he works, making me fall.

I can't let myself.

When he turns me to face him, he lifts my chin with his fingers. "There's a lot of power in submission."

My brows pull together in confusion. "What?"

"Last night, you said you wanted to feel powerful. Submission is powerful."

I'm not entirely sure what that means, but I let the idea bounce around in my head while we finish up. I get my hair washed, and he lets me wash him, only once complaining about feeling like a child.

It's not until we're back in the car on our way to campus that I check my phone.

> COLIN: Who the hell is this construction guy in our bathroom?

> ISAAC: I put in a request to the dorms to fix our water pressure. Maybe they're finally fixing it?

> COLIN: Uh. No. This is not a guy from the school.

Turning to Oliver, I lift a brow and wait for him to notice I'm staring.

"Do you have something to say or are you trying to read my mind?"

"There's construction happening in my dorm bathroom."

Oliver checks his watch like he's not surprised by this information.

"I love a punctual man." Oliver nods and goes back to his scrolling through his phone.

"What? When did you have time to find someone to fix my hot water?" I quickly replay the morning in my head, and while I was in the shower a few minutes before him, he'd ordered us breakfast.

"I called before I ordered room service. I asked the maintenance man from my building to take care of it," he says, like this is a completely normal thing to do.

I don't know how to respond to that, so I just blink. He puts his phone in his lap and turns to look at me, pinning me to my seat with his gaze.

"Do you not want me to get things done in an orderly and timely fashion? Stop acting so surprised I do things you ask me to."

"You do realize that's not normal, right? Most people have to find a plumber or whatever and it takes days for them to come take a look, then they have to order parts and find another time to come out." Does he really not know how things work for everyone else?

"Why am I being penalized for taking care of what you asked me to?"

"Who said you were being penalized? Now you're just being dramatic," I huff.

"I would call your attitude and doubt a penalty and an affront on my character."

"Your ego is plenty big enough to take the hit." I roll my eyes and turn back to my phone.

"I won't be sorry for having loyal employees who work efficiently and quickly. I'll save you the trouble. No need to apologize, kitten. You're welcome for getting your shower fixed so quickly." The tone in his voice says he's won something, but I'm not entirely sure what it is.

We're silent for the last few minutes of the drive. Checking the time, I see that I only have a few minutes to change before I have to hustle to class or risk being late. I hate being late.

Oliver gets out of the car when we pull up in front of the dorms and leads me inside. On my floor, there is construction stuff everywhere. Wood, tools, plastic tarps. What the hell is going on?

Colin steps out of our room and meets us halfway down the hall. "What the hell did he do to warrant a new shower?" He nods toward Oliver.

I'm not really sure how to explain what happened last night since I'm not sure either. "Uh, we got into an argument . . ."

Oliver ushers us into the room so I can get changed.

"That's a lot more than fixing a water heater . . .," I mumble when I see the chaos that is my bathroom. Two by fours and pipes are exposed, there's dust everywhere.

"It's disgusting. How am I going to fuck you in there with mold growing in the grout?" Oliver says, pushing me toward my dresser for clothes.

"How do you know there's mold growing in my shower? You've never been in there." Colin raises his eyebrow at Oliver. "Right?"

"It's not a far leap to assume you're living in squalor, Colin," Oliver deadpans.

Colin pops a hip, putting a hand on it. "I'd say something mean, but I'm just happy to have water pressure."

"You're welcome." Oliver turns to me. "Your new MacBook will be here this afternoon."

"What? I didn't ask . . ."

"You should really dream big. You're worth so much more than just a shower." He leaves without another word, and I'm left with Colin staring at me.

"Do you have like a magical dick or something you need to tell me about?"

Twenty

Oliver

W hen I stroll into practice later that day, Colin has Isaac in a corner whisper yelling at him. I open my locker but don't change, lingering to eavesdrop.

Isaac meets my eyes over Colin's shoulder, which makes Colin look over, too. He scowls and turns back to Isaac.

Who pissed in his corn flakes?

"Trouble in paradise, ladies?"

Isaac shakes his head while Colin ignores me.

How badly do I want to know? I strip off my shirt, still trying to listen, but they are just out of hearing range.

I watch the interaction for another moment, but witnessing the way Colin speaks to him sparks my anger, and I interject myself. "Pardon me, but as a captain I feel like I have to inquire as to what this is about?"

"Go away, Oliver," Colin says between his teeth.

"I don't think I will. It's my responsibility to make sure we don't have tension in the ranks."

"There's none." Colin's short, and his voice carries attitude.

"With competition fast approaching, I am tasked with keeping our team dynamic healthy, so I don't think I'll be doing that. What's going on?" I move closer, almost shoulder to shoulder with both of them, forcing Colin to take a step back.

"It's a private conversation. Butt out." Colin isn't just mad. He's seething.

Isaac pleads with his huge puppy dog eyes for me to drop it. I won't be doing that.

"Not so private when it's happening in the team locker room." I step between them, putting my back to Colin to confront Isaac. "Are you okay, kitten?"

Isaac crosses his arms over his chest. "I'm fine."

"You don't look fine." His entire demeanor from this morning has changed. "What happened?"

"It's a personal matter," Colin interjects, moving from behind me to try and get between us and elbow me out of the way.

I glance from his elbow to his face. "Respectfully, and by respectfully I mean with all the respect you don't deserve, Colin, fuck off."

"You fuck off. You're the one who got in the middle of this." Colin holds my gaze with pure disgust.

"Is the shower not to your liking, or did I emasculate you by taking care of it when you couldn't?" I ask, done with his fucking attitude.

"I put in a maintenance request. It would have been fixed." Colin rolls his eyes.

"Did you drop Daddy's name when you put in that request, hoping you were important enough to get it fixed before you moved out, and now your grand gesture for Isaac has backfired?" I can't figure out why he's so angry.

"Not everyone needs to throw money around to get things done, Oliver." His voice drips with disdain.

"No? Then why wasn't it done, and I didn't have to drop money to get it done? I asked my maintenance man. He wasn't expecting anything more than his usual salary, but I did pay him extra because I believe in treating employees well."

"So you threw money around?" Colin doubles down.

"Sure, sweetheart, if that's what you need to hate me. Are you finished yelling at Isaac? Now we really do need to get to practice. I'd hate to see Coach Kennedy single him out for being late." I sit on a hair trigger when it comes to Isaac, and I hate the way Colin spoke to him.

"He's not yelling at me," Isaac says quietly.

I lift a brow. "It didn't come off that way. You seem upset."

"He wasn't. We were—" He breaks the eye contact to look at his shoes. There's something he isn't saying.

I have half a mind to throw Colin into the lockers and threaten his life. "You were?"

"Having a heated discussion. It's fine." Isaac still won't meet my eyes.

I glance between them. "We have to be warming up in five minutes. I suggest you two get changed."

Colin scowls while Isaac turns to get dressed.

I return to my locker, needing to change myself. Quickly changing, I spot my brother and grab him as he walks by. "Did I cause offense?"

"Huh?" Owen asks. "I'm not upset. Well, not any more than normal."

I lift my chin in Isaac and Colin's direction. "These two. Colin is acting like I've caused some grave offense."

"Why would I know?"

"Because you're the sabre captain." Why does it feel like everyone in the room is gaslighting me?

Owen closes one eye like he's trying to remember. "He hasn't said anything, but we don't really run in the same circles."

"There's only twelve of you."

He shrugs. "I don't pay attention. I have too much existential dread to worry about what's going on with someone I'm not even friends with!"

I pinch the bridge of my nose. "Can you do some recon for me? As a personal favor."

"These personal favors are adding up."

"I told you to pick a night and I'll cover."

Owen looks at Isaac and isn't even subtle about it. "Why do you care so much? Do I need to do an intervention or something? You've never been like this. It's making me uncomfortable."

"Why is it making you uncomfortable?"

"Because I am used to getting the version of Oliver I know, and then you do this, and now it kinda seems like you like that kid, but that can't be right. But you're obsessed with him. It's like my entire world doesn't make sense anymore. I do not like it."

I sigh dramatically. "We have to go out there. Can you just see what you can suss out? Please."

Owen shudders.

"What?" I ask, unable to help myself.

"You said please."

"I'm being nice."

"Stop. It makes me uncomfortable when you're nice."

I hold up my middle finger as I walk out of the locker room.

At least practice gives me two hours of Colin free access to Isaac, even if we'll be working.

I begin stretching us out and stand next to Isaac. "Care to fill me in on your roommate's sudden change of mood?"

"Colin is moody?"

"I guess I'll go talk to him myself." I call a water break.

"No." Isaac looks panic-stricken. "You doubling down is only going to make him more mad."

"I'd love to know what I did to make him angry in the first place?"

Isaac gestures at all of me. "Existing basically. He doesn't like that you kidnapped me."

"I don't seem to recall you ever telling me no . . ." I act like I'm going through the previous night's events. "Nope, not once. Does Colin have a thing for you?" Jealousy would explain his behavior.

"No! Not at all." Isaac is adamant, but I'm not buying it.

"Something is bothering him."

Isaac shrugs, but he's still cagey.

"I will get to the bottom of this." I pick up my water bottle and squirt some into my mouth. "I'm going to ask him unless you tell me." I lift a foot like I'd cross the gym to the piste they were doing drills on.

"Please don't."

"So secretive." I cross the space and nod to my brother. "Water break time."

Owen calls it, not even questioning my motives. Sometimes I wonder what goes through his mind.

"I feel like we need some cross competition to ease the tension amongst the ranks."

Owen scrunches up his nose. "Is this about . . .?"

"Sure," I reply. "Let's pick relay teams. What do you say, Owen?"

"Okay . . ."

I gesture for him to go first.

He starts to say Eliot, but I elbow him. He stops and looks at me. "What?"

"You pick Colin and I pick Eliot."

"Why don't you just divide us then," Owen says flatly.

"Perfect. I will."

Isaac tips his head back and groans. "Can we please just drop all that stuff and focus on practice?"

"What stuff?"

"The sexual stuff," Isaac mutters so no one else hears him.

"You want to drop the sexual talk to go play a sexual sport?"

"Sword fighting isn't sexual." Isaac acts like I've offended his sensibilities.

"What sport have you been playing this whole time? Surely not the one the rest of us are, kitten."

"It's not sexual. It's combat."

Colin bursts out laughing. "You are literally crossing swords."

Isaac blushes.

"Let's cross swords, Colin. First match. We can fight it out. Which weapons would you prefer?" One of them could tell me, or I'd beat it out of Colin.

Twenty-One

Isaac

After practice, Colin is furious. He's been in a mood all day, randomly venting about The Godfrey family throwing money around to get what they want but not really making any sense. He's warned me to stay away from Oliver. I've been interrogated about why I slept with him a second time and asked if I was kidnapped. Pretty sure he told me to blink twice if I'm in danger but he hasn't told me exactly what's happened to piss him off.

Getting his ass handed to him at practice by Oliver didn't help.

When we get done with showers and changed, he's still fuming, but by the time we get back to our dorm, he's got a dangerous smile on his face.

"Isaac, you're taking ECON UA, right?" Colin asks as I drop down onto my bed.

"A *friend of* mine is also taking it but is not doing well. I volunteered you to tutor him." He shrugs like it isn't a major inconvenience. "I gave him your number. He'll text you."

"Seriously? What if I wasn't taking the class?" I glare at my only friend. Who does that?

Colin rolls his eyes and waves it off. "You left your schedule on the desk, I already knew you were taking it."

"Listen, I don't know what your deal is today, but leave me out of it."

My phone pings with an incoming message.

> UNKNOWN: Hey, this is Tyler. Colin said you could help me with Econ. I really appreciate it, man. When can we meet up?

I glare at Colin again, but he just smiles at me.

"Trust me, you need to make nice with people who aren't related to the devil." Colin drops down onto his bed, typing a message out on his phone. "Plus Tyler is cute, sweet, and does this thing with his tongue–" Colin moans while biting his lip, and my face heats.

"I'm not interested in what Tyler can do with his tongue." I try to sound stern, but I am clearly embarrassed.

"Baby bird, you need to date, to see what else is out there, to find a *nice* guy whose family isn't in the business of ruining others' lives just for the hell of it." The longer Colin speaks, the more agitated he becomes.

"Are you going to tell me what you're so worked up about so that what you just said makes sense?"

"Not if you can't keep it a secret."

My phone chimes again, but this time it's not Tyler.

> OLIVER: After consideration, I can't fathom a good reason as to why you're covering for Colin.

I swallowed thickly at the threat. I'm sure whatever torture he would use would be orgasm inducing. I can feel the heat climb up my neck, and my hands shake just a little. The very idea of what he could do to me . . .

"Are you even listening to me?" Colin snaps his fingers in my face.

"Are you going to tell me why you're so mad at Oliver? Are you mad about the shower?" I hadn't thought about that being the reason he's upset until Oliver had said it. Maybe it's a rich guy pride thing?

"That's the straw that broke the camel's back!" Colin yells and gets up to pace our room. "You aren't going to understand what I'm about to say because you aren't part of our social circle, but that's not a dig at you. Honestly, I kind of envy you for not having to deal with this bullshit."

He's quiet for a minute, spinning one of the chunky rings he has on his fingers. It's so odd to me that he's rich but dresses in distressed jeans, tank tops, big rings on all his fingers, and boho bracelets. His hair is long and makes him look like a surfer most of the time while everything about Oliver and Owen screams money. It's like Colin is rejecting it. Just walking on campus you can tell whose parents are rich by the way they dress and the brands on their stuff, but not Colin.

"My father is a money hungry, soul sucking, little man trying to play with the big boys." He keeps moving like in order to get through this he has to move. It's making me nervous, twisting something in my gut. "Marriages are more about political gain or business transactions than anything else. It's one of the reasons I'm so glad to be gay and make sure *everyone* knows it. I will not be trapped into a marriage with a woman to make my father's life better."

Political gain or business transactions? What the hell?

"But my sister is another story. She's a year younger than me and a dutiful daughter. All she's ever wanted is to make Father proud of her." Colin's hands are shaking, and it makes me want to give him a hug, but I don't dare touch him right now. I don't know what he would do.

"My father has somehow convinced the goddamn Godfreys to marry off my sister to one of the twins! Probably Owen because he's easier to boss around. That would be my guess anyway." Colin scrubs his hands over his face and through his hair. "I don't think she's been told yet, and that pisses me off even more."

My head is spinning with the very idea of arranged marriages. I know some countries still practice it, but not here. I didn't think that was ever really a thing here.

"Wait, your dad is setting up an arranged marriage for your sister? Is she going to be okay with that?" I finally speak up.

"Will she like it? Who knows, but she's too young to know what she wants. But will she do it to make Father happy? Yes." He sighs and runs his hands through his hair again. "She doesn't understand my need to stand up to him like I do. She follows along quietly, doesn't want to make waves. She's too damn nice for her own good. I know she has a backbone in there somewhere, but I swear she doesn't know how to use it against my father."

Colin turns and pins me with a look. "I don't know if Oliver and Owen are aware of this. Our parents are just . . . like this. They know it as well as I do, but they also don't make waves often. At least, not publicly." He shakes his head like it doesn't matter. "They are dangerous people. Not in the they'll murder you and hide the body type of way, but they don't have the same moral code you do. They aren't playing by the same rules, not to mention he's basically bought you with a new shower. He's turned you into a literal whore." He stops in front of me and puts his hands on my shoulders. "I'm begging you to go on a few dates with someone else."

My stomach is in knots. I knew I couldn't keep Oliver. We're too different, come from two very different worlds, and this just proves it. I hate it. It feels wrong, but I know he's right. My heart splinters at the very idea of not being able to have Oliver, but if his parents arrange his marriage, there's literally nothing I can do about it. I've gotten to enjoy him, now it's time to move on, I guess. Maybe we can be friends?

Doubtful. Anytime he's in the same room as you, you want to jump him.

Seeing him with someone else will shatter me, but it has to be done, I guess.

Swallowing thickly, with tears burning the back of my eyes, I look into the eyes of my only friend. "Okay, I'll go on a date."

The smile Colin gives me is sad. He knows I have feelings for Oliver. I'm sure they're written all over my face, so I appreciate him not gloating about it.

"Do the study thing with Tyler. If you hit it off, I'm sure he'll ask you out. He's a big flirt and super sweet with a *dirty* mind." Colin squeezes my arm. "And if you aren't feeling him, I have a whole contacts list to try out."

I shake my head and blush in embarrassment. I've never been on a date.

There's a dull pain in my chest that I rub at with my hand. A part of me is hoping Oliver will keep his word and take me out on a date, but now I know it won't mean anything. Not really. It would be another way for him to get access to my body, which is what he really wants in the first place. I have to be more careful to protect myself.

Two hours later, I'm sitting in the coffee shop on campus with my economics stuff, waiting on Tyler. Nerves are tingling my stomach, and I want to puke.

It's just studying. Relax. He's not going to grope you here in front of everyone.

But what if Oliver comes in and sees? Will he make a big

show of it like he did at the bar? Make some claim he won't back up later?

My knee is bouncing, and I've chewed my thumbnail back so far it's bleeding and sore when a cute man with short black hair and a big smile approaches.

"Are you Isaac?"

I stand and offer my hand like my parents trained me to do from a young age. "Yes. Tyler?"

He takes my hand and shakes it. It's a firm shake, but his hands are soft. He certainly looks nice. There's something about him that makes me want to trust him, and I find myself smiling back.

"Thanks so much for this, I really appreciate it. This class makes no sense to me." He drops down into the chair next to me and gets his stuff out.

"Where did you get lost? Maybe I can help bridge the gap." I take my seat and open my notebook.

A little blush pinks his cheeks, and it's so cute. No wonder Oliver likes to embar–*stop it!*

Forcing myself back to Tyler, I look at his notes and chuckle. He has three lines of chicken scratch on his paper while mine is color coded and highlighted.

He sees mine, and the blush deepens to a red. "I see you are a professional note taker."

"Yeah. I like notes." I smile. "It's a skill that we aren't taught though, so most people struggle when they get to college because they don't know how to find the important information in the text-books. We have to teach ourselves how to do it."

I shrug and attempt to read his handwriting, but I'm pretty sure it's not English.

We get into it, and I walk him through what we've learned so far in class. He copies from my notes and seems to be getting it.

After about an hour, he sits back in his chair and scrubs his hands down his face.

"I need caffeine if I'm going to keep my brain active." He stands and pulls his wallet out. "You want something?"

"Oh uh," I stumble over my words, not really knowing what to say. Do I want a sweet, hot coffee? Yes. But does he actually want to get me one, or is he being nice?

"Come on Smarty Pants, what's your coffee order?"

"Vanilla latte, please," I blurt out the words.

He winks at me and walks away. He's cute. Colin is right, but he does nothing for me. There's no pull. No excitement.

My phone pings, and I pull it out of my backpack.

> OLIVER: If neither one of you wants to fill me in, I'll have to give Colin a reason.

> ISAAC: What's going on with Colin is not my story to tell. Please, just leave it.

> OLIVER: It's interfering with me, therefore it's my business. So I won't leave it.

> OLIVER: So if you don't want to tell me, I'll take matters into my own hands.

> OLIVER: And what happens when I want something, kitten?

I sigh a bone-weary breath.

> ISAAC: You always get what you want.

Twenty-Two

Isaac

When my alarm goes off the next morning, I groan. I don't want to be awake yet. Why did I think an eight a.m. class was a good idea? Past me was an idiot.

I reach for my phone to shut it off and sit up. Colin starfishes over his bed, with the blankets bunched up around his knees, in only short shorts. I shake my head and stretch before smacking his butt to wake him up.

"If you aren't going to fuck me, you don't get to spank me," his muffled words make me laugh as I go to the bathroom to piss and brush my teeth.

I've found a comfortable friendship with my roommate. I know I can tell him off without backlash, be vulnerable, make jokes. This type of friendship was sorely missing from my previous life.

Once I'm done, Colin is standing at the door waiting to get in with sleep still heavy in his eyes. He is not a morning person. I pat his cheek and ruffle his hair on my way past him.

"Fuck off, church boy," he grumbles, slapping at my hands.

I chuckle and get dressed for class. I have ECON this morning, and since I had a study session last night, I should be just fine in class today. I'll have to text Tyler and see when he has it and how it goes. Hopefully, better than the previous classes.

I can see myself being friends with him too. Am I finally going to have a friend group that I can be myself with? That would be cool.

And a first.

It takes Colin no time to get ready for class. He does some kind of magic in the bathroom that has him looking alert and ready to take on the day. He quickly gets dressed in ripped jeans, boots with buckles, and pink shirt that says, "Spreading Cheeks Not Hate." He grabs a "Kenough" hoodie and we're out the door.

It's cold this morning, and I regret not grabbing a jacket, but the lecture hall is always boiling hot, so I know I'll be fine once we get there.

In the hallway outside our lecture hall, Oliver is standing with a to-go cup. He looks so good in dark jeans that probably cost more than my tuition, a dark green button-down, and black wool military style peacoat with bright gold buttons. His hair is perfectly done, and he looks like he just stepped off a runway or a magazine cover.

This man is so far out of my league. Everything I own is secondhand. The faded blue polo and khakis that are a size too big because I needed clothes and couldn't afford to be picky. I'm a mess in comparison.

Colin tenses beside me, clearly readying himself for a fight when he sees Oliver. I try to mask my emotions, but I'm sure he can read me. He always does. There are no secrets I can keep

Oliver flicks his eyes to Colin, takes in what he's wearing, and huffs.

I stop when I'm in front of him, hoping he won't make a scene if I give in to him.

"Good morning, Oliver."

He hands over the to-go cup, and I take it, surprised.

"Oh, thank you."

"Trying to buy him off with coffee? Buttering him up for something? Haven't you whored him out enough?" Colin snaps.

I jerk my head toward him, hurt that he called me a whore in public. I know that technically, he did buy my virginity and placate me with a shower. I already feel weird about it, but that's not hallway conversation.

"Adorable that you seem to think of yourself as the authority on sexual immoralities." Oliver's voice is like ice. "I didn't see you assisting your friend with his expenses, thus giving him no other choice."

"Sexual immoralities?" Colin scoffs.

"Do you need me to explain it to you? Or should I remind you that you can't judge anyone for sex work, as you're the product of the practice? Since your mother is thirty years younger than your father." Oliver sips his latte.

"At least I'm not in the business of arranged marriages!"

"Arranged marriages?" Oliver lifts a brow, giving Colin a curious look.

Colin doesn't reply. He stomps into the lecture hall, letting the door slam closed behind him. Oliver has a pensive look on his face, the wheels in his mind clearly turning before he focuses back on me. He steps closer to me and drops his voice to a whisper. My entire body buzzes with his nearness.

"Kitten." Oliver corners me.

I try to suck in a breath, but all I can smell is his damn cologne, and it fogs my brain. "Yes, Oliver."

"Do you know what he's referencing?"

I swallow past the lump forming in my throat. I don't want to try to lie to Oliver, but I can't tell him either. It's not my story to tell.

"Yes."

"I see." He lifts his knuckle to my chest and runs it down my sternum. Immediately, I'm bombarded with memories of being naked at his penthouse. Of being hand fed and groped and forced to orgasm over and over. My body responds like that damn dog experiment with the bells.

"Thank you for the coffee. I have to go."

I expect him to stop me, but he lets me go. I let out a relieved breath when the door closes and I find my seat next to an angry Colin. He turns on me.

"You didn't tell him, did you?"

"Of course not. It's not my secret to tell." I take a sip of my coffee and fight back a moan. Only twice have I had coffee with him. Did he really remember how I like it? That seems odd . . .

After class, Colin hustles me back to our dorm.

"What the hell is wrong with you?" I all but shout as he shoves me inside and closes the door.

"I need a favor." Colin heads to his closet and starts pulling out stuff I've never seen him wear before. Suits. Waistcoats. Ties. Belts.

I lift an eyebrow at him and wait.

"I have a charity dinner tonight that I could not get out of, and I need you to come." He's talking so fast it takes me a second to process what he's said.

"What? Why?" I cross my arms and wait while he starts stripping.

"Blah, blah, blah, rich people's problems, okay? But a good friend of mine needs a date, and I already have one, so I need you to be his date. You don't have to do anything but sit there and eat what's put in front of you." He looks me over for a second. "I have an outfit that should work, and you'll need to shower."

He grabs my hand and sandwiches it between his. "Please, I am begging you. Plus, it'll be fun. Sort of. Once all the boring shit is over. You don't have to stay the whole time, either."

I sigh, but I've already agreed in my head. I can't tell people no when they ask me to help. It's just not in my nature.

I huff out a "Fine," and he grabs me in a hug.

"Thank you! Thank you! Thank you!" He steps back and rearranges the clothes on the bed. "Hurry and shower, I need one too."

When I get out of the shower, Colin hops in and tells me to get dressed.

He's left an outfit for me on my bed, and it's the nicest outfit I'll probably ever put on my body. I find a pair of underwear and steal an undershirt from Colin since all mine are stained.

The shirt is soft as butter against my skin and the slacks fit so well I'm surprised by my own butt. I feel so grown up in this outfit. It's weird how clothes can change how you feel about yourself. Black suit pants and a cream dress shirt. I haven't added the tie or jacket or shoes yet, but I already feel different.

I get the shirt buttoned and tucked into the slacks, then add the belt. I'm buckling it when Colin steps out of the bathroom in underwear and an undershirt.

"Damn, look at that ass! It's unfair how good your ass looks in my pants." He smacks my butt as he passes me, and I blush but smile. He's so over the top.

He gets into his own clothes. Charcoal gray slacks and a pale pink dress shirt. It's subtly Colin, and I like it.

"Do you know how to tie a tie?" he asks me while he does his own.

"Uh, I can do a single Windsor . . . sometimes." I pick up the colored silk and lift the collar of my shirt to place it, but Colin bats my hands out of the way.

"This tie is too wide for a single. I'll do it." With competent hands, he wraps and flips and pulls the tie into a knot, folds over my collar, and adjusts it. "Jacket and shoes, let's go."

He puts on black dress socks and slides his feet into black dress shoes and ties them. I do the same, surprised we wear the same size in basically everything.

I reach for the jacket when Colin stops me. "Hang on, did you put any product in your hair?"

I shake my head no, and he pulls me toward the bathroom. He spritzes me with cologne, then grabs some mousse and gel and does something to my hair. I don't know, I can't see it.

"There, jacket."

He slicks his hair back into a small knot at the back of his head, and it's weird. I don't think I've ever seen him pull his hair back before.

"What?" he asks when he catches me staring.

"You look weird with your hair like that." I shrug on my jacket, and he does the same.

"That's kind of the point. I have to put on a persona for these things, so I make myself look as different from my everyday self as possible."

We make our way downstairs, people staring as we pass. I feel so confident in this suit. I'm not used to it, but I like it. Maybe I'm putting on a persona too. I can be anyone I want tonight, and no one but Colin will know.

A car is at the curb with the driver at the door waiting for us when we leave the dorms. It's giving me flashbacks of Oliver. Colin nods at the driver and slides in, so I do the same.

We drive for a while into a neighborhood that's familiar. A sinking feeling drops into my gut, and I turn to Colin. Are we in Oliver's neighborhood?

"Um, where are we going?"

He looks up from his phone and shoves it into his pocket.

"We're meeting up with our dates so you can meet him and we'll arrive together."

My phone chimes, so I pull it out and see a message.

> TYLER: Dude. Thank you so much for yesterday! Today actually made sense!

I smile at the message, proud that I'm able to help.

> ISAAC: That's great! I'm so happy for you!

> TYLER: Any chance we do a study thing like once a week? I want to make sure I don't fall behind again.

> ISAAC: I'm sure we can do that.

"Whatcha smiling at, baby bird?" Colin leans over my shoulder to look at my phone.

"Tyler just said studying helped."

"Aww, look at you, like a proud little papa bird."

I roll my eyes and shove him off me. "Shut up.

"Uh, Colin?" I'm scanning the buildings, looking for one that I recognize but they all look so similar it's hard to tell.

"What's up?"

"Isn't this where–"

"Come on, we're here." The car comes to a stop, and he

scrambles out before I can finish my question, which probably means he knows what I'm going to ask, and he doesn't want to answer.

Oliver lives, I finish in my head. *Crap.*

We run across the street, a taxi honking at us, but Colin flips them off as I hurry after him. There's a coffee shop tucked away on the bottom floor of a high rise. The gold framed sliding doors open with a quiet whoosh, and Colin strides in like he owns the place. For all I know, he does. Or his father does. I don't actually know what his father does for work. Maybe it's the suit that gives him the confidence?

We head straight for the café, but just being in this building makes me feel under dressed. Why do I always feel like the token poor kid everywhere I go? Like I'm being judged all the time?

The shiny stone floor gives way to rustic wood. It's a classy kind of rustic, as if they want to pretend that everyone is welcome, the blue-collar construction worker type of guy, but really if you don't own Burberry or a Louis Vuitton, you don't belong here.

The whirring of coffee beans being ground and the scent of espresso fills the air. There are a few people sitting in comfortable leather sofas or at the bar-height counters on wooden stools.

Standing inside are two guys about our age also wearing suits, so I assume that's who we're here to meet.

"Alton, Douglas," Colin says when we come to a stop. "This is Isaac."

I shake hands. The two are impeccably dressed, very similar to us, only with white and grey shirts. Alton has jet black hair that's slicked back to the side, giving him a very professional look while Douglas has longer light brown hair that hangs in his eyes. Both are gorgeous though, and taller than both Colin and me. What is it with rich people being beautiful? It's really not fair.

"Douglas, why don't you ride with me and Isaac can ride with

Alton. Give you two a chance to talk for a second before we arrive." Colin grabs Douglas's hand and leaves before I can object. Awesome.

Alton chuckles. "That boy is a force to be reckoned with sometimes."

He puts his hand out, offering for me to go first up the steps next to me as we exit the building. As we wait for Douglas and Colin to leave, Oliver and Owen get out of a sleek black car. Oliver freezes when he sees me next to Alton. Even from across the street, I can see the promise of retribution in his eyes.

Alton sighs and places his hand on my lower back. "Don't worry about them. They have their own things to deal with tonight."

What the hell does that mean?

Twenty-Three

Oliver

"Y ou don't have to go if you want to use this as your pay back. I'm sure I can come up with some excuse." I fix my bowtie in the mirror while my brother sprawls on the floor of my room.

"I am saving it. Plus, if I'm not there, it will turn into a thing with the press and Mom's friends. It's not worth causing the drama, even if you came up with a good excuse."

I toe him as I check my Patek Philippe Celestial watch. "We need to leave or we're going to be tardy, and you know how Mother will react."

"Do you know she said she's introducing me to someone tonight?"

I freeze, going back over Owen's and my recent interactions. "Why would she do that?"

"You tell me." He waves a hand in my direction. "You're the one who's poised to take over for dad and have the wedding of the century, so why am I being singled out."

It didn't make any sense. I feel disjointed, after missing the last family dinner, and come to think of it, I haven't received an update call from our sister in ages.

"I don't know. I'll see what I can find out tonight. Do you know who she is?"

"No, Mom just said she has someone she'd like me to meet and not to bring a date." Owen rolls to lie face down on the oriental rug. "Like I've ever brought a date."

I wrinkle my nose and toe him again. "She didn't request I not bring my usual date." Ruby Walton and I had had an agreement since high school to play each other's beards. Since she's a lesbian and her parents would never accept it, while I didn't want to give my family nor a girl any idea about what bringing them to dinner with my parents meant, it worked out perfectly for us.

"Interesting. I can't speak to her motivation, but I will find out tonight."

"Thanks," Owen mumbles into the rug.

"I am leaving without you if you're not dressed in the next two minutes, and then you'll have to deal with traffic getting uptown."

"Fuck you. It will take over an hour at this time of day." He bangs his head against the floor a few times, then pushes to his feet. "Do not leave without me."

"Two minutes." I click the timer on my watch, walking into my closet to pick a cologne. I select the custom Tom Ford I had made for me while in Paris over the summer. It drives Isaac wild, and after seeing him in a coffee shop with someone else, I've decided to pay him a visit after the dinner tonight.

Owen somehow jogs up to the helicopter mostly dressed before the two minutes is up. He's barefoot and his bowtie isn't tied, but I'm impressed. "Tie this for me," he says after he gets his shoes on.

"It's a wonder Mother thinks you can get married. You can't even take care of yourself."

"I know. I can't even speak to women. How does she expect me to marry one?" Owen brushes his hair out of his face, putting his headset on.

The ride to the American Museum of Natural History is less than ten minutes. As a backdrop for a charity event, it's one of my favorites. Who didn't love to be in a museum after dark? There is something forbidden and erotic about it. And I've always wanted to climb the blue whale model that sits over the tables for dinner.

My parents' gala isn't the type with fanfare and influencers who wanted the attention of cameras. They hate those kinds of new money wealth flaunters. So the event isn't publicized, except for a few tabloid shots of attendees arriving.

Owen and I make it inside without any issue, where Ruby is waiting for me.

I pull a black box with a simple bow out of the inside pocket of my coat before I pass it to the attendant. I press it into her hands. "Happy anniversary, darling. What is this, eight years?" It's our little inside joke since our first "date" was at this exact event.

"You're so thoughtful. You shouldn't have." Ruby pulls the delicate bow, meeting my eyes. "I didn't get you anything."

"Wearable symbols are less important for men."

She gasps when she opens the box. "I cannot believe you! Mom and Dad are going to cry when you don't propose. I hope you know."

I take the Cartier love bracelet, and she holds out her wrist for me to slip on. "Are we doing a dramatic break up then? Do put it on my calendar so I don't forget."

Ruby rolls her eyes. "If you want to break up you need to

initiate it. Mother will just ask me why I didn't fake a pregnancy to keep you."

I shudder. "Please don't. I'm not ready to be a fake father."

"Do not even speak to me. I don't want to even pretend I let a penis near me."

Owen laughs. "Me either."

"Not even Rachel's silicone one? Shame for her," I say cheekily.

Ruby smacks me lightly. "Do not speak her name in this room of sharks."

"My apologies." I don't envy her. She'd fallen in love with one of her radical feminist leftist professors, and her parents would never approve. It would be worse than me bringing Isaac home. At least his parents' political views aligned with my parents' agenda. We'd all be better off when the whole lot of them died and left us to be the freaks they'd raised.

"Can I get you a glass of champagne?" I ask as I pull out her seat.

"Please." Ruby sits and lets me scoot her in.

"Owen, do you want to get a drink with me, or do you need to find your mysterious date?"

"I'm drinking. Mom can wait. It might be the only way I get through tonight."

Ruby grabs me before I leave. "Oliver, can I ask a favor?"

"Always." I lean in.

She drops her voice to a whisper. "Can we leave early, and can you cover for me?"

"Only if you don't get arrested again. I swear your dad would have killed me if he could have."

"I promise I won't."

I kiss the top of her head before going to the bar. I need something much stronger than champagne to get through tonight.

I stop in my tracks halfway to the bar when a hint of his voice catches my ear.

It can't be.

"Did you hear that?" I scan the tables.

"Huh?" Owen asks.

"Go get your drink. I'll meet you there," I say when I find Isaac sitting with Colin on one side and the guy he was with at the coffee shop on his other.

"Is that a good idea?" Owen grabs my sleeve, his gaze following the direction I face.

"I don't care."

"As your brother and the only person who knows you at all, what the fuck?" He keeps ahold of me. "What does that guy have over you?"

I don't have an answer for him.

Owen searches my face. "This isn't like you."

"What would you like me to say?"

"I think you like him," Owen says carefully.

I pull my sleeve out of his grasp. "I am not allowed to like him. I'm enjoying myself until I'm told who to marry, which sounds like isn't far off because of what mom's doing to you."

I try to make my escape again, but Mother steps in front of me. "Good evening." I fake a smile.

"Good evening, dear. Where's your brother?" she asks.

"He was right here?" That rat bastard. "Do you need me to fetch him?"

"No, I'll speak to him later and explain, but I have someone I want you to meet."

"Me?" I ask. Alarm bells go off in my head.

"I know you've had a date for ages, but after hearing the rumors last year . . ."

I sigh internally. After Ruby was arrested protesting with a group of lesbians, there were quite a few rumors. I thought my parents had missed that bit of gossip since it had been a year, but clearly it had been a false sense of security. "Awful rumors and not a hint of truth."

Mother narrowed her eyes. "No, but you know your father . . ." She didn't have to say "would never approve." "So he gave Owen's plus one to Cassandra Covington. He and your father are becoming such great friends . . ."

I stop listening to her, trying to place Cassandra . . . I know Colin has a couple of sisters, but Cassandra didn't ring a bell.

"Your father would love for you to come meet her and be her escort for the evening, as she doesn't know anyone."

Why wouldn't she know anyone? My ears buzz as I try to make sense of what my mother is getting at.

"I can't just ignore Ruby. It would be rude."

"No. We'd never expect you to do that." She links her arm through mine. "Come meet her. I'm sure you'll love her."

My gaze flicks back to where Isaac sits, laughing with his date. Colin meets my stare and glares. Is this why Colin is acting like a bitch? He has to know it means nothing. This is standard practice for our families. What am I missing?

As soon as we approach my father and Colin's and I see the girl standing between them, it all clicks into place.

Twenty-Four

Oliver

"Oliver, so good to see you." Mr. Covington holds out his hand.

I take it in a firm grasp. "How are things?" I despise fake pleasantries.

"Couldn't be better." He releases my hand and places his on the girl's shoulders, standing between him and my father.

"This is Cassandra. My youngest." Mr. Covington smiles, meeting my father's eyes. "Say hello, Cassie."

"It's a pleasure to meet you," Cassie half whispers. She looks no older than eighteen, and I'm irate.

"The pleasure is mine," I reply, digging for even a spark of nicety to fake to my parents.

My father and Mr. Covington seem giddy, and I can't help but feel like they think they are giving me some sort of prize in this girl. I hate the way our families do things, but for the most part arranged marriage is still very much alive and well in these social circles. But this seems low even for them.

"I hope you don't mind showing Cassie around, helping her get to know people." Mr. Covington winks at me. He actually fucking winks.

I barely swallow a gag. "I don't mind at all. This is your first gala?"

"It is. It's lovely. Your parents do such a good job." She must have been in boarding school or something before this.

"Are you going to university in the city?"

"I don't . . . yet . . . I graduate in May."

I cough. "Pardon me?" I meet my father's eyes. "You're how old?"

Cassie blushes. "Seventeen."

These motherfuckers. No wonder Colin is so mad. Not only is this his fucking baby sister, but she's a child. I glance between my father and Mr. Covington again. The wink makes even more sense. They actually believe they are handing me a prize in this innocent girl.

My father knew about my proclivity for new and not letting people get attached, but why they thought this . . . I don't want to know, and now I have to find a way to shut it down without giving them the opportunity to shop her off to someone else in the room. Fuck my life and fuck Colin for assuming this bullshit about me.

"Want to take a turn with me?" I ask Cassie, offering my arm. "I'll show you around the museum if it's okay with your parents."

"Excellent," Mr. Covington proclaims, and I have to get out of here before I punch him in the face.

"Where do you go to school?" I ask as soon as we are out of ear shot of her parents to get an idea of how worldly this fucking seventeen-year-old is.

"I'm homeschooled," Cassie admits. "I got in with a bad

crowd at fourteen, and they pulled me out of school." Worst-case scenario.

"And now they're auctioning you off before you turn eighteen and get pregnant?" And making it my fucking problem.

Cassie makes a face. "Oh . . ."

"Oh, is right. Let me guess, Colin isn't happy you're here."

"He did seem pretty upset." Cassie bites her lip.

Thank fuck I do not have a younger sister. Just a pain in my ass younger brother to manage. I spot Owen hiding behind a fake plant next to the bar.

He holds up his hands when I near, but he has nowhere to go with the wall and bar blocking any hope of escape. "Did Mom and Dad put you up to this?"

"No, they brought her here to set me up with her, not you."

Owen instantly looks relieved. "Thank the lord. May you have many happy years or whatever."

"She's seventeen, and I need you to babysit. You're the only one here I can trust to actually keep an eye on her."

Owen makes a face. "Ew. Is Dad trading bulls and goats for her? What is this?"

"Thank you. They've lost their fucking mind. So will you watch her?"

He looks her over again with a disgusted curl of his lip. "Is she gonna try to run away or something?"

We both turn on Cassie.

"If you get me a drink, I won't."

"I'm okay corrupting the youth when her parents are trying to sell her." He points at her. "But only wine, and one glass."

"Deal." Cassie holds out her hand.

Owen takes it, and I'm already gone, seeking out Isaac.

Thankfully, Isaac is still sitting at his table with Colin.

"I need a word with both of you."

"Where's my sister?" Colin snaps.

"With Owen, drinking behind your parents' back. Thanks for the fucking warning."

"What?" Colin shoves to his feet.

I block him in. "Will you stop being an insufferable hot head?"

"I told my parents not to leave her alone with you."

"Let's level set for a minute. Your own fucking father winked at me after asking me to show her around."

Colin shakes with anger. "She's seventeen fucking years old."

"Can we take this somewhere else so we aren't making a scene?" I say, under my breath.

Colin glances around, then fixes his shirt with a nod.

"You too," I say to Isaac when he doesn't move.

"Why?"

Colin glares at him, and he gets up.

We duck under velvet ropes into an empty hallway.

"Where is Cassie?" Colin demands immediately.

"I told you. Safe with Owen."

"Where?" he says through his teeth.

"Will you stop thinking either of us wants your baby sister? I'm fucking your roommate, in case you forgot."

Colin crosses his arms over his chest. "What do you want?"

"Why didn't you warn me?"

"I assumed you knew."

"Why would I know?"

Colin shrugs.

"I knew nothing of our parents' nefarious plan to set me up with your sister. I'm appalled and disgusted. I'd much rather fuck your roommate."

"They won't stop. We both know they won't."

"I know." I hate telling Colin he is right, but he is.

"Then what are you going to do?"

"I don't know, but I will figure it out." I didn't have the brain capacity for this right now.

"Give me your word," Colin says.

"I give you my word, but you better stop setting up Isaac on dates."

"Where is Cassie? A location, Oliver."

"With my brother at the bar." I don't let him escape. "I want your word."

"Not one second before this is called off." Colin shoves past me heading toward the bar.

I growl, turning on Isaac.

"I didn't know it's a date-date. He said it was a favor."

"I'd love to believe you, but as you are on a date, I'm going to make sure you think of me all night."

Isaac's brows furrow. "I'm not interested in him. It's just a favor."

I lean in, putting my lips next to his ear. "If he's not interested in you, enjoy explaining why you can't sit down and why my cum is leaking out of you all night."

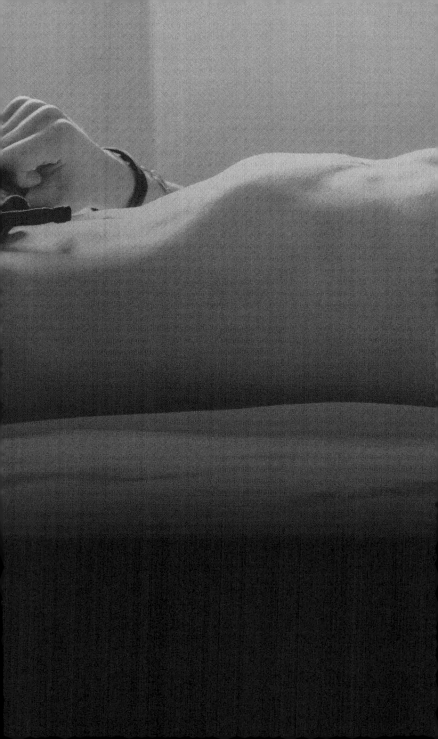

Twenty-Five

Isaac

My entire body clenches both with fear and lust. He doesn't have to speak, just look at me with that fire in his eyes, and I melt. But when he stands over me, whispers dirty words in my ear, I don't want to fight him.

A needy whimper escapes my throat, and Oliver smirks. He's won. He always does.

I'm needy for him, and I hate myself for it. Every time I let myself fall into him, it digs him deeper into me. When he walks away to marry whoever that woman is he brought with him, it will destroy me.

"Here kitty, kitty." He curls a finger at me.

It's almost condescending, but I crave it.

I want to be wanted by him.

My breath catches in my throat, but I nod. In a place like this, he can't hold my hand. Nothing so obvious. While we might be kind of tucked out of the way for our conversation, we're easily stumbled upon.

Oliver leads me deeper into the museum where there are no guests, and the lights are dim. I'm not paying attention to what's around us despite always wanting to have visited this place. Maybe I can convince Colin to bring me back during regular hours.

Oliver finds a dark corner and spins on me, gripping my jaw and crashing his lips to mine in an angry, hungry kiss. His free hand splays across my lower back, anchoring me against his body. I moan into his mouth, and he swallows it, thrusting his tongue between my lips like a man starved of affection.

His fingers dig into my cheeks hard enough I'm afraid he'll leave bruises that I can't explain away.

"Oliver," I mumble against his lips.

"You're on a damn date." He growls against my mouth.

"It's not a real date," I try to argue, but Oliver spins me around and pushes me against the wall. "Colin asked me to come as a favor."

"I wish I believed you," he says against my ear. There's a sound of a buckle being undone. My stomach tenses, fear and arousal fighting.

"What are you doing?" My words tremble in the dark with my face against the plaster. He pins me tightly against the wall so I can't move, not that I've tried very hard.

"Marking what's mine." His hand slides down my back to my butt, cupping the muscle and ` his fingers in. "Have you ever been spanked, kitten?"

"Yes," I whisper, and close my eyes. My dad is no stranger to corporal punishment while reciting scriptures.

"Good." Both of his hands wrap around me, opening my belt and pants, then shoving everything down to mid-thigh.

stay still. Whatever he's planning will be worse if I fight him on it.

"Hold your shirt out of the way and stick your ass out while I turn your ass a beautiful shade of red."

He moves to the side but faces my back and smacks my butt cheek hard. It startles a squeak from me, and I clench on instinct.

"Hush. You don't want anyone to come back here to investigate, do you?"

He slaps my other cheek, then doesn't stop. One side, then the other, back and forth, up and down to make all of the skin sting and heat. I try not to squirm, but it hurts while also turning me on. My dick is half hard, like my body is confused.

Do I like this?

I don't know, but I also don't want him to take his hands off me. After a few smacks, I start to drift, almost like I'm not in my own head but floating. The heat of my angry skin dulls, the sting isn't as sharp.

"You're so hot like this. Bent over for me." He rubs my cheeks, massaging the ache into my muscle. "I love when you do what I ask."

His reassurance hits deep. I crave those parts of him, too. In a room full of anyone who would have him, he picks me. I'm high off the power of being his choice.

I close my eyes and let myself go. Oliver will take care of me, I know that much for sure. In this situation, I can trust him.

I do trust him.

I can't keep track of time...has it been five minutes or thirty? I don't know, but eventually he stops, and I realize I'm panting. I'm not as hard, and my butt burns enough that I don't want to pull my clothes back on. Is his hand as sore as my skin?

"Good boy." Oliver kisses my neck. "Now your punishment can begin."

Punishment?

I whimper, but don't really understand what he's saying. My brain isn't firing on all cylinders. What is he going to do? Punishment? For what? What did I do this time?

He fidgets with something, his belt maybe? But I don't open my eyes to look. It feels good leaning against the cool wall in the dark with Oliver's hands on me. He's leaving marks on my body again. Marks I crave.

Something smooth drags up my thigh, and I flinch.

What is he doing?

Do I get to orgasm this time?

"So jumpy." He keeps rubbing my skin with what I'm pretty sure is his belt until I relax again. "Stick your ass out farther."

I comply and wait.

"Your skin is a beautiful shade, kitten, but I think it needs some stripes." Slowly, he drags it up the inside of my thigh and against my balls. "Don't tense up, that will only make it worse. If you're good for me, I'll let you come when I fuck you."

I groan and try to relax, but the way he's playing with me is making me hard. He waits, ever full of patience and control until I've calmed down before removing the leather from my skin.

The first strike catches me off guard. The smack echoes in the room and steals the breath from my lungs. My body reacts, instincts driving me to protect myself, but my brain isn't involved. It's offline.

"Breathe." Oliver's voice is there in my ear, grounding me as I gasp, then he puts a hand over my mouth as I yell. I have no control over the sound. It's ripped from my soul through my chest, forcing my back to arch and hands to slap against the wall. I have been spanked before, but it was nothing like this.

"Shh, breathe. You're okay." Oliver is rubbing his hand over the abused skin, taking some of the sting out of it. "So beautiful."

A tear rolls down my cheek, but he brushes it away with his finger.

"Ready?"

I whimper. "How many more?"

"Two."

I suck in a deep breath and nod. I wasn't expecting it the last time, but now I know, and I can control myself better.

Why do I want him to be proud of me? Of the way I take his spanking.

The second strike hits, and I suck in a deep breath and jerk away. Not that I can go far. His hand is there, rubbing my skin, and it's comforting. I let out a sob and bite my sleeve to muffle my sounds.

The third slap hits, and I jerk up onto my toes, forcing my body straight and no longer pushing my butt out for him. It's more like I'm trying to climb up the wall to get away from the pain.

"Shh." Oliver slides against my back, his hand not stopping its stroking of my painful skin. His other hand reaches around my hip and wraps around my soft cock. "I will never get enough of how you react to me. I wish we could hide away the rest of the night together." There is an ache in his voice.

I moan at his touch, my dick perking up quickly at the attention. "Why can't we?"

"They'll notice." His tone is sad.

"Who?"

"Everyone." He rocks into me, the soft fabric of his slacks abrasive against my ass. "You wear my marks so beautifully, kitten."

His hands disappear from my body, but he's still close enough for me to feel his nearness. There's rustling of clothing and the opening of some kind of packet before slick fingers slide between my cheeks and over my hole.

I suck in a surprised breath and groan, pushing back against them. "Please." I don't care what I'm asking for.

"I'm going to fill you with *my* cum to take back to your date."

I shiver at the image his words put in my head, but I want it, I want him. Tomorrow I'll hate myself for it, but in this moment, he's the only thing I want.

"You want that, don't you?"

"Please," I mumble when his fingers leave my body. He didn't warm me up much, and I think that was part of the point. Is this part of the punishment, too?

"Remember who you belong to, Isaac."

The thick head of his cock pushes against my hole, and I relax to let him in, leaning back into it and crying out at the burn.

He doesn't slow down or wait for me to adjust, just takes me. Pulling me from the wall, he grips my throat and makes my back arch while he thrusts. There's no softness here, only his carnal need to prove to himself that I'm his.

If only he knew how true it is.

"I'm yours, only yours." The words tumble from my lips, and his fingers dig into my hip with bruising force. I want it to be true. So badly it hurts.

"I know. All mine."

The burning stretch gives way to pleasure, and even the sting when his hips meet my heated flesh doesn't take away the high of him. It's hard, deep, rough. A claiming in the most primal way possible.

"I love being inside you. Stretched around my cock, so filthy and needy." He twitches inside me, grinding and staying deep, while his hips rub against my stinging skin. I feel more alive than I ever have.

Every part of me is on fire. I'm throbbing and on the verge of coming in a matter of minutes.

"Oliver," I sob his name and cling to him. "More." More what? I don't know. All of him. Every touch, and kiss, and stretch. How did he lay me so bare?

His lips find my ear. "No one will ever make you feel like I do."

Tingles explode across my skin, and my dick pulses in his hand a second before cum shoots from me, covering his hand, and dripping onto the floor and my pants.

My eyes roll back in my head and my body sags.

"Such an agreeable cumslut." Oliver groans into my neck as he tenses and slams into me one more time before stilling. I love feeling him twitch inside of me and the warmth of his cum. "*My* slut."

I let him hold my weight and drop my head back on his shoulder with my eyes closed, letting myself just feel.

His hand leaves my dick, and he swipes cum across my lip. I open my eyes to watch him lick it off his hand, then turn my face toward him to suck it off my lip. He kisses me, thrusting his tongue and my taste into my mouth. It's slower than earlier, lazier, but just as potent.

He lingers for just a minute before he releases me and slips from my body. I pull my clothes back to right and realize he barely opened his pants. He's putting his belt back on as I'm tucking my shirt in.

Once he's dressed, Oliver watches me for a second until I meet his gaze.

"Enjoy feeling my cum inside you while finishing your date. Wishing I'm taking you home to fuck you again instead of a guy who will never know what you need."

I don't want to go back to my date.

"Isaac," he calls over his shoulder.

"Yes?"

"If he touches you, I'll kill him."

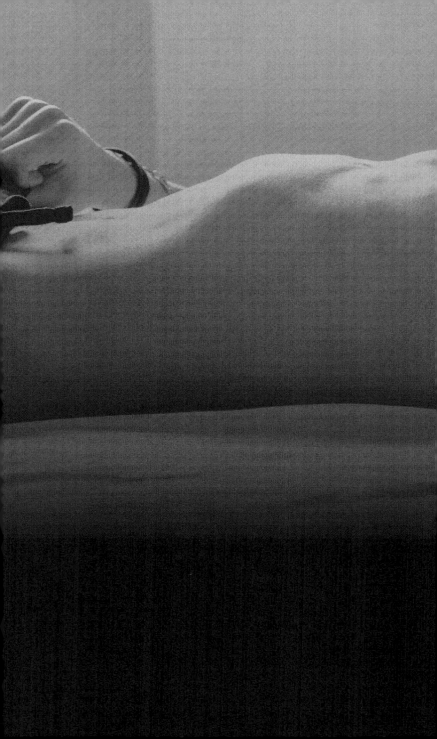

Twenty-Six

Isaac

When I get back to the main area, it takes me a minute to find Colin, Douglas, and Alton, but I hear Colin laugh and head in that direction.

Moving my way through the crowd, my eyes lock on Colin who lifts an eyebrow at me. I blush but continue.

"Isaac, there you are." Alton hands me a glass of something, and I don't bother to ask what it is before taking a big drink and coughing.

"Whoa there," he says and slaps my back. "That's a rum and Coke."

"Yes it is," I wheeze. And a strong one.

Colin scans my body, probably finding evidence of the tryst I had with Oliver, but I do my best to ignore him and not squirm as my skin smarts from the brush of cotton over the abused flesh.

"So what normally happens at these things?" I ask before Colin can start in on me.

Douglas looks at his fancy watch. "They will announce it's time to find our seats in about three minutes. Then there will be speeches, probably some kind of entertainment or slide show of pictures from whatever charity we're donating to, then dinner and dessert. Another speech and dancing or mingling."

Sounds boring.

Alton puts his hand on my lower back. "Should we head in and find our seats, then?"

Crap. I really don't think I can sit down. The chairs are not very comfortable, and I'm sore in more than one way.

In the corner of my eye, I catch a glimpse of either Oliver or Owen, I'm not sure which, with Colin's sister Cassie talking with who I think are the Godfrey parents. I've seen Colin's parents and it isn't them, but I guess they could know other people as well.

Cum is trickling down my thigh, and it's all I can do not to squirm at the tickling sensation.

"I need the bathroom. I'll meet you in there," I say and hand him back the glass before turning to march away. I don't know if the bathrooms are this way, but I don't care. There wasn't one between where Oliver took us, so they have to be over here somewhere.

Thankfully, I find one and hustle inside to clean up some. I wish it was a single and I could take a look at the damage he inflicted on my skin, but maybe it's better that I can't.

I clean up as well as I can without taking a suspicious amount of time and hurry back to my table. My skin feels like it's on fire every time I move, but I have to find a way to deal with it. There's no way I can tell *anyone* about my discomfort.

Distracted by my underwear rubbing on my sensitive skin, I get lost for a minute, so by the time I get back to the room with all the tables, the doors are closed.

With a huff of embarrassment, I find the door I think is close to where we were sitting and open it carefully to slip inside. The lights are dimmed so the brightness from the hallway is very apparent. Embarrassment has me apologizing to the tables near the door as I skate along the edge of the room in search of my table.

Finally, I catch a break, and it's only two down from where I came in. Alton looks up as I get to my chair and smiles before turning back to the man at a podium in the front of the room. I pull out the chair but hesitate. I really don't want to sit, but I also can't just stand here like an idiot.

"What's wrong with you?" Colin hisses across his date at me.

With an internal groan, I force myself into the seat and can't hold back the hiss when my weight is pressed against the seat. I'm almost sweating from the effort of not sitting too fast but not taking too long that it's weird.

"Dude," Colin whispers again. "What's your deal?"

"Nothing," I hiss back and pick up the glass Alton must have put in my place for me. I've never really had access to alcohol, but I think I'm going to need it tonight. Anything to dull my senses will be welcome.

I chug my glass, not caring how it looks, and lean back in my chair with a groan. Oops.

Alton leans in and puts a hand on my knee. "Are you okay?"

"Yup," I say a little too high pitched and lean over to pour myself some water from the pitcher in the center of the table. Forcing myself to take a deep breath to calm my nerves, I close my eyes and drop my shoulders, too.

But that's when I hear it.

A voice I haven't heard in months. Well, not in person, but it lives in my head.

"God gave us two sons because he knew the first one would fall victim to perversion."

With horror coursing through my veins, I turn and find my parents sitting at the table next to mine with the Godfrey family.

No.

I know it's written all over my face for anyone who looks my way to see. Tears welling up in my eyes while my gut is clenched so tight I want to puke. My father's face shows sadness to those who don't know him, but I can see the anger, the betrayal, the hatred.

My lungs seize, and I feel like I can't breathe, but I can't look away either. Does he know I'm here? What are they even doing at the gala? How do they know Oliver's parents? I'm so confused.

Homes for Heroes flickers onto the screen behind the podium, and it all starts to click into place. I know my father is involved with this charity, he talked about it a lot and how much it was helping the homeless veterans in our community find God, but I didn't pay much attention to it. Too lost in my own head and hiding who I was. Who I am.

My entire life, I was told we had to live in poverty to prove our faithfulness to God. If that is true, then how the hell did they get here? I don't want to know what the tickets to get in cost, much less what clothes they're wearing cost.

The names of the CEO and other important positions are put up on the screen, then the board of directors. My father is the third name down under that title, and it hits me like a freight train. My entire life was a lie. Everything they ever told me was *bullshit*.

Father turns, and I spin in my seat so he can't see my face. I'm more afraid of him seeing me and making a scene, showing Colin and Oliver just how undeserving I am to be here.

A lump forms in my throat, but I don't let myself fall apart. Not here. Not now.

Leaning against the table, I take a minute to ground myself.

Ignore them. They don't exist in this world. You are here with Colin, Douglas, and Alton. Focus on our table. If they say something to me, Colin will defend me.

I hate that I don't know if Oliver will stand up for me or not, but I don't know how he is around his parents. Maybe keeping the peace is how he is with them. If my parents have found a way to befriend his parents, it would be in his best interest to go along with them.

Flicking my gaze back to their table, I find Oliver sandwiched between Cassie and another woman with no expression on his face. Nothing to give away what he's thinking. Owen is chugging a glass of something, scotch maybe? Whiskey? Hard to tell.

The longer the speeches go on, the more exhausted I become, the more I'm sure this was the last time Oliver will touch me.

He has a female date, for Christ's sake. Possibly two. Both of them fit in better with these people than I do. There's not a chance in hell he'll come out and claim me to his parents if they're friends with my parents. Why would he? Look at them, they're beautiful. Cassie is underage and Oliver said he isn't interested, but the other woman he came in with is gorgeous.

Finally, the lights turn up, glasses are raised in a toast, and people stop going up to the podium to talk. Wait staff bring out trays of food to serve. I don't question how they know what everyone wants. It doesn't matter.

Chatter in the room rises, Colin and Douglas are laughing about something, and Alton chimes in, but I'm checked out. I pick at the food on my plate, not paying attention to what it is.

"You have a son in college?" a female voice I don't recognize asks behind me.

"Technically, yes, but he's no longer a part of our family. He chose to walk a sinful path in life instead of staying on God's path." The knife in my heart twists at my mother's words.

I put my folk down and stare at nothing in the middle of the table.

I will never be able to outrun my past if I stay in this city. I will never be good enough for Oliver to accept long term. I'm the charity case on the fencing team and was probably only accepted to the New York Gods as part of some statistic requirement.

"Oh, I see," Mrs. Godfrey says and clears her throat. "Our boys graduate this year, and Oliver will take over the business from his father. We're expecting a wedding to follow soon after." Her tone says this is not a negotiation, and that's all I can take.

Pushing back from the table, I mumble an excuse and leave the room. I wander the space aimlessly, just needing to get away from everything to lick my wounds and cry. Why does getting the confirmation of what I knew make it so much worse?

I find a darkened corner and slide down the wall to sit on the floor. The cold tile is soothing as I cover my face with my hands and sob as quietly as I can manage. Tears stream down my face, and my breathing hiccups as the fantasy I've built comes crashing down around me. I knew I couldn't keep him. I *knew* it, but having the truth shoved in my face makes it so much more agonizing.

It feels like my heart is bleeding out onto the floor and no one cares because I'm not worth caring about. The shattered pieces of who I am are sharp and slice through my chest as I attempt to pick them up and put them back together. But I'll never be whole again. How can I be? First my parents turned on me, and then I threw myself at the most unavailable person on the planet.

I'm the common factor here. I'm the problem.

Footsteps echo in the empty hallway, and I quickly wipe my face and scramble to my feet. I sniffle back the tears and hope the low light helps hide my red splotchy face from whoever it is.

Of course, it's Oliver that appears and stops inches from me.

"Isaac—"

"Don't." I hold up my hand and push him back so I can get away from the wall to not get trapped. "I can't do this anymore."

Oliver stands a little straighter and watches me carefully,

assessing me like he always does. "Please enlighten me. What are we not doing anymore?"

"Whatever this is. I can't do it anymore. You're nothing but a bad habit I desperately need to quit."

For the first time, I walk away from him, but I haven't won. I don't have the upper hand like he normally does. All I have is a broken heart and nothing to show for it.

Twenty-Seven

Oliver

I saac's reaction sits with me for days, and I can't focus on anything else. No one has ever held this kind of power over me, and I hate it. His words replay over and over in my mind, clouding my classes and even practice. My toy he is no longer. He won't even look at me. I don't want to isolate him, and it wouldn't work anyway, because he isn't trying to interact with anyone. He just sits in the corner scribbling in a notebook until we start practice.

Coach is going to get mad if he doesn't integrate into the team. He lets me have a lot of liberty with the guys, but I can't ostracize Isaac completely, and I don't want to. I hate knowing this sad, depressed mess he's turned into is my fault. I want to put the fire back in his eyes.

I'm not ready to face what this says about me either.

"You're my drill partner today. Come on."

"It's not time to start yet." Isaac doesn't look up from his notebook.

"We're getting an early start. You're here and dressed." I playfully try to snatch the notebook from his hands.

He snaps it closed and shoves it in his bag, reluctantly getting up.

"Why am I a habit you need to quit?"

"Because," Isaac snaps.

"I'm not settling for because. What upset you at the gala?" I press as he gets his foil and mask.

"Everything. Nothing. I see you're not available."

"What are you talking about?" I run through the night, trying to figure out what could have set him off.

"I'm a toy, nothing more." He avoids my eyes going to the mat.

"You like being a toy." I get in his face, sliding a finger under his chin.

"Don't touch me. You're just using me until you marry your *girlfriend*." He pulls away, sharply.

"Why are you upset I brought a date? You brought one."

"It's different."

"How?" I ask.

"What drills are we doing?" He lifts his foil.

I lift my foil. "Footwork. Yours still needs work when you get flustered."

"Fine."

I advance on him, and he backs off. We do it five or six times before adding in blades. "Why is my bringing a date different than you bringing one? Ruby isn't interested in me. She doesn't like men."

"I heard your mom, and I know why Colin's upset. You're going to marry a woman, so this isn't going anywhere. I don't want to talk anymore."

I keep trying to engage him in conversation during practice, but he is either silent or gives me one-word answers. I can't even get a second with him in the locker room because he leaves without changing. He knows if I corner him, we'll fuck, and it's clear he doesn't even want to be forced.

Anger burns in my gut.

But I'm not angry at him.

I'm angry for the first time with the narrow path I must tread.

I corner Colin in the locker room after practice a week later. "We need to talk."

"I have nothing to say to you."

"What are you going to say at dinner tonight when our parents make their intentions known?"

Colin stiffens. "They didn't tell me you would be at dinner."

"So they are doing this behind your back?" I ask.

"Dinner could be for any reason. Our dads are friends and have been for a long time."

I scoff. "No, they aren't. My dad uses yours when he needs something, and this is bigger. Did you think we were having dinner with both our families for anything else?"

"It's just my father wanting to not deal with Cassie. The second you say no, he'll get it out of his head," Colin says like a delusional asshole.

"My father would never put a marriage on the table if it wasn't big. This isn't convenience. I'm his heir apparent. Use your brain."

"I will kill you."

"I don't want to fuck your sister, you imbecile. I'm trying to find an amicable solution that doesn't involve marrying her." If

211

there is one thing I despise, it's people who stick their head in the sand and get mad instead of finding a solution. "Pouting and attempting to make my life hell won't make this go away."

"It will make me feel better." He moves to step around me.

I block his exit. "It's wiser to have me as an ally than an enemy. Do you want your sister sold at auction to the highest bidder when I refuse to marry her?"

That gets his attention. Colin's eyes meet mine. "Fuck you."

"It's the truth of it. And if your father wants to get rid of Cassie that bad, the second I tell my parents no, they will find someone else. I see the determination in your father's eyes to make her someone else's problem."

Colin's jaw flexes. He knows I'm right.

"What do you suggest?"

"I don't know. Do you think there's any changing his mind? Because if he's this determined . . ."

"I don't know." Colin wrings his hands.

"You need to make sure you're at dinner so we can make this a recon mission. Gather as much information as possible."

"Fine. But we aren't friends."

I laugh, shaking my head. "Whatever you need to tell yourself. I'm not offering friendship, merely an alliance."

"I'm not helping you with Isaac."

I consider his statement. "I don't need help, just for you to stop interfering."

He holds out his hand. "Fine."

I take it. "Answer one question."

"Depends on what it is."

"The notebooks he's always writing in. What are they?"

Colin narrows his eyes, clearly deciding if he should tell me. "He's drawing. He's always drawing. He wanted to go to art school, but his parents wouldn't let him."

"Thank you."

Colin shudders. "Don't do that again?"

"What?" I ask, confused by his reaction.

"Be nice to me. It's off putting and not right."

I hold up my middle finger.

Dinner with Colin's family carries a weight over it. My parents and his both act normal, but I feel their silence. Cassie sits next to me, and she talks nonstop, which Colin takes the brunt of. I'm waiting for the bomb to drop.

"I can't hold it in any longer." My sister shoves back from the table.

Mother glances around, looking confused. "What are you talking about, Olivia?"

"I can't sit here another minute like this. Greg and I broke up." Olivia takes her ring off and tosses it at Greg. "We broke up three months ago, and he doesn't want to tell his parents, but I can't keep planning a wedding until he gets up the courage to tell all of you."

"You're getting married in June. We have everything booked." My mother gasps, staring at Greg. "What happened?"

"Don't look at him!" Olivia shouts.

"Can we discuss this when we don't have guests?" Father asks.

"No. You keep inviting him over and I can't stand to look at his face." Olivia picks up Greg's plate. "Leave."

Greg makes a sheepish face, glancing between my parents and Olivia. "My apologies."

"Olivia, honey, I know you're upset, but Greg loves you. We have almost everything planned and the Four Seasons booked for June! It's your dream wedding."

"I don't care. I can't marry him!" Olivia puts both hands on the table and leans in toward my parents. "Either he's leaving or I am."

"Olivia, do you have to be so dramatic?" Mother sighs.

"I'm serious," Olivia says through her teeth.

My father flexes his jaw. "Greg, I'm sorry to have to do this . . . but we'll discuss this at the office Monday."

"I understand." Unceremoniously, Greg stands and leaves the room.

An awkward silence settles over us. Olivia hadn't breathed a word of this to me. I don't know what could have happened.

"Maybe you don't have to give up the deposits," Colin's mother says coyly. "If there were someone else who hit it off . . ."

"I hadn't thought of that. It might be a good idea to hold on to it for a little while." Mother smirks over at Colin's. They are thick as thieves.

I put my napkin to my mouth, hiding my grimace.

Colin outright gags.

We finish dinner with small talk before moving to the library for after-dinner drinks. Easier to avoid Cassie in this setting. Thankfully.

I'm not in the mood to play my part.

The Covingtons leave, and now it's time for the real inquisition.

I'm not the first victim. My parents corner Olivia trying to get out of her why she and Greg broke up.

She's tightlipped, which means it's bad or embarrassing. I feel bad for her. She's been the shining beacon of everything my parents want in an oldest child for so long and still they favor me over her. I don't blame her for finally getting sick of it, even if it puts more pressure on me.

"I'm taking a job with my law firm in London," Olivia says

after more pressure from Mom to go to counseling with Greg and to keep the engagement ring.

My father stops mid drink. "What?"

"I'm moving in a month. Greg and I are done for good."

Owen and I exchange a glance.

Mom sits stunned, and Father picks up the paper.

"Good for her, honestly," Owen mutters under his breath so only I can hear him.

I nod, happy Olivia is doing what she wants but annoyed because I know this means I will be the focus.

"Oliver," Mother calls when she gives up on trying to talk sense in to my sister.

"Yes?" I get up to make myself another drink. I bring one to Mother and hand it to her before sitting next to Olivia.

"I have something for you."

"Oh?" Maybe this isn't going to be about Cassie.

"I thought you'd want Grandma-ma's ring to give to someone special when the time is right." My mother presses a box into my hands.

I open it to find an ornate ruby ring. The center stone is at least seven carats. It's gaudy but sophisticated. Nothing I'd ever give anyone I wanted to marry. "It's lovely."

"It's important you make the right choice when it comes to the woman you're going to marry. This woman will be your foundation. She will curate the right company and social engagements. She will run the charity after I'm gone . . ."

I hold up a hand to cut her off. "Mother, I understand, but I am much too busy with school and fencing to think about this right now . . ."

"We'd like you to get to know Cassie. I'm sure you can either cut fencing or figure out how to work around taking her out," my Father says without looking up from the paper. It isn't worded as a threat, but I know what he means. He'd make a call to have me kicked off the team if he sees fit.

"I'll find time."

I seethe the rest of the evening, trying to figure a way out of this. If I give in to what they want, I'll piss Colin off and Isaac won't forgive me, and they'll probably use my sister's venue to marry us in June. I can't let it get that far, but I also can't figure out a solution.

I'm a caged animal, backed into a corner.

My sister claims work in the morning, and Owen and I use the same excuse for school to leave.

"Can we have dinner before you move? No pressure." I stop my sister at the elevator before we part ways.

"As long as you're not on their side," Olivia replies. Hard as steel. She is more like Father than even I am.

"I'd never be on their side. The three of us have to stick together."

"Okay, I'll have my assistant get something on the books."

"I love you. I have your back with them, whatever you need."

She wraps me up in a hug.

Owen gets in on it. "Me too. Anything you need."

"I love both of you. I need to get out of this city, out from under their thumb, to find my own peace. It's not you."

"We'll come visit." Owen squeezes us.

Olivia breaks away and gives me a long look. "Don't let them make you marry Cassie. You won't be happy. After trying to fit in their box for too long, I know I'm not."

"I couldn't. Maybe six months ago I could, but I think I have feelings for someone else."

Shock colors Olivia's face.

"I fucking knew it!" Owen shouts. "I've been trying to get him to say it for months!"

Olivia smiles. "Who is she?"

"He," Owen corrects.

Olivia gives me a look.

I shrug. "His name is Isaac."

"Bring him to dinner when we set it up." Olivia hugs me again.

"If he'll speak to me."

"I know you. You don't take no for an answer. Go charm his ass off." Olivia steps into the elevator, leaving Owen and me to the helicopter.

"What are you going to do?" Owen asks.

"I have an idea."

Twenty-Eight

Isaac

Drawing has always been my escape. It's how I process and get lost in my own world. After the gala, I splurged and got myself a sketch book. I needed it badly.

When I can't sleep, I draw. When I don't want to think, I draw. When I'm supposed to be studying, I draw.

Unfortunately, it's all Oliver. His eyes, his lips, his hands. The way he holds a foil. This damn sketchbook is full of him. Maybe it's my brain's way to getting him out of my system and I'll light it on fire when I'm done.

But I doubt it.

I know it's coming, the day that whatever I'm doing with Oliver will be over, but the amount of physical pain is overwhelming. My body aches and not just from the welts he left on my skin. For days, it ached to sit or lie down, but it's faded now. Part of me is glad but part of me mourns the loss. I think there's still some kind of mark I just can't see in the mirror because of the sore spots that are lingering. I don't know. Maybe it's just me wishing.

It's been weeks since he touched me, months maybe, since I felt connected to anything. All day every day is the same. The holidays were a blur of sleeping and drawing but since classes started again my days are just class, fencing, sleep. Even in my dreams I can't escape him. Probably because I don't really want to. How did I get so wrapped up in him when we weren't ever really together? It's not fair how fast my heart clung to him or how dependent I became when he's walking around like the world is still turning and his heart is intact.

He acts like nothing is wrong, like nothing has changed, but I can't manage it.

"Okay, Debbie Downer, it's time for you to get out of this dorm room." Colin puts his hand on his hip and stands over me.

"What?" I glance up from my drawing of Oliver's lips in a smirk.

"You. Need. To. Get. Out," he enunciates every word. "Go hangout with a friend. Find a casual hook up to blow you. Text Tyler for coffee or dinner. Text Alton. I'll give you his number. I don't care who you go out with, but you need to go get your flirt on and find yourself again."

I close the sketchbook and sigh as my stomach grumbles. When was the last time I ate?

"I'm telling you, Tyler's tongue will cure what ails you." Colin waggles his eyebrows at me, and I sit up.

"Fine. Anything to get you to leave me alone."

I send a quick text to Tyler, asking if he wants to meet for coffee or pizza or something. While I'm not interested in having sex or anything like that, maybe Colin is right and I need to get out of this room, shower, get dressed, and be with someone who flirts with me.

After a quick shower – since I'm not sure when my last one was – and getting dressed, Colin fusses with my hair. I'm pulling on a hoodie when there's a knock on the door. I smile to myself and open it to see Tyler standing there with two to-go cups in his hand.

"It's cold out there, so I thought coffee would help keep us warm." His charming smile as he holds out the cup to me has me smiling back.

"That was sweet, thank you."

"You two kids have fun." Colin pats me on the back and hustles me toward the door. "Make sure you have him back by midnight."

I turn to glare at him. "Thanks, Dad."

Tyler chuckles and ushers us down the hallway to the elevator. I ask him about ECON since I haven't met up with him in a few days, and we make mindless small talk for the ride down.

"There's a really good pizza place right off campus if you're okay walking a few minutes," he says as we exit the building.

"Sure, that sounds good." I take a sip of my coffee and groan when it's perfect.

Tyler's eyes are alight with amusement, and my cheeks heat. That's embarrassing. Crap.

"I'm so sorry," I rush out. "That was so embarrassing. I didn't mean to do that."

He puts his hand on my lower back to get us moving. "It's okay. I'm glad you're enjoying it."

"I can't believe you remembered how I take it."

"It's not complicated, so it's easy to remember."

There's still some color on the trees, despite it being January, and the chilly air has our breath fogging in front of us. Some people hate winter, but I enjoy it. I like the drastic change of seasons and snow.

The pizza shop is a hole-in-the-wall type of place with sports stuff all over the walls. The scent of fresh bread, melted cheese, and garlic permeates the air, and the tables are full of college students. I like it.

For once, I don't feel out of place.

The menus are under the plexiglass coverings on the tables, the cups are red plastic, and look like they've been around since the '90s. It's not fancy or expensive, but I bet the food tastes amazing.

"Come on." Tyler grabs my hand and pulls me through the crowded space to a table in the back. It's loud with TVs playing games and the chatter of conversations.

"How did you find this place?" I ask as I slide into a booth with blue vinyl benches.

"My roommate is from around here, and he showed it to me."

I'm going to need a slice of cheese and a Coke for sure. There's a nostalgic feeling to it. This could be the place down the street where I grew up where Mom would get me and my little brother, Noah, a slice sometimes.

Thinking of Noah makes my chest ache. I've tried to text him, but it looks like my parents changed his number. I hope he's okay.

"What are you gonna get?" Tyler asks, leaning on the table.

"A slice of cheese and a Coke. You?"

"Pepperoni and a Coke."

A man with a thick New York accent and a dirty black apron comes and asks what we want and brings it back a few minutes later.

I pick up my slice, folding it in half to take a bite. It's. So. Good. The mozzarella and spices in the sauce combine with the perfect amount of crust. It's a perfect bite and a perfect pizza.

Tyler groans and nods at me when he eats his slice. "It's amazing every time."

I'm about to take another bite when my phone pings. I reach for it and see Colin's name.

COLIN: Have you discovered his tongue yet?

I blush and type back.

ISAAC: We're eating pizza, stop it.

Tyler nods towards the seat where I drop my phone. "Everything all right?"

"Yeah, just Colin being Colin."

He laughs and nods.

"Have you known him long?" Tyler asks, leaning on the table.

"Just this semester. He's my roommate. You?"

He blushes a little, which is extremely cute. "Uh yeah, I've known him for a bit." He picks up his cup and takes a drink. "You guys aren't—like—together or anything, right?"

"Oh God, no." I shake my head. "He's definitely not my type."

Tyler chuckles. "But guys are . . . your type?"

It's my turn to blush as I nod in confirmation. It's weird to acknowledge it, especially in public. Oliver and Colin know, maybe Owen? I don't know what Oliver tells his brother, but I assume he does. Now Tyler. No one else on campus knows unless Colin blabbed to his friends. It's weird and kind of scary but also freeing.

It's part of who I am. A part of myself I don't want to hide anymore. Isn't that what I told myself when I moved here? That I wouldn't hide who I am?

We finish eating and learn more about each other. He tells me about his family, his crazy cousins, and the family dog he misses. This sweet guy is nothing like Oliver. I hate that I compare everything he does to the man I want to strangle and cuddle up to at the same time. I want to like him. I wish he gave me butterflies and all I could think about is him touching me or kissing me, but that's not the truth. He's cute, adorable even, but I will never find out what he does with his tongue.

But this is a real date. I've never been on one before. I went out with Tim a few times, but we had to be careful not to be seen, and most of the time we spent together was at church or one of our houses.

It's getting dark, and the temperature is dropping quickly, so we head back to the dorms.

My phone chimes again, and I groan at Colin's name.

> COLIN: Let me know when you're on your way back so I can leave the room for a while so you guys can have some alone time. *winky face*

My face heats. There will be no alone time. Not in the way he means, anyway. I can see us hanging out and watching movies, but nothing more.

Tyler holds the door open for me, and I shiver as I walk into the warmth.

"Thank you."

"You're welcome."

The elevator opens when we push the call button, and we step inside. It's not until we're heading up to my floor that I realize I've had more fun tonight than I've had in a really long time. I've laughed, joked, been at ease, and just been . . . me.

"Do you want to come in and watch a movie or something?" I can feel the blush crawling up my neck when he looks at me with a raised eyebrow. Crap. "Just watching something. To hang out."

He cracks a smile and nods. "Yeah, that sounds good."

I sigh in relief and lead the way to my room. I check the handle and roll my eyes when it's unlocked. Colin is horrible about remembering to lock it.

Opening the door, I stop in my tracks when Oliver is standing in the middle of my room.

"Good evening, kitten."

Oh crap.

Twenty-Nine

Oliver

"Now what?" Owen asks when we get back to our apartment.

I strip off my dinner jacket and toss it over the back of a wing-back while I pace. "I don't know."

"Admittance is the first step, or something or other."

"I blacked out talking to Olivia. I don't remember admitting to anything."

Owen takes a seat and leans forward, resting his forearms on his knees. "You said you have feelings."

"I can't. They'll never allow it. Can you imagine if I'm disinherited?" I lace my fingers behind my head, rethinking every choice I've ever made.

"They won't do that. Can you imagine Dad trying to make me his heir apparent?" Owen shudders. "I'm too mentally ill for that."

I roll my eyes. "You could do anything you want to."

"I don't want to." Owen sits back and rubs a hand over his mouth.

"I know." Which means all the weight is on my shoulders. "What does someone do with feelings? This is terrible. Do people feel like this all the time? I knew I was better off never getting attached."

Owen stares at me.

"What?" I ask.

"You really aren't good. Jesus Christ, I don't think I've ever heard you like this." Owen makes a face and shakes his head. "I never thought I'd see the day you weren't in control of yourself. Maybe you are a real boy."

"If you tell anyone, I swear I will kill you and gaslight Mom and Dad until they believe I was never a twin."

Owen bursts out laughing. "So what are you going to do?" he asks when he gets a hold of himself.

"I don't know. He doesn't even want to speak to me. He's probably out with that fuck." I tip my head back, massaging my temples.

"Ask Colin?"

"Do you really think he's going to help me?" I exhale, trying to regain some sort of composure.

"With your new found alliance over not wanting his sister, maybe."

I grab my jacket. "I have a better idea."

"Don't tell me you're going over there." Owen shakes his head, but is wearing a grin.

"I won't tell you then."

I walk. It's not far, and I need the time to clear my head.

I have to find a way to win myself back into his good graces, and I don't think it will be easy. He's stubborn, and doesn't trust easily, and while I think he trusts me for a fuck, I don't think he trusts me any other way. I probably deserve it, but that doesn't make it easier. But I want him to trust me. I want him to know he can.

A student holds the door open for me to slip through, and it's a wonder these buildings even need key cards to enter.

I knock on their door and step back.

"Why are you here?" Colin asks when he pulls the door open.

"Is he out with that fuck again?"

"I don't see how it's any of your business." Colin crosses his arms.

"When are you expecting him back?" I press, not taking no for an answer.

"I don't know." Colin is playing coy, and I want to hit him. "He might be out all night."

I growl. "Get out."

"What?" Colin asks.

"You heard me."

"This is my room." Colin steps back when I step forward.

I shove the door open farther, making sure he's not just covering for Isaac.

"He's really out." Colin backs off, shoving his hands into his pockets.

"Because of you?" I ask coldly.

"What does it matter? He wanted it."

"You don't want me fucking your sister. You better get out of my way with Isaac. Call off your dog. I don't want him going out with that fuck again." I step into his space, looking down at him.

"He's his own person. He can do what he wants."

"So is Cassie. So am I. You don't want to play this game with me. I've been on your side with your sister." I press closer, putting us chest to chest. "Isaac is mine, and I'll destroy anyone who interferes."

Colin doesn't back down, and it makes me respect him more.

"Isaac is his own person. Even without me setting him up, if he doesn't want you, he doesn't want you."

"If that's his choice, that's his choice. But no more getting in the way."

"Fine." Colin looks into my eyes.

"I want your word." I step back, holding out my hand.

"You have my word." He takes it.

"Now get out."

"Where the fuck am I going to sleep?" Colin asks.

"I'm sure you can find something to do for a couple of hours." I open my wallet. "Do you need beer money?"

Colin scoffs. "I don't need your money."

I stare him down, waiting for him to leave.

An hour later, far too late for anything good to have happened between them, I hear a key in the door. I stand in the middle of the room and when the door opens, Isaac freezes in the doorway.

"Good evening, kitten."

Isaac is frozen with his hand on the doorknob.

"Tell him to leave," I demand.

"What? Why would I do that?" Isaac sputters, crossing his arms.

"Tell him to fucking leave, Isaac."

He drops his eyes down my body, drinking in my stance, and back up to the set of my jaw. He squirms, but just barely, before stepping into the hallway, closing the door behind him.

I wait.

This would be my answer. Would he leave or return?

The door opens less than thirty seconds later, and he slips inside, pressing his back to the frame.

I wait.

He shifts, then crosses his arms, finally speaking, "What are you doing here?"

"I want you." I stalk forward, trapping him against the solid wood.

"No, you don't. You just want to use me."

"No. I want you. All of you."

"I don't want to *talk* anymore! I want you to tell me I'm yours. Only yours. Then I want you to prove it!" He breaks our eye contact, looking at his feet with frustration radiating off him.

I slip a finger under his chin. "Do you think I chase anyone?"

He lifts his shoulders noncommittally.

"How can I prove it to you?" I ask, knowing an answer would be too easy.

He shrugs again.

"Will you allow me to?" My lips hover over his.

"Maybe."

"I'll take it." I part his lips with mine, slipping my tongue into his mouth.

Isaac moans.

"That sounds like more of a yes." I deepen the kiss, demanding more.

He opens up, sliding his arms around my neck. I hook an arm under his thigh, lifting him up to wrap his leg around my hips. Isaac whimpers and rubs against me. So perfectly needy. Fully picking him up, I slam him into the door to get as much friction as possible.

"I need to be inside you."

"I like you needy," he mutters into my mouth between kisses.

"You have me there, and now I'm going to tie you to the bed so I can have you as long as I need."

Isaac whimpers out a moan, which I take as consent and carry him to the bed. Tossing him onto the soft surface, I loosen my tie. He drags his teeth over his lip.

"Like that?"

He nods. "I like watching you undress."

I leave the tie loose and slip my thumbs under my suspenders, drawing another groan from him. I take them off my shoulders and let them hang, returning to my tie. "Take off your shirt and lie back."

Isaac pulls the hoodie over his head and does as I ask.

"Arms above your head." I straddle his hips.

He slowing lifts them, holding my gaze. I lean forward and loop my tie around his headboard, binding his wrists to it. I sit back, teasing my fingers over his throat. He arches, but with his hips and arms locked in place, he can't do much more than squirm.

"My beautiful boy." I tweak his nipple, then lean forward and find his other with my mouth.

His eyes roll back, and he pulls at the bindings, trying to use his hands.

I smile against his skin, laughing softly. "Nope. I get to do what I want tonight after you spent a night out with someone else."

"If this is a punishment, I'm going to keep going on dates."

"You're not going out with anyone else ever again." I pick up my head to make it known. I mean it. "Never again."

"What does that mean?" His voice trembles.

"You're not allowed to go out with anyone else." I plant a hand next to his face and brush my lips over his.

Isaac processes the information for a moment, not kissing me back. "You're serious. You can't ask me to do that . . . not when you're—" He cuts himself off.

"Not when I'm?" I ask.

He shakes his head, closing his eyes to withdraw into himself.

"Don't do that," I whisper over his lips. "Come back. Talk to me."

"You can't be mine. You're going to marry a woman. Even if it's not Colin's sister, it will be someone else."

"I'm not going to."

His eyes snap open. "What?"

"I'm going to tell them I'm not going to marry anyone. I know my mom won't like it." I close my eyes, dropping my face to rest against his chest. "I don't know what my excuse will be, but I'm not going to let them set me up with anyone else."

"Will that stop them?" He doesn't seem convinced.

"I don't know."

"Look at me." He bucks into me.

I pick up my head, somber, forcing myself to look at him. "Yes?"

"What does that mean . . .?"

"What do you want it to mean?"

"Are we—" He trips over his words.

"Say it," I demand.

"Are we together? Like, dating?"

"Haven't we been dating?" I want him to say it.

"Are you only seeing me?" he clarifies.

"I haven't been with anyone else since the first night." My words are stern. Serious. No waiver, so he believes me.

I hope it's enough.

Thirty

Isaac

Is *he telling me the truth?*

My pitiful heart wants to believe he is. Wants to trust that he'll find a way to make this work. With his lips and hands on my body, I can believe anything he tells me. It's when he's gone that the illusion falls apart.

"Why?"

Oliver covers my body with his again. "Why what?"

"Why . . . me?"

Oliver trails his fingers down my side, and I jerk away when it tickles but can't get far. "You aren't like anyone else I've ever experienced. You stand up to me while also giving in. You balance this push and pull. You're soft when I need it, and stubborn, which I hate, but also need. And most of all, I can't stop thinking about you, but I've come to realize I don't want to. I want you stuck in my head right where you are."

Oh my poor heart. I don't know what to say to that, but tears knot in my throat. That's the sweetest thing anyone has ever said to me.

"Kiss me," I whisper. "Please."

"Whatever you want." He brushes his lips over mine.

The wheels in his mind work for a second longer before he takes my mouth again, slower this time but just as deep, just as breath stealing.

"Whatever I want?" I ask when we finally break apart.

He taps my nose. "Don't get greedy."

"I want you to f-fuck me," I manage to say without a blush, or too much of one.

"I'm going to spend the rest of the night so deep you can taste it while I mark every inch of you with my mouth, so there is no doubt who you belong to."

I pull at the bonds on my wrist, wanting to grab him and hold him to the promise.

"Lube?"

"I-I . . . Um . . . I don't have any." I can feel the flush heat my entire body, and he pulls back in surprise.

"Every gay man should have a bottle of lube, kitten." He gets off the bed and finishes stripping off his shirt, then goes through the drawers next to Colin's bed. I love watching how he moves, how the muscles bunch and relax under his skin.

Finally he finds a bottle, looks at it with disapproval but brings it with him back to the bed. He strips my pants off without ceremony, leaving me bare under him.

Slapping my knees apart, he bends over me to bite and suck on my skin. Across my chest, down my stomach, over my hips. I can't stop my hips from rolling in desperate need of him to touch my dick or the panting of my breathing when he moves around it. His words meet reality, and I'm in my head. He's leaving hickies that will get questions tomorrow if I change in the locker room. What will he say to the guys who ask me about them?

Will he say they're his?

"Please, Oliver," I whine when his cheek barely brushes my cock.

"Please what?"

"I need you inside me."

He smiles, not moving to do as I ask. "Eventually."

"You said whatever I want!" Frustration creeps into my tone.

"I'm going to give you what you want, but you did go on a date with another man, so I'm going to make you earn it."

I whimper and bury my face in my arm as much as I can. He's going to kill me.

My back arches as he brushes his hand lightly over my straining dick, and my breath catches in my throat. Oliver cups my balls, lightly tugging on them and rolling them around in his palm. The click of the lube bottle opening has me looking at him to see what he'll do next. Anticipation tightens my stomach as I watch him add some to his hand, then close the bottle and toss it away. He's purposefully taking as much time as possible. The jerk.

With his eyes locked on me, he reaches for my cock and strokes. Hard, fast strokes that push me to the edge in a matter of seconds. It's so quick I can't breathe, all my muscles tighten up, my skin tingles, then nothing. He releases me and goes back to cupping my balls and lightly scratching his nails over my taint.

"Noooo! Please!" I sob and pull on the restraints, but it doesn't do me any good.

"I have all night."

All night? I'll never survive.

His slick finger circles my hole and presses against it but doesn't enter. I want him inside of me so badly it hurts. I want him to take me. To use my body and put a claim on me that everyone will see tomorrow.

"Never again, Isaac." Oliver leans over me with a hand next

to my head. His finger breaches my hole, and I open my mouth on a silent moan. "No more dates."

I shake my head almost violently, my eyes never leaving his.

"Say it."

"No more dates."

"Good boy." He thrusts his finger in and out of me, just slow enough to drive me to the brink of insanity but not enough to push me over. "You're going to show me just how sorry you are for letting other men touch you."

"No one touched me. Only you."

He looks at me like I'm an idiot, but my brain can only focus on so much at once and whatever he's doing with his finger is taking all my mental power.

"No hand holding, brushing of arms, hand on your leg?"

Crap.

"I'm sorry. It'll never happen again. I swear."

"He's lucky that's all he did. Because I already want to kill him." Something primal flashes in his eyes, but he quickly schools his features, taking my mouth again. It's hungry and deep. I groan into it and try to wrap my legs around him, but he slaps my knees back open. "You'll be on full display while I use your mouth, kitten. I want to see what's mine."

Erotic flutters tingle low in my belly, and I nod.

He withdraws his finger from me, strokes me one more time, then stands and opens his slacks. Standing next to the bed, he tugs me as close to the edge as he can with my hands still tied and pulls his glorious cock out.

"Look at me." The demand in his voice is sexy. "Open your mouth."

With no hesitation, I do what I'm told. He brushes my lips with the tip of his dick, the smooth skin caressing my flesh almost like he's painting something on me. Testing him, I stick my tongue out enough to sweep across him, and his eyes turn molten.

Oliver thrusts between my lips, and I revel in the feel of him. I like giving him pleasure, knowing he's taking what he needs from me. His hand grips my hair as he uses my mouth. In, out, in, out. He watches me watching him for a minute before sliding his gaze down the rest of me. Completely naked, knees wide with everything I have on display. From the right angle, you can probably see my hole too.

"Such a sweet mouth."

Saliva is dripping down the side of my face onto the bed, I probably look a wreck, but he likes me this way. He makes me messy.

"I love watching myself glide in and out of your lips." Oliver's free hand reaches for me, and he pinches my nipple when a key jingles in the lock.

Horror and shock war within me. Oh my God.

It clicks open.

On no.

The door creaks as it opens.

Oh my God!

Oliver's furious eyes snap toward the door while I'm trying to cover myself but can't get anywhere due to the tie. My body doesn't seem to care though because I keep pulling and thrashing around like that will fix this. *Jesus, fix this!*

"Colin!" Oliver growls. "Get out!"

"Holy fuck. If I knew what the Godfrey boys were packing, I would have been a lot nicer."

Did he just?

My face heats like I've spent the last eight hours in the sun with no sunblock.

"It's astonishing you're surprised." Oliver tosses a blanket over me, but doesn't move to cover himself. "Why do you think I have the reputation I do?"

"Bravo, baby bird, for taking that thing as a virgin." Colin takes another slow look down Oliver's body and starts a slow clap.

"We aren't letting you watch. Get out."

"And you two are *identical,* right?" Colin coughs. "Too bad Owen is straight . . ."

I'm going to perish. Spontaneously combust.

"He most definitely is. Not that I think he's dated anyone in a long time."

Are they seriously having this conversation right now while he's NAKED?

"Maybe I'll double check, for science."

"Your roommate is a size queen? Who'd have known?" Oliver deadpans.

"Oh my God! Untie me!" I damn near scream.

He strokes over himself, distracting me from my mission for a moment and reminding me why I like his cock so much. I'm so glad no one else is going to see it ever again.

And I will never be able to look Colin in the eye.

Ever.

"Colin!" I all but scream. "Go away!"

He rolls his eyes but backs out of the room. "We'll be discussing this later."

Once the door is closed, Oliver lifts an eyebrow at me while he studies me.

"Untie me."

He looks like he's going to argue for a second but puts his dick away and pulls on one end of the tie, letting one of my hands loose.

"Colin has always had the worst timing."

I lower my arms and attempt to get my other wrist free, but it's useless. With a disgruntled huff, I hold it up for Oliver to deal with, which he does in about three seconds. Jerk.

He takes both my hands in his and slides his thumbs over the angry red marks on my wrists.

"A testament to how badly you wanted to get away and how good my knots are." Oliver lifts my abused wrists to his mouth and kisses over the pulse point. "I will prove how serious I am about you."

"Okay." I swallow thickly not sure I believe him.

Oliver cups my face and kisses me again. A lingering, breath-stealing kiss.

"I promise I will."

I want to believe him, but it's terrifying.

Oliver presses a kiss to my forehead and finds some pajamas for me. Before he leaves, he tucks me into bed with another kiss. "Good night, kitten. I'll see you tomorrow."

I can't help the smile that turns up my lips. "Good night, Oliver."

He opens the door, and Colin's voice filters through. I'm really hoping to be asleep when he came back.

"Sad, I was hoping for a show."

"I knew your anger was a mask for how much you want me."

Colin grumbles loudly and comes in, immediately changing for bed while I hold my breath. I know it's coming. He's going to say something, and it's going to be embarrassing. Colin surprises me and jumps on my bed like we're sixteen-year-old girls at a slumber party.

"You did not tell me how good the d was." He looks at me disapprovingly. "But I guess since you don't have anything to compare it to, you probably don't know just how glorious that thing is."

I'm fully aware . . .

"I guess I understand why you keep letting him fuck with you . . ." He taps his chin and purses his lips. "Listen, I don't know how he's going to get out of marrying Cassie, but I'm sure it'll be dramatic. You should steer clear of him for a while so you don't get dragged down into his bullshit."

"He's my fencing captain. I can't exactly avoid him."

Colin smacks my forehead. "Stop letting him fuck you, dumbass."

My face heats, and I'm glad it's dim in here. "I'm done with this conversation. Get off my bed. I'm going to sleep."

He sighs a big dramatic sound but does. "Fiiiiine." He climbs into his bed. "Were you introduced to Tyler's tongue?"

"Good night, Colin!"

Thirty-One

Oliver

> OLIVER: No, I won't have a threesome with your roommate and you.

> OLIVER: Top of my list of nonnegotiable.

I laugh as I send the message then add.

> OLIVER: Along with me picking you up for practice tomorrow.

Has he fallen asleep so quick? He must be talking to Colin.

> ISAAC: I can walk. It's on campus.

> OLIVER: I know what you can do.

> OLIVER: I'm not asking.

> ISAAC: My last class is college algebra in the Hensen building. It finishes at 2.

> OLIVER: I'll see you at 2.

I toss my phone onto my nightstand and shove a hand into my hair.

I have to figure out how I'm going to get out of marriage. It seems like an impossible task.

Owen knocks on the doorframe. "Is it safe?"

"Yes, I didn't bring him home with me."

Owen peeks around the ornate wood. "Are you feeling okay?"

"I can't make him move in here immediately." I give him a flat look.

"Again, are you feeling okay?"

"First, what would Mom and Dad say, and second, I have to convince him I am serious before he'll do any of that. Even if every one of my instincts is to lock him in my room so no one else can even look at him." I take my tie out of my pocket and toss it in the hamper. It needs a good washing and press after being used tonight.

"Right. I forget they pay our butler to spy on us. Fucking nosy ass bastards." He sprawls out on my chaise lounge. "So next week, then? Poor Colin."

"Don't you start with the poor Colin thing. That's how he'll get you into bed." I give him a look.

Owen picks up his head, opens his mouth, closes it, then says, "I'm going to need some context."

"The short version is Colin walked in on us, saw my cock, and wants a ride. As I am seeing his best friend and he hates me, you are clearly the next eventuality."

Owen's expression turns pensive. "I mean, it's probably just like anal, which I've heard is good and one time might be worth exploring . . ." He pauses and purses his lips.

What the fuck am I witnessing here?

"No, I don't think I could do it even if anal sounds fun."

I blink. "Have you never had anal?"

"That would be what you focus on instead of me considering sleeping with a man?"

"Because everyone is a little bisexual when they think about it long enough."

"That's not true."

I shoot him a look. "Go to bed."

"Not everyone has had anal."

"You're a fucking Godfrey. Women drop their panties at the sight of you."

"And?" Owen seemed offended.

"Next, you're going to tell me you're a virgin."

"I'm not a virgin. I slept with Cindy Drescher."

I stare, narrowing my eyes.

"What?" Owen asks.

"You say that like you've only slept with Cindy . . ." He'd dated. At least a few people. Not that I paid that close attention.

"Time for bed." Owen is on his feet and exiting my room before I can get another word in.

I put it out of my head, needing at least a couple of hours sleep before I deal with Isaac's anxiety tomorrow.

Isaac looks like he's been having a panic attack all day when he climbs into the back seat next to me.

"Well, aren't you a pretty wreck." I hold out a cup for him.

"What's this?" he says when he takes it.

"A vanilla latte." I sip my quad espresso.

"How did you know I like vanilla latte?" He has dark circles under his eyes, and I'm glad I brought caffeine.

"Isn't it your boyfriend's job to know what you like?" I say flatly.

"That doesn't tell me how you know," he shoots back. "I was distracted last time and forgot to ask how you knew."

"It's called stalking, kitten."

He smiles into the drink. "Did you call me boyfriend?"

"Is that not what you are?"

He keeps smiling, and I love his happiness.

"Now why do you look like that?" I ask, ready for a long, drawn-out thing from him.

"What?" Isaac looks down at himself. "Did I spill something on myself?"

I look at the roof of the car. "Not your clothes, your face."

He wrinkles his nose. "What's wrong with my face?"

"It looks like you've been having a meltdown all day."

"Since last night, actually," Isaac mutters.

"Why?"

He lifts his shoulders and won't make eye contact.

"I know you know why." I unbuckle his seatbelt and force him into my lap.

He yelps and blushes.

"If you spill your drink on me, I won't be happy."

He tries to scramble off, but I dig my fingers into his thighs, keeping him in place.

"Nope."

"I could die. Then how will you feel?"

"We are going one mile an hour in traffic. Try again."

He huffs, but I don't relent. "What will people think?"

"What people?"

"Everyone at practice," he says into my skin, making me harden instantly.

"Does it matter?"

"To me it does. You aren't exactly nice to me." His warm breath fans over my collarbone.

"If you keep that up, I will be fucking you in this car in front of my driver, and while I'd enjoy it, it would leave me open to a lawsuit, so I'd rather not."

Charles laughs from the front seat and meets my eyes in the rearview mirror. He'd never sue me. But he would expect a premium to look the other way. Thankfully, Isaac is too worked up to notice Charles's reaction.

"Keep what up?"

"Your lips on my neck."

Isaac pulls back enough to give me a smirk. "I'm going to remember that."

"Please do." I rock his hips over my hard on. "See what you do."

He groans and grinds against me. "You're so distracting."

"Likewise, kitten." I still his hips. "Now tell me what the problem is before we walk into practice."

"I don't want the team to know. About us." Isaac bites his lip and looks like he's going to cry.

"I figured as much. Why?" I struggle with softness. But I know Isaac needs it. I cup his cheek.

"Because I–" He takes a deep breath. "I don't want to be known as Oliver Godfrey's five-minute fling."

"Help me understand what you need to be comfortable. For me to pretend like I hate you?" I rub my thumb under his eye, wiping away the hint of moisture there.

"I don't know." The show of emotion makes me want to fuck him more. There's something seriously wrong with me.

"I can't know unless you try to put it into words, kitten."

"I need to know this is real before we tell them. So I guess." He presses into my touch.

"Stop being so sexy. It's hard to take you seriously," I say playfully. "We can keep it between us until you're comfortable." It would give me more time to figure out how to manage my parents. "But don't you dare, for a minute, think I will let anyone look at you or touch you."

He squirms in my lap, making me impossibly harder. Goddamn, he'll be the death of me. "I don't know how to pretend to hate you in front of the team. Plus, it's not like you went easy on my skin last night. How am I supposed to explain those without mentioning you?"

I grab his hair, tipping his head back to nip at his Adam's apple. "Tell them you're dating someone? You don't have to mention me if it makes you feel better."

He puts a hand between my lips and his neck. "Behave for a minute."

"Make me."

He lets out a long, drawn-out groan. "Okay. But we can't walk in together. At least I don't have to explain it to Colin. He already knows I have a weakness for you."

"Fine." I sit back dropping my hands.

"Just like that?" Isaac asks, carefully getting off my lap.

"Give me your best hate. Make me believe it."

Amusement flickers in his dark eyes. "I'm going to make everyone believe it."

I lean in lowering my voice. "If you do a good job, I'll fuck you like I hate you." I flick my tongue against his ear. "Just like a bully would, shoved against the cold tile in the showers after practice."

Thirty-Two

Isaac

I try to change quickly and not turn away from my locker to limit how much of my torso is exposed, but of course the loudmouth of the team sees the hickies.

"Goddamn, Becker, did you find yourself a Hoover?" Adam says loud enough for the guys outside of the locker room to hear.

"Shut up." I pull a shirt over my head but turn to see Oliver hiding a smile. "Some of us have class and don't kiss and tell."

He laughs along with half of the guys in here. "Class? Right. Was she ugly? Are you embarrassed to tell us who she was?"

I really dislike this guy. Thankfully, he's a sabre, and I get breaks from him every once in a while.

"You jealous?" Colin turns on Adam and pops his hip. "I've told you before I would gladly take one for the team if it made you shut up for five minutes."

I finish changing into my practice clothes, grab my foil, and leave without another word. Adam has never been shy about giving Colin a hard time about being gay, which is why Colin flirts with him. It makes Adam uncomfortable, which makes Colin happy.

"Let's go boys, I don't have all night!" Coach Kennedy barks, and the stragglers start hustling. We're all lined up on one side of the practice space to wait for directions. "We have a tournament coming up, and if you want to participate, you will be focused. Seriously. I will not have you embarrassing me or this school by showing up to it only to fall on your face." He meets all our eyes in turn. "Do you understand?"

We all say "Yes, Coach," and he starts leading us through stretches and warm-ups.

"Break up into disciplines and spar. Captains, take note of who needs to work on what. Let's start fine tuning this team."

I smile internally. Good. Oliver will be a jerk like usual, and I won't have to fight that hard to be mad at him.

As we break off onto different pistes, grab the equipment we need, Colin gives me a knowing look. If only he knew what's really going to be happening . . .

"Everyone pair up, let's start with footwork."

I find myself the only one without a partner and stand aside to wait.

"Isaac, do the directions not apply to you?" Oliver says loud enough for everyone to hear.

"I don't have a partner. What would you have me do? Drill with the ghosts of fencers past?"

I can feel everyone's eyes on us, but I don't look away from Oliver.

"You'll just have to partner with me then."

I swallow thickly but square my shoulders.

Fine.

I can do this.

"How are you going to be watching everyone else if you're sparring with me?" I take my starting position.

"You aren't a challenge," he says casually, and my face burns.

Oliver makes the first move but instead of trying to make contact that would score him a point, he hits my hand. On purpose.

I hiss and jerk back.

"Lift your foil, you're too low."

I grit my teeth and reset.

Before he has a chance to come at me, I lunge but step too far forward and almost lose my balance. Oliver smacks my shin as he blocks my advance.

He lifts an eyebrow at me, almost like he's asking me if I want him to let up on me. Yes but no.

We go back and forth a few more times, and he finally calls for everyone to switch partners when he gets me in just the right spot that my hand goes numb and I drop my foil. My hand tingles for a second, and I shake it out, then grab for my foil.

"Sorry not all of us had Daddy's money to pay for private lessons. Some of us had to learn from the bare minimum."

"Blaming your ineptitudes on others will not make your skills improve."

I hate him for embarrassing me in front of the team, but I'm also kind of turned on? What the hell is wrong with me? This can't be normal. Or healthy.

"Stupid, know it all, show off," I'm mumbling under my breath as I pair up with the other freshman, Ben.

"He's a real dick, huh?" Ben says as we get set.

You have no idea.

"Yeah. Pretty sure he gets off on making us cry." I almost laugh.

Ben smiles, but I attack, and he isn't able to parry correctly.

Instead of hitting my blade, he cracks the back of my hand, and I hiss.

"Shit, sorry. You all right?"

I nod, and we reset.

This time I'm able to make contact and would have gotten a point if we were sparring for real. That makes me feel better, but Ben cracks the back of my hand and my knuckles almost every time he tries for me. I can already tell I'm going to have bruises under my glove. Drawing is going to be difficult the next few days.

"Water," Oliver calls, and someone cheers, but I'm not sure who. Taking off my mask, I push my damp hair off my sweaty forehead and chug water. It's hot in here, and I'm exhausted already.

My hand aches, so I pull my glove off to inspect the damage. I'm not bleeding yet, so that's good, but the back of my hand is turning purple. Fantastic.

Heading into the equipment room, I find our first aid kit and grab a pad of gauze and wrap tape around my palm to secure it, then shove my glove back on. It's not much but will give me just a little more padding. Flexing my hand, I make sure the tape won't interfere and head back to the floor.

We get set up with different partners. This time I'm with a junior, Leo, who is just as good as Oliver. Watching the two of them spar is really fun, but Oliver thinks faster on his feet, so he normally beats Leo. He just has to work for it.

I'm not going to lie and say I don't enjoy watching him have to work for it for once.

We set, and he makes quick work of kicking my ass. With every touch of his foil, I get more frustrated until I'm making stupid mistakes because of knee-jerk reactions. I'm not keeping my cool at all.

"Take a deep breath, dude. Don't let me get in your head." We reset, and I force myself to suck in a deep breath and lower my shoulders. "Attack me."

I lunge, and he parries perfectly, turning what should have been my point into his.

"A split second before you lunge, you lift your arm. It gives you away." We reset, and he tells me to attack again. This time I think about where my body is and work on holding my arm still when I lunge.

We do that a few times before Oliver calls for another water break. Leo lifts his mask and is smiling at me as we head toward the bench with our stuff.

"You've already made an improvement. Good job." He claps me on the shoulder.

"Thanks, I really appreciate your help." I grab my water and chug the rest of the bottle, but I'm still thirsty.

I head to the hallway to refill my water, but I'm not alone. Oliver follows me out.

"Getting awfully chatty with Leo." Oliver steps up behind me close enough for me to feel his presence.

"Scared he's going to teach me enough tricks to beat you?"

Oliver's snort makes me smile.

When my bottle is full, I turn to face him and am surprised by just how close he is to me.

"I would be happy to have you beat me on the piste." He runs his ungloved thumb over my lip.

"Are you jealous, then? That another man is helping me?" I lean in a little closer. "Smiling at me?" Raising up onto my toes until our mouths are almost touching. "*Praising* me?"

"Do you want me to be jealous?" He wraps the cold indifference around himself like a cloak, but I'm starting to see it for what it is. A mask. "Do you want to delight in my suffering? Or do you want a reaction? I could hurt him—or you—maybe both."

I watch him for a minute to see if the mask will crack, but he holds firm. "Do I want you to be jealous?" I purse my lips a little like I'm thinking about it. "Maybe a little." I shrug, but the idea flutters low in my stomach. The idea that I could be worth being jealous over is a bit intoxicating.

"Murder. I can already feel my hands around his throat for even daring to look at what's mine." He gets the same look in his eyes he gets when he's thinking about how to make me pay. I recognize it now.

"Is it bad I like it?"

"Be very careful what you wish for, kitten."

I suck my bottom lip between my teeth to keep from kissing him. But God, do I want to.

"I'm sporting enough bruises from you at the moment that I think I'm all good on the hurting part." I take a deep breath and put some distance between us in case anyone wonders in here. "And don't hurt him. He hasn't done anything wrong."

I move to walk away and am surprised when he lets me, but as I enter the practice space, I hear his voice.

"Yet. One toe over the line . . ." He doesn't have to make it a threat.

Oliver takes position against me again. I expect my hand to be even more bruised. But he lets me go a few rounds without smacking the back. We move back and forth, but my feet tangle in a retreat. He doesn't stop, he keeps coming.

I fall on my ass and find the tip of his foil under my chin.

He uses it to lift my face. "Your footwork needs work."

I know this is what I asked for, but it sucks.

We go again, and he springs forward, catching me off guard. He never fights so openly and aggressively. He's usually guarded. He chases me back to the line. Over and over.

I stand my ground the next match, and he gets in my face with crossed foils. "I'm not letting you win."

"Do you know how bad I want to fuck you right now?" His words catch me off guard.

I stumble.

He redoubles his attack, and I fall again. This time he steps over me and drops one knee to my chest. Pinning me there. "All I can think about is fighting you, disarming you, and then having my way with you while you try and fight me off."

I barely hold back squirming as my cock gets so hard it hurts.

"You'd like that, wouldn't you?"

I nod, slowly, not trusting my voice. Knowing we are too exposed.

He lifts. "Get up."

I do, and we reset.

I charge him, wanting to feel some sort of vengeance against his words. We clash, and I gain some ground, scoring a touch. But only one. Because after that he makes it a personal mission to destroy me. I've never seen this side of him. He's faster than I ever imagined, scoring point after point.

In another face-to-face clash, he whispers, "I can see your hard-on under your cup." He brushes his fingers over my tip, so quickly I doubt it even really happened, but I blush and back off.

Hiding him is a new kind of hell, but I want more.

Thirty-Three

Oliver

"I saac," Coach Kennedy says after he dismisses practice.

The rest of the guys head to the locker room while Isaac looks around like he can't believe the coach asked for him directly.

This kid. As mature as he could be, his innocence shows through sometimes, and it endears him to me further. I should hate him for it. But I don't.

"Yes?" Isaac steps forward when the Coach gets annoyed by his freeze.

I linger, nosy and protective. Ready to step in if anything has been said to Coach Kennedy about us fraternizing.

"Kinsey is out for the rest of the goddamn season. Broke his fucking leg." Mirth soaks through Coach's voice as I listen in. "Which means you're being moved up from the JV to the Varsity relay team this weekend." He holds up a hand before Isaac can get a word in. "Yada, yada, yada, you're not ready. You'll let everyone down. This isn't my first turn around the sun. Nor my first year coaching. I've heard all the excuses. You'll do fine."

To Isaac's credit, the only outward sign he shows is a slight knee wobble.

"Got to earn that scholarship." Coach Kennedy looks him over. "All right?"

Isaac swallows hard and nods.

"Great. Keep up the good work." He turns his back, and Isaac looks like he's going to pass out.

"Now I have even more reason to ride your ass to get you ready." I step forward, sure Isaac isn't aware of my presence.

He jumps, grabbing his chest. "What kind of riding?"

I laugh, scratching my temple. "In practice, of course."

His heated gaze drops down my body. "And?"

"And after."

A smile curls over his mouth.

"And any time I want you."

A blush creeps up his throat. "Anytime?"

I cross the space between us. "You heard me. If you want it all, you want it all." I wait for a reaction, but he doesn't speak. "Is that a problem?"

"You're asking me?" His smile spreads.

It makes me want to fuck his face. "I am. Isn't that how relationships are?"

"Yes." He touches me, right there in the open. He blooms into his confidence, and I love watching. "I want it all."

"It's going to be so hard to not touch you when others are looking at you." I slip a hand between us, grabbing his cock. "It's agony."

"I love when you tell me how you feel." He rocks into my grip, sliding his hardening cock through my fingers.

"I'll keep that in mind for when you behave."

"Is this not behaving?" Isaac's words carry a coy tone.

"This is, you were pushing it at practice." I squeeze his cock, eliciting a moan from his lips.

"I have to keep up appearances."

I scoff. "Right."

"I bet everyone is gone . . . do I get my reward now?"

"Do you deserve it?" I walk him backward by the dick.

He nods vigorously.

I push him through the doorway, watching over his shoulder for any sign of activity.

It's silent, but I still check. I free his dick while we stand in the middle of the locker room, brushing my thumb through the pre-cum pooling at his tip. Isaac groans, eyes falling closed. I keep it gentle, working him up, until I grab his jaw, dragging his mouth to mine. He eagerly kisses me back, and I let him for a minute, and then I flip him around and shove him into the wall.

He hits it with a grunt, palms pressing into the tile. He rests his cheek between his hands, arching his back.

"Such a needy little slut for me, aren't you?" I hook my thumbs under my sweats, dragging them down to free my erection.

He presses back, rubbing his ass against my tip. "I can't help it."

"Can't you?" I spread him and spit, massaging it into his hole.

He clenches and shivers. "Do you want me to?" He twists enough to make eye contact. Entirely sinful and wanton.

I trade my fingers for my tip, sliding it over his opening, teasing. "No. Never change." I pull a packet from my pocket and rip it open before pouring lube over my cock. "How badly do you need me in inside you?"

"Oliver . . ."

I force myself inside of him, taking him in one stroke.

He wraps an arm around mine, digging his nails into my skin. "Harder. Please . . ."

"Don't worry, I'm going to fuck you like my whore, and then I'm taking you to dinner like my prince." I slam into him relentlessly, stretching him wide open, owning every inch of him.

He tries to argue, but I fuck him until he can't speak.

I grind into him, putting my lips against his ear. "I won't be taking no for an answer."

He melts into me, coming and half collapsing. I wrap my arm around his chest to keep him upright, taking his weight while I fuck him into incoherent bliss.

My kitten.

Isaac tries my patience the rest of the week. He pushes a toe over the line, dancing back and forth over it, pushing every button I possess. Then I spend the rest of the night taking out all my pent-up aggression on his ass.

If ever the idea of believing in a higher power came to mind, it would be dealing with Isaac. He was put on this earth to test me. I swear to fucking god.

By the time we are leaving for our tournament, I am entirely too keyed up.

This might kill me.

Isaac is enjoying it.

He loves pushing me and challenging me and getting me all worked up until I take him.

Isaac didn't stop at practice either. He finds ways to tease me in every manner every place we went.

At restaurants and at bars, in elevators and stolen minutes, in my penthouse and the backseat of cars.

I watch him find a confidence in his sexuality I never imagined.

"I want to devour every inch of you."

He flashes a coy smile. "We don't have time."

"Kiss me before you get out of the car." There is no question to my tone.

He releases the door handle, turning back to face me with a glint in his eyes.

I snap my teeth. "Do you know how badly I want to force my cock down your throat when you look at me like that?"

"Do it." No hesitation to his words.

I growl and slam my head into the rest. "If you put another toe out of line, I'll have you in the bathroom on the plane."

Scarlet colors his cheeks. "They'll notice!"

"Maybe, maybe not." More than forty of us because the women's team is also competing in the tournament this weekend, plus coaches on a chartered jet is risky, but I've lost all control around Isaac.

"You'll have to wait until after the tournament." He is giddy with it. "We have curfew, plus I'm rooming with Colin and you're with Owen."

A growl builds in my chest, and I grab him by the jaw, kissing him thoroughly. "You love this."

He nods, moaning into my mouth. "Maybe . . ."

"Maybe my ass." I tighten my grip when he tries to pull back. "I'm going to pay Colin to let me into your room, and you're going to wake up with me inside you."

"Don't threaten me with a good time."

I narrow my eyes, and he uses the distraction to hop out of the car.

We make it to Massachusetts, the home of our biggest rivals. The Monsters.

They are the only team who stands in our way for the division title come March.

We have a team dinner and then strategy meetings for the rest of the night. Isaac and I don't speak. He's overwhelmed. I see it in his body language. In every interaction.

I catch him the next morning when he slips into the conference room for breakfast.

He squints at me.

I curl a finger at him.

He glances around before coming over. "Hi."

"No one will be up until they have to, and Owen I'll have to drag out of bed." I grab him by the back of the thigh, forcing him to walk forward until he's standing between my knees.

"He's lucky to have you as a sibling."

I shrug it off. "It's what we do for people we love."

He nods, looking over his shoulder. "I should eat." Isaac isn't himself.

"Are you stressed about today?"

"A little." He is stiff in my arms.

"You need to put all of that out of your head. It will get into your weapon. Swords feel doubt when they are wielded. You have to have all of the unbridled confidence of a nineteenth century nobleman."

He rolls his eyes. "You just made that up."

"If you think the Godfreys haven't been fencing long before the nineteenth century, you'd be wrong. We are steeped in tradition, and I was raised on it, even if my parents think it's a silly sport. My grandmother was an Olympic fencer, and she gave me my first foil."

Isaac softens. "You better not have made all that up. It's making me feel bad for you."

"Why is it making you feel bad?"

"Because I'm pretty sure you don't have a heart or feelings, so when you say things like that, it means you do, and then I have to treat you like a human."

I give him a flat look. "So I shouldn't tell you how she died in a fiery plane crash?"

Isaac's eyes widen. "Are you serious?"

"I am." I laugh. "She was on her way to see her secret boyfriend my grandfather didn't know about. It all came out at the funeral when she left her medals to Aldéric. It caused quite the international scandal too as they were on rival Olympic teams and their affair started during their games."

Isaac stares at me. "I cannot tell if you're being serious or not."

I smirk. "It's all true. I'll show you her things when you come to dinner at my parents' house."

"Dinner at your parents' house?" Isaac morphs into a deer in headlights. "Let's put that off as long as possible."

"Are you scared of my parents?"

"I don't think they'll like me."

"Why not?"

"Because I'm a peasant."

"Hardly with lips like those." I skim my thumb over his lower one.

"Stop." He playfully pushes my hand away. "Someone is going to walk in."

I drop my hand but don't release his leg. "You need confidence. I want you to embody it."

"What are you two talking about?" Colin asks.

Isaac jumps back and spins around.

"I'm telling him not to fuck up."

Colin looks between us. "He'll be fine."

"I know he will be, if he finds some goddamn confidence," I reply putting on a bored tone to keep our cover. "He'll lose the relay for us if he doesn't."

"He better fucking not. Little prick," Sebastian says as he walks in.

263

"Shut the fuck up, Sebastian. Or need I remind you and everyone else on the team what an embarrassment you were as a freshman?" I shoot back.

Sebastian's head snaps to look at me. "What the fuck? I'm allowed to be pissed he's in our lineup and not Kinsey."

"No, you're not. You get to be supportive. He's on your team. I'm the captain, so I'll be the only one giving pep talks." I shove to my feet, so he knows I'm serious.

"Fuck this. I'm eating outside."

"Why did you defend me?" Isaac asks when Sebastian takes his food out of the conference room.

"Because I get to bully you. No one else does."

"That doesn't even make any sense," Isaac replies.

Colin holds up a hand. "No, I think he's on to something."

"Go eat. You need to have something in your stomach before you puke it all up. Puking up bile sucks."

"How do you know I'm going to puke?" Isaac sounds defensive.

"Are you ready for your first tournament on a national stage?"

"No," he mutters, toeing the floor.

"I didn't think so."

Right on cue, Isaac looks green as we walk into the guest locker rooms.

"Your turn," I say to Colin when Isaac goes into a stall.

"Why are you being so nice to him?" Colin asks, looking me over.

"Because I want to win?" I fix him with a glare.

Colin makes an annoyed sound and goes to Isaac.

He's still green when he walks out of the stall, having changed into his team warmups.

I make eye contact and loosen my tie. Team rules say we have to dress up in and out of matches, so we change into matching team warmups here. Isaac falters in his step when he sees what I'm doing. I strip off the tie and undo the buttons on my shirt, one by one. He swallows hard, and my skin prickles.

I love when he watches me.

I let the fabric fall off my shoulders, grabbing a hanger to slip it on. I slide my tongue over my teeth. Isaac shakes his head, but keeps watching. I strip off my slacks next and take my time standing in my compression shorts while I hang them. I grab my cup and face Isaac while I push it into place in my jock.

He lets out a soft groan.

Colin grabs him by the arm, trying to drag him out of the guest locker room. He doesn't budge.

I mouth, "Good boy."

He scowls but doesn't move.

I laugh to myself, pulling on my fencing pants, then my team warmups over them. I leave the suspenders dangling while I pull on my sapphire undershirt.

"I think our colors are nepotistic. Why is it only rich people look good in blue and white?" Isaac half says to Colin, but I know it's directed at me.

"Do you really not know our team colors?" I ask in disbelief.

"I know them. Blue and white," he says, side-eyeing Colin to check.

Colin laughs.

"Our colors are diamond and sapphire," I correct.

"So white and blue."

"No, no. Do you see the diamond glint in the fabric?"

"Diamond isn't a color."

"It is when you're rich enough." I smirk, knowing he'll hate it.

He sighs and pinches the bridge of his nose. "I'm not sure which is worse, that all of you actually think the school colors are diamond and sapphire or that I might actually be too poor to understand it. This is some rich person math crap, isn't it?"

"I'm baffled you cannot tell the difference between white and diamond, nor differentiate between shades of blue. I thought you were gay."

"He's peasant gay. They don't know fashion," my brother mutters, but doesn't try to be quiet at all.

I laugh. "Peasant gay. That's some *Devil Wears Prada* shit. I like that."

"How come he gets to make fun of me. You said no one but you could!" Isaac gestures at Owen.

"He's my brother. He's basically me. He's allowed."

Isaac gets closer and drops his voice. "Does that mean he can fuck me too?"

I snarl, barely stopping myself from grabbing him by the shirt to slam him into the lockers. "Careful."

His pupils dilate with lust. He shakes it off and steps back. "Is everyone in our division like this? Don't tell me I'm going to learn a new host of colors?"

"Only the teams in the Myth League. You should study up. You're one of us now."

We walk out, and Coach Kennedy directs us to stretch out.

I scan the stands for my parents. They are in their normal seats, and Mom is decked out in gaudy diamonds and sapphires like the rest of the parents. "She's so embarrassing with her foam finger." I lean over to my brother.

"Do your parents travel to every tournament?" Isaac asks, squinting at the stands. "How many parents are here?"

"Eavesdropping?"

"You're not exactly quiet."

"I'm not trying to be." I open my legs in a suggestive manner, half stretching, half teasing.

"Then answer me." Isaac pulls an arm over his chest.

"Yes, most of them travel. Do you not expect yours to be here?"

He shook his head sitting next to me. "They won't come."

"You don't think they would to keep up appearances?" Even if mine were threatening my life, they'd be here so their friends wouldn't gossip.

Isaac gives me a look, then awkwardly laughs. "I told you. They've disowned me."

"I know what you said—" I shake my head. "Even if my parents disinherit me, I just . . ." I don't know what to say. I could not imagine my parents doing that, even as much as they try to control us with money.

He lifts his shoulders. "I no longer exist to them."

The tone of his voice is a dagger to my chest. How he managed to elicit these feelings, I'll never know. I have a sudden urge to scorch the earth in Isaac's name. I reach for him, but he cringes away from my touch, meeting my eyes with panic written in the lines of his face.

I drop my arm.

"Sorry," he mutters quickly. "I'm sorry, but everyone will see. Your parents included." He doesn't want anything to do with me in public.

It hurts. The fear in his eyes hurts. The hesitation hurts. Knowing he doesn't trust me.

The feeling instills a rage into my bones. I know it's my fault.

"I understand." I step away, giving Isaac space while a plan forms in my mind.

Thirty-Four

Isaac

W hy the hell am I even here?

My body is vibrating like someone is running electricity through me. Everyone's parents but mine are in the stands, watching, waiting, whispering.

Oliver wrapping his arms around me is the only thing I want in this moment, but I can't have it. This can't be the moment his parents find out or even suspect he's slumming it with me. And that's what they'll think. I'm so far below them I'm basically the gum stuck to his mom's fancy high-heeled shoe.

I see the hurt in his eyes when I flinch away. I hate myself for it, but I'll have to make it up to him later. Right now, we have to focus on the match.

I turn my gaze to watch the Monster's team warmup, hoping to catch a glimpse of a weakness I can use against them, but I find nothing. I'm going to be the reason we lose, and Sebastian is going to lose his mind.

I can't wait for the berating that's coming from it.

Everyone warms up, and we're sent back to the locker room to get out of our practice kits.

Coach Kennedy goes over the schedule with the men's team, telling us which order we'll go in, and against which teams. Everyone else seems to be excited, and Coach does his best to pump us up, but nerves are eating me alive.

We grab everything we need and head out to our first competition. Sebastian glares as he shoulders past me. I stumble a step but catch myself and ignore him. I don't have the energy to worry about him right now. My boyfriend's parents are sitting in the stands and don't even know my name. If I do badly here, I'll be more of an embarrassment to Oliver than I already am.

Team relay fencing competitions are nine legs or rounds of three minutes or five touches and the points stack making every round more important.

I'm second in our first match, Oliver giving us a solid 5-3 lead. I just have to hold it. Both teams are trying to make it to ten points in the second round, and I have a two-touch advantage.

"Don't fuck it up," Sebastian growls when I stand.

"I won't." Grabbing my mask and foil, I head to the piste to get connected to the body wire and prepare.

Oliver walks by as the exchange happens and snaps at Sebastian, but I don't hear it as I head to the line.

I let out a quick breath as I face my opponent. I can do this.

We walk toward each other, tapping our foils to our lames to make sure they're working and head back to our sides. Sliding my mask on, I wait for the referee.

"Ready?" he says, looking at both of us. "En garde!"

We approach slowly, taking account of one another. My heart hammers in my ears drowning out everything else. We exchange a few taps, and then my opponent immediately lunges. I parry and retreat.

He gives chase, quick on his feet, and even quicker with his weapon. The metal-on-metal rings out multiple times before he's backed me up to the edge of the strip, he fakes another lunge and gets a touch.

The referee calls it and we both head back to our lines.

"Ready? En garde."

This time I advance and spring into a lunge, trying to get the upper hand before he's able to form an attack, but he's able to see it coming and get the touch on my lower left side.

He's makes up the lead Oliver gave us. I press my eyes closed hating myself, knowing how mad Sebastian is going to be. I can't let him get any more touches.

We set again, and I'm breathing hard. The weight of this competition is heavy. I shouldn't be here, and the team is counting on me. I'm letting them down.

He comes for me again, and we battle, our weapons clashing over and over until I see my opening a split second before he gives it to me. I reach for the touch, my foil bends and snaps into three pieces.

Humiliation colors my face under my mask. I only have three foils. That's it. This was my best one.

The match is paused until a spare from the coach is brought to the strip. In order to qualify for a match, you have to have two pieces of all equipment at all times.

I'm so wrapped in my head all I can hear is a buzzing when the referee comes over to take my broken foil. I walk to the back of the strip to get my spare from Coach Kennedy. I'm sweaty and frustrated and filled with shame, but I don't have time to dwell on it. Everyone is looking at me, I can feel it like a physical weight on my shoulders.

The poor kid with bottom tier equipment broke a foil. Surprise, surprise. He shouldn't be allowed to compete with the other guys. Don't they have a poor kid league he could play in?

But when I look up, it's not Coach waiting. Oliver is standing there, and not with my blade. I can't look him in the eyes.

"I can't take that."

"Yes, you can. I have a dozen of them."

"I might break it." I keep my eyes on my feet.

The ref calls for me to come back.

Oliver shoves the foil at me. "Break all of them. I'll buy more. I'll buy you a dozen."

Reluctantly, I take the weapon from him. "I don't want you to just buy me things or think that's why I'm in this."

"It never crossed my mind. Go before you get a fucking penalty."

I test the new foil and head back to the line uneasy about his weapon, and the relationship, and what I thought I was doing taking a spot on one of the best college fencing teams in the country.

When the timer runs out, we're 6-8. I fucked up our lead, leaving a huge deficit for Sebastian. He's going to hate me even more. And I broke a damn foil, which means I only have 2 left, and I really don't want to spend the money to buy a new one. There's still some left from what Oliver gave me, but I'm trying to save it for an emergency. I guess this is one. I can't keep using his. I don't even want to know what the ones he uses cost.

I pull my helmet off angrily.

"Way to not blow it, loser." Sebastian pushes past me, and it's all I can do not to hit him with my foil. I need a minute to breathe, but I can't leave in order to do so.

I pinch the bridge of my nose hard enough to leave an indent and close my eyes.

Focus.

Calm.

Breathe.

"There are more matches. You're fine. It's only two points to

272

make up." Oliver is standing too close, looking too tempting for our current situation. His parents are watching along with everyone else's. I can't have rumors going around about us if it's not going to last. I don't want to field the questions while trying to mend my shattered heart. Because there will be questions.

"Sebastian hates me. There is no way Coach Kennedy keeps me on the relay team. He'll go for anyone Sebastian hates less."

Oliver growls. "If Sebastian doesn't get his act together, he's about to be the one off the team."

"You can't do that. He's too good."

"I'll do whatever the fuck I want. He has no reason to act like he is. It's not your fault Kinsey broke his fucking leg."

"There has got to be someone better than me. Why did Coach Kennedy even bring me?" I'm not ready.

"I don't know, but he's the gold medalist. He knows what he's doing. He's been leading this team to win nationals for over a decade." Nice Oliver makes me feel weird.

I would feel way more comfortable if everyone called me stupid. I blame my dad for that.

We make it through the next few legs of our match, neck and neck in points with the Monsters. The strain is getting to Sebastian, and Oliver is over his snippy remarks.

"We wouldn't be in this position if Kinsey was here." Sebastian shoots me a glare.

Thank you, captain obvious.

"If you don't shut the fuck up, I'll make sure you're not at the next tournament." Oliver doesn't raise his voice, or even sound threatening. It's just a fact.

I have to turn away from them to hide my smile.

"He shouldn't be here. He's not varsity material!"

Oliver gets into Sebastian's face this time. "If you were better, we would be in a better standing too. This is not his fault."

Sebastian pushes Oliver back a step. "What's your deal with

him? Huh? Why are you so protective? He your little bitch or something?"

"It sounds like you want to be my bitch." Oliver gets a familiar glint to his eyes. It's his, "I dare you to step over the line so I can make an example out of you", look.

"What are you talking about?" Sebastian asks. "I asked if he's your fucking bitch."

Oliver steps up to him, dominating the space. Holding himself with an air of confidence only he can pull off. "Maybe you're misunderstanding the situation. You're here because I allow it. I'm protective over everything of mine. That includes our legacy, and championship. If you can't be a team player, get the fuck off the mat and let the alternate fence." Oliver leans in and drops his voice to a sinister whisper. "Make no mistake, if you keep acting like a bitch, your spot on this lineup will evaporate."

My back stiffens, and I whirl around, done with everything. Done being the only one without family, done being the poor kid, done being the verbal punching bag for this jerk.

"Are you jealous no one cares enough about you to stand up for you?" I get closer to him so I don't have to yell. "Maybe if you weren't an insufferable know-it-all, someone could stand your presence for more than thirty seconds."

Oliver mouths *atta boy,* and I shake my head. He grabs his mask and foil and heads back to the line for his last match.

"Listen here, you gutter trash," Sebastian comes at me, but I turn on my heel and leave the strip. I'm not supposed to, but we have an alternate if we really need it, and I just can't take it anymore.

Coach Kennedy calls my name, but I don't stop walking. I've done my final match, and if I don't get away from Sebastian, I'll hit him.

I storm through the room until I get to the locker room. Since everyone is still out on the floor, it's empty, and I have room to pace while no one asks me questions.

Coach is gonna be pissed. Parents are going to whisper about me. I'm a damn embarrassment. Sebastian is right, I shouldn't be here.

Thirty-Five

Oliver

Monday morning I ditch my classes, a much more important engagement on my calendar. I'd fallen into a rabbit hole the night before when I looked up Isaac's family. I don't know how I'd never put two and two together, but Isaac's father is on the board of directors for my family's charity. Them having a connection to my family makes me more irate.

Did Isaac know? Why hadn't he told me? Either way, they weren't being honest with Isaac, and that makes me even more enraged. They have more money than Isaac knew, and they left him to rot and be taken advantage of at school for months. Had I not stumbled upon him that day . . . I didn't want to think of where he'd be. Probably dropped out of school and back in their clutches.

After that, finding where they live isn't hard. The drive takes me out of the city, about ninety minutes north. I try to get home-work done on the way, but I can't focus. I see Isaac when I attempt to do anything. The way he cringed from me. How he looked after breaking his foil. When he realized the entire team's parents were there except his.

It works me into a murderous rage.

And I keep stoking the fire all the way there. Much like my father, I don't lose control when I get angry. It burns like coal in my belly, and it's a tool. Like any other emotion. Harnessing the tools we were born with is so much more fun than calling them curses.

I tell my driver to wait as I slip out of the car and walk up the sidewalk to the white house. It's not new or shiny, but it's kept up well. It has a good-sized yard and a swing set in the back. What a quaint little place to grow up. It explains some of why Isaac is so sheltered. We came from fundamentally different backgrounds.

It makes him who he is, so I like it. Even if his parents are on my shit list.

I rap my knuckles on the oak-finished door and step back.

"Can I help you?" Mrs. Becker says when she opens the door.

"No, you can't. But you're going to want to hear me out. Go get your husband and tell him Oliver Godfrey is here to speak to you both."

It takes her a second, but she recognizes the name. I see it flash in her eyes before she scrutinizes me. "Your father—"

I cut her off. "Is not someone you want to upset? I can assure you. Now ask me inside before you piss me off."

She pulls the door wide, and I step inside, looking around. I'm nosy about Isaac's childhood as much as the mission I'm here for.

"Honey, Oliver Godfrey is here to see us," Mrs. Becker says as she walks towards the kitchen.

I slip my hands into my pockets of my slacks as I wait.

"What? Why?" Mr. Becker asks way too loud.

"I don't know. He didn't say," Mrs. Becker whisper yells.

They argue in hushed tones, which I can't make out, before reappearing around the corner.

"What can I do for you, son?" Mr. Becker holds out his hand.

I drop my gaze, but don't move to take it, flicking my eyes to meet his. "Don't call me son. I'm not here for social niceties or to be treated like a child. I'll buy your church and turn it into a parking lot."

The air between us shifts, and I feel him searching his mind for any offense he might have given. I'm enjoying his squirm far too much.

Mr. Becker shifts his stance. "Okay . . . then, why are you here?"

"I found it quite curious that your son started on the varsity relay team this past weekend and you were nowhere in sight." I keep my hands loosely in my pockets, not showing any signs of aggression—yet.

"We don't have an oldest son anymore," Mrs. Becker sneered.

My attention moves to her. "So he's emancipated then?"

"No," she says.

"So on top of being awful parents, you're leaving him destitute. Am I hearing that correctly?" I fling my words at them.

Mrs. Becker stammers a half-assed defense, but her husband cuts her off.

"His own choices left him destitute."

"So God said abandon your children? God said punish them? God said cast off your sons . . . No . . . I don't seem to remember reading that in theology class. But I went to a Catholic boarding school so maybe I'm wrong. Please tell me what your text says."

"It says in Leviticus—"

I don't let him finish. "What does that have to do with abandoning your child? Nothing. Correct me if I'm wrong but I believe it's Matthew seven-three which says 'Why do you see the speck that is in your brother's eye, but do not notice the log that is in your own eye?' and I think we read the same verses that amount to God telling you, you are not fucking qualified to judge others. In fact, it goes so far as to say if you take God's role away from him, you will be judged with those acts."

Mr. Becker stares at me, and Mrs. Becker's face twists in a scornful scowl.

"Furthermore, what did we learn in the story of the prodigal son? It's a little sad I'm having to teach a preacher and his wife the bible. It's almost like this is a phony act you two put on to be disgusting, hateful cunts."

"What would your father think?" Mr. Becker finds his voice. "He obviously gave you a good Catholic education. What would he think about you defending a homosexual?"

"He's smart enough to know that even if he's made uncomfortable by something, blood matters. Family matters, and he wouldn't risk embarrassing himself or his company with a personal belief." My voice carries no emotion to convey how silly and trifling their ideas are.

"Are you saying you're a homosexual? Should we test the theory and tell him you're gay?" Mrs. Becker says like she's pulling one over on me.

I laugh. "It's cute you think you can threaten me. Tell them—no—better yet—" Their threat gave me an idea. I pull my phone from my pocket and hit my father's contact. When he answers, I go right into it. "I'm gay, Dad. So I can't marry Cassie. Hope that doesn't mess anything up."

My dad doesn't reply right away. "Thank you for telling me, son. Have you spoken to your mother yet? She was hanging her hopes on this June wedding." He isn't mad. He's annoyed he'll have to deal with Mother not getting to plan a wedding.

"No, I'll call her next."

"Thank you. We can discuss it further at dinner this week."

"Sounds good." I hang up the call and glance between them.

"What does any of this have to do with you? Why do you care?" Mrs. Becker snaps.

"What your book didn't teach you, but my father did, is I don't enter arguments I can't win." I want to tell them because I plan on being balls deep in their son for the foreseeable future, but as Isaac isn't ready to come out as a couple, so I bite my tongue. "I'm the captain of the Gods fencing team. And I wanted to see why our new varsity star's parents were deadbeats."

"We aren't deadbeats. We have morals—"

"Ones based on nothing, I guess, which makes you look foolish. But continue if you like to look idiotic. Now that I have my answer, where are Isaac's sketch books? He said you didn't let him leave with any of his things. Give them to me." I told out my hand, and Mrs. Becker looks like she's going to object, so I go on. "Don't burn your social life and your church to the ground. I'll ruin you before lunch, and I'll enjoy every fucking minute of it. Do not tempt me."

Thirty-Six

Oliver

I phone Mother on the drive home, and her reaction dumbfounds me.

I sit in disbelief as she squeals and begins to spew about always wanting a gay son. I don't correct her about being bisexual. If I want her to drop the stuff about Cassie, I have to sell it. My parents didn't need to be in my business anyway.

"I've always wanted a gay son . . . We are going to be able to bond so much more over this . . . I can't believe you waited so long to tell me . . . Have you known long? I don't know how your father and I didn't notice . . . It's so nice to get to have this with you . . . It's too late now because all the best hotels will be booked, but we need to spend spring break in Paris shopping . . . I'm calling our travel agent now . . ." She doesn't even take a breath between her run-on sentences.

I don't interrupt, knowing her well enough to give her time to burn out.

"Does Olivia know? I can't believe you told her before me . . . Is this why she and Greg broke up? Did you have a feeling about him? You know my psychic never liked him. She tried to warn me about his family . . . You know I wouldn't be surprised if they were intimidated. What am I always saying about new money?"

By the end of the drive, I'm ready to kill her. Maybe both of us just so I never have to hear her treat me like another stereotype again.

"I have to go, Mother. Class starts in five minutes."

"Oh no, we have so much more to talk about," she whines like we haven't been on the call for ninety minutes without her taking a fucking breath. "I guess we can talk on Thursday at dinner. I love you, honey, and we support you. Always."

I hang up the phone and think really hard about abducting Isaac to go live in another country on the lam with me for the foreseeable future, at least until my parents die.

I need a drink. I check my watch. It's not even noon.

I decide I don't care and pour myself a drink as soon as I set foot in the penthouse.

"Isn't it a little early for that?" Owen walks out of his room looking like a functioning member of society in slacks and a crisp blue button-down tucked in.

"Isn't it a little early for you to be so dressed up?" I look him over.

Owen and I are opposites. I like to get up and all my classes done before noon, while Owen never begins classes before noon if he can help it.

"I have an interview."

I make a face. "What are you talking about?"

"I'm applying for grad school."

I blink. "Excuse me?"

He shrugs.

"What will Mom and Dad say?"

"I'm banking on them being too distracted by your wedding to Cassie and subsequent downfall when you back out last minute. They won't care what I do." Owen wears a smug smile, and it looks good on him. I like when he's up. I sometimes forget how good it can feel to have my brother around when he's not doing well. How much I miss him. I try to block it out because I don't want him to feel bad about his lows.

"I love you, and I'm sorry I'm about to burst your bubble, but I'll do everything in my power to distract them so they don't pay attention."

A crease forms in his forehead. "What did you do?"

I laugh and pour him a drink. "I told them I'm gay."

He shakes his head when I offer it to him. "You what? You're not gay."

"I told them I was gay so I don't have to marry Cassie. I am bisexual."

"Really? Are you?" He gets a thoughtful expression.

"I'm dating a man."

"Are you two actually dating now?" Owen doesn't seem convinced.

"I told you I liked him." I run over our interactions, sure he was there when I told him. "I told you in front of Olivia. Do you not remember?"

"I wasn't aware you could actually 'have feelings'," Owen says before breaking out into a laugh.

I hold up my middle finger, then down the drink I poured for him. "Fucking asshole."

"You're screwing up my life plans with your romance. I had to get you back." He grabs a bottle of water from the fridge. "So you're serious about him. Are you telling Mom and Dad who you're dating?"

"I don't know. He doesn't even want to acknowledge me in

public. I doubt he'll want to rock up to dinner with our parents if he won't even touch me in front of the team."

Owen takes a sip from the bottle. "He'll come around. He seems to like you despite all your red flags."

"He will. I just have to see how much groveling is required."

"Groveling will be good for you."

"I thought you were on my side?" I refill my glass and then cross the room to fix his tie.

"Thanks," he says when I finish. "I am, but that doesn't mean I can't see when something will be good for you."

"Just be warned dinner will be insufferable Thursday. Mom is already threatening to make me go to Paris with her for my fucking gay opinion on shopping."

"Enjoy that." Owen checks his watch. "I have to go. Don't tell them."

"You know I would never."

"I know. But it feels better saying it." He pauses after he puts his coat on. "Isaac will come around."

"I know."

Thirty-Seven

Isaac

S oft kisses on my neck stir me from my dream. The scent of Oliver engulfs me in his bed as I try to dig deeper into the soft sheets and comfortable mattress. I don't know what magic his sheets are made of, but they feel amazing on my bare skin. A cold breeze makes me shiver as the blankets I've cocooned myself in are lifted, and a cool hand slides around my ribs and up to my throat.

"Mmm I like finding you warm and naked in my bed, kitten." Oliver's mouth brushes my ear as he speaks.

"Your bed is the best part of this arrangement." I smile at my snarky response. We've gotten to a place where I'm comfortable being a bit sarcastic with him, riling him up a little.

"Oh really?" He bites at my shoulder and pulls me flush against his fully clothed body.

"The orgasms are right up there, though. A solid second place."

"I should turn your ass red for that." The hand at my throat roams down my body to grip my ass cheek. "Then use your throat and leave you wanting."

My dick perks up at the idea, and I whimper.

"But that will have to wait. Get up. I have something for you."

I groan when he releases me and quickly roll over to grab him.

"Wait." I throw my leg over to straddle his hips, dragging my most sensitive skin against his slacks. He watches me with lust filled eyes but doesn't move. I know this game well. He's given a direction and expects me to follow.

With our gazes locked, I unbutton the top few buttons of his shirt before leaning forward to brush my lips along his collarbone. Oliver shudders under me, and his hand comes up to tighten in my hair.

Using his own weaknesses against him is one of my favorite things to do. Along with using my body to distract him. That's a powerful feeling, knowing I can break his concentration by grinding against him or moving a certain way.

His cock is thick under me, and I smile into his skin when I roll my hips against him again, and his breathing hitches. I lick up his throat, stopping to suck on his Adam's apple before continuing up to his jaw where I bite softly.

"Kitten." The word is a growl. He has a mission, but he is close to giving in. Before I fell asleep, however long ago that was, he fucked me on the bathroom counter, then carried me to bed. I wouldn't need any prep to take him again now and God do I want to.

"Yes?"

His hand tightens in my hair, and he pulls my face back.

"Stop distracting me."

I smile and sit back on his lap. Clearly, he has something important to say, or he would have taken over and be buried inside of me by now. My Oliver only lets me get so far before his need to control and dominate becomes too much and he snaps. I love when he snaps.

"Kiss me, then show me why you woke me."

With one hand tight in my hair and one gripping my jaw, he crashes our mouths together in a hungry kiss. The way he takes from me while giving me what I asked for is intoxicating. *He's* intoxicating.

Once I've been thoroughly ravaged, Oliver slows our kiss, turning sweet and sensual. It's a sharing of air and space, intimate and delicate. Almost like he's hesitant or nervous.

"All right, you've had your fun. Get dressed."

I smile and press one last quick kiss on his lips before climbing off the bed to pull on some joggers and his T-shirt. I love that it smells like him.

"Okay, I'm dressed." I lift my arms up to show him as if he couldn't already see for himself. "Show me."

Oliver takes my hand, threading our fingers together, and leads me down the hall to the room I now refer to as the Beast's Library. Mostly because it annoys him and makes Owen chuckle.

This penthouse is mind-boggling. It's bigger than the house I grew up in. Probably four times as expensive too.

There are bookshelves atop cabinets and trophy cases, awards, and framed pictures on the walls. It's all very pretentious but my favorite chairs are in here, so I study and draw in here. Plus, the lighting is amazing with a huge wall of windows. Oliver didn't even complain when I moved one of the overstuffed chairs to the windows, just lifted an eyebrow and smirked at me.

I love the mood of this space, its dark green walls and books, a few vining plants, shiny gold accents, and soft comfortable chairs. It reminds me of foggy mountains.

Looking around the room, I see he's rearranged some of the furniture. Both chairs are now by the windows, with a small table next to each of them and a wall-mounted light overhanging the chairs when it's dark.

His desk has been pulled more toward the middle of the room where he can dominate the space where a cardboard box sits with the flaps folded.

He leads me to my favorite spot, and I settle into it, pulling a cashmere throw into my lap and criss-crossing my legs.

Oliver picks up the box and brings it to me. His face gives away nothing as I take it from him. It's heavier than I expected, about a foot square and six inches tall.

"Open it."

Confused by what could possibly be in here, I pull open the flap and gasp. My eyes shoot back to Oliver as my heart pulses in my ears and my stomach falls to the floor.

"How? When? How?" I look back into the box, at my sketch-books, pencil box, and pictures that had been on the walls of my bedroom.

I'm almost afraid to touch them, like if I do, they'll disappear.

"I got them from your parents."

There's more to it than that, but I don't care what it is in this moment. Maybe later I'll care enough to ask how he managed to get them to agree to give him this, but with trembling hands and a knot in my throat, I lift the top pad and cradle it to my chest.

Tears fall down my cheeks when I look back at him. "Thank you." The words are barely a whisper and full of gratitude. "I don't know what else to say."

"This space is yours." Oliver opens the cabinet door closest to me. "You can keep your art supplies or whatever else you need. I won't touch them or look. I promise. If you need more space, I'll find it."

Setting the box down, I launch myself at him, jumping up into his arms and wrapping myself around him. I bury my face in his neck and cry. I never expected to see these again, these pieces of my soul that I bled onto the pages. And to know he went out of his way to track down my parents and convince them to give them to him means more than I have words for. I'm overwhelmed.

Oliver holds me just as tightly and sits us in one of the big chairs. He pets my hair and rubs my back with one hand, holding me with the other. Anchoring me to him, to the present. Maybe I am worth something.

"Was this proof?"

Not understanding his question, I peel myself from his neck and look at him.

"What?"

He cups my face and wipes my tears from my skin.

"Was this proof that I want more from you than just your body?"

He's got that mask on his face that he uses to protect himself, but I've learned that when he looks at me like that, he's hiding a vulnerability. He's not sure if he's done the right thing or if he did enough.

"It's—" I cut myself off and try to think of a way to describe what this means to me. "It's everything."

ISAAC: Meet me for dinner.

COLIN: Nice to know you can think past Oliver's dick.

ISAAC: Your jealousy is showing.

COLIN: *Eyeroll emoji* only a little. Where and what time?

ISAAC: The pizza place right off campus, in like an hour.

Leaving the bathroom attached to Oliver's bedroom, I go in search of Owen. It's so strange to see how different the two of them are. In public, it's hard to tell them apart unless they're looking directly at me, but here in the apartment, it's very obvious. Oliver is always refined, controlled, put together. Owen is dramatic, often frazzled, and messy. Both physically and mentally. I adore him.

I find Owen draped over the couch in the living room, one arm and leg hanging over the edge onto the floor with his other arm over his face. It's very seventh century delicate woman of him.

"Good afternoon, Owen." I sit on the coffee table in front of him and lean on my palm. "What are we contemplating today?"

"Life is meaningless. We all suffer, then die, but to what end?"

I do not have the brain power for this. No wonder Oliver is always at his best. How does he manage this?

"Well, I don't have an answer for that, but how about you get up, maybe brush your teeth and put some jeans on, then come out for pizza with me?"

Slowly, the arm covering his face lowers and he stares, stock still. It's an expression I'm familiar with on Oliver, but I don't know what it means from Owen . . .

"Where is Oliver? Did he put you up to this? Why are you asking me out?" He sits up, back straight, and folds his hands in his lap.

"Oliver is in Beast's Library doing whatever it is he does in there. I'm hungry, and we're friends. Ish." I shrug.

"You could just Uber some food or go look in the kitchen. I'm sure the cook left something for us to reheat."

The fact that he says that so casually still blows my mind. Who the hell has a cook?

"Go put pants on."

"Excuse me?" Oliver's stern question has words falling from Owen's mouth before I have a chance.

"He asked me to go out with him. I don't know what's happening, but I am not touching your fuck toy."

My cheeks heat, and my mouth falls open.

"Owen!"

"Kitten . . ."

Owen hops over the back of the couch and disappears down the hallway to make me face his brother alone. Coward.

"You're letting him get away!" I point down the hallway after Owen and huff.

Oliver is standing a few feet from me with his arms crossed and an eyebrow raised, waiting for an explanation.

"I just want a slice of pizza, and he looked like he was two seconds from slitting his wrists. Plus, I don't think he's eaten today." I take in his tailored slacks and green button-up shirt that's still tucked in, but the top buttons have been loosened. I lick my lips thinking about tasting him there.

"If you wanted pizza, why didn't you tell me? I would have had the cook make some."

I stand and walk over, holding onto his hips and lifting onto my toes to lick the hollow of his throat.

Growing up, I didn't think I would be an overtly sexual person. Probably because I couldn't imagine a time I would be able to be with a person I truly wanted, but being in the same room with Oliver gets my blood pumping.

"You were busy, and once I got Owen moving, I was going to tempt you to leave with us."

Oliver cups the back of my head and kisses my forehead.

"Thank you for looking after him. Nothing is more important to me than you and my siblings."

Meeting his gaze, I can see the truth in his words, and they heal a broken part of me.

"What's important to you, is important to me."

Oliver nuzzles into my hair and kisses right behind my ear.

"Come out to dinner with me, please?" I kiss his mouth softly. "A simple slice of pizza and soda. I know of a place." There's a softness in his eyes. It makes me want to show him a part of me that no one else has seen. "Come here."

I grab his hand and lead him back to the library. Pointing to the chair I usually sit in, I tell him to sit. He raises an eyebrow but does it. Opening the cabinet he gave me for my drawing stuff, I take a deep breath and reach for my most recent sketchpad to hand it to him.

He looks at the book, then up before he takes it. Oliver looks almost hesitant like he expects me to snatch it back.

"This is what I've been drawing since I met you."

Opening the book, he flips through the pages silently. The lack of response has me wringing my hands.

"They are lovely." He looks at me for a long moment, lips barely parted like he considered his words. "Since the first night, or only since you decided you liked me?" A smile plays on his lips, the hint of a tease.

I smile the same way. I want to mess with him but I'm too emotionally raw.

"I bought this sketchbook after the gala but I've been drawing you in my notebooks since the first night." I drop my gaze to my hands and chew on the inside of my lip. "When I had proof that you couldn't be mine, I hoped that if I drew you enough, I could get you out of my system."

"I don't think it worked very well, but as the outcome benefits me immensely, I'm glad."

"I think it actually made it worse. I started obsessing over every little detail."

"And now? Do you still draw me?"

"Yes," I whisper. I don't know why I'm embarrassed to admit that.

A genuine smile stretches over his face. Not his typical smug one.

Closing the book, he sets it on the table and reaches for me. I climb into his lap, straddling him. He pulls my lip from my teeth and brushes his thumb across it.

"Good. I want you to be obsessed with me. That puts us on even ground."

By the time we get to the pizza place next to campus, Owen has a public face on, Oliver is pretending like he didn't have to threaten his brother to put jeans on, and I am so confused that I'm just laughing.

"This is where you want to eat?" Oliver looks around the space with a very different expression than I do.

"He's a peasant, brother. This is fine dining."

Owen isn't wrong, but I don't take offense.

"Yes, cheese pizza and a Coke, please and thank you." I look around and find Colin sitting at a booth with his face in his phone. I slide in on the opposite side of him and take my jacket off. Okay, it's Oliver's jacket and too big, but I don't care. It's warm and smells good. I'm trying really hard not to think of what it costs.

"Look who decided to—" Colin looks up, catching a glimpse at the coat before I get it shoved to the side, then looks back. "I was pretty sure I knew where you were when you weren't coming home, but now I know for sure."

Owen and Oliver come over, both looking surprised to see Colin, but they take their seats with Owen sitting next to Colin.

"Isaac . . .," Colin drags my name out. "What is this?"

He rakes his eyes over Owen, his thoughts clear on his face. He wants to know if he can turn Owen.

"I'm dating Oliver."

All three of them turn surprised faces on me, and I grin.

"For fuck's sake, this is not going to end well." Owen sighs.

"Oh, eww," Colin sneers like he's smelled something gross and sits back with his arms crossed. "Have you hit your head? Has he rattled your brain with his dick?"

"My dick has hypnotic powers," Oliver deadpans, but puts his hand on my leg.

"Only to those who aren't used to dealing with your kind." Colin rolls his eyes and Owen snickers before he turns back to me. "Seriously, you don't have to date him to use him."

"No one asked you, Colin, fuck off." Oliver growls, and I lift his hand from my leg to thread our fingers.

"Just be glad you have the room to yourself *and* a shower that works."

Oliver lifts my hand and kisses the back of it. I can't drop the smile on my face. I'm trying to not let my poor ever-hopeful heart get ahead of me. I want this, with him, so badly it's physically painful to think of him changing his mind. Maybe if I want it bad enough, I can keep him?

Thirty-Eight

Oliver

"T his is weird, right?" I look over at Isaac. "It's not just me." We stand in the doorway of my brother's room, but I can't believe my eyes. Instead of the usual sight of Owen dragging his feet to get ready he's—playing air guitar.

"No, you're right. It's really weird." Isaac wrinkles his nose. "Is he okay?"

"What do you mean?" I ask unable to look away. "It's like a train wreck."

"It is." Isaac shakes it off. "I mean, not to sound insensitive or anything, but is this like a sign he's more mentally ill?"

"Or is it a sign he's better?" I'm not sure. "I wonder if it's in that drug store pamphlet they always give you but I just throw in the trash."

"You don't read it?"

"Absolutely not. I'm not taking it. I just put the pills in his muffin every morning, then try to coax him out the door with an iced coffee."

"You put his pills in freaking muffins?" Isaac stares at me.

"He asked me to. Calm down." I half glare. "I'm not drugging my brother against his will. He doesn't remember to take his meds."

"We are never living on our own, are we?"

I shake my head. "Not unless we can find a nice girl to adopt him. But I've lost hope. Women want puppies, not grown-ass dogs."

"I can hear you two," Owen says, but doesn't stop his air guitar.

"That's the point. I'm trying to shame you to stop."

Owen holds up his middle finger. "I'm having a good day. Is that a crime?"

"Yes, obviously, I need five to seven business days' notice so I can properly mentally prepare," I say, giving him a playful shove. "You have to get dressed. It's really nice to see you happy."

He shoves me back, then shoves his hand into his sweaty hair. "I got really into this new 2nd Star album." He lifts his shirt to wipe his face. "Oliver making sure I take my pills is actually the nicest thing he does for me. I'd never remember, and probably wouldn't get out of bed to take them if he didn't."

"You do have a heart, baby."

I shoot him a glare before the word triggers. "What was that?"

Isaac gets a bit of a panicked look. "Baby . . ."

I grab his shirt and drag him closer. "Say it again."

"Before you two start fucking, can one of you tell me when we need to leave?" Owen calls.

Isaac groans, trying to answer Owen, but my tongue gets in the way. He laughs, play fighting.

"Now. The car is waiting," I manage to get out between kisses.

"I need to shower."

"We'll be late for our reservations!" I pick up Isaac by the backs of his thighs to slam him into the doorframe.

"And now you're putting on a show," Owen mutters.

"Go get dressed." I grind into Isaac. "You're going to make me cum in my pants."

"No, I will not take responsibility for that," Owen calls out aggressively.

Isaac groans and then starts laughing.

"Thanks for ruining the moment!" I say, not really mad.

"You said we have to leave. I was just trying to save your reservation."

"The one you're making us miss by showering?" I reluctantly put Isaac down and smooth a hand over my shirt, trying to fix the wrinkles.

Isaac sticks out his lip, dragging his gaze down my body.

"Evil."

"What?" He plays innocent.

"I can't believe you two are making me watch this!" Owen says from somewhere in his room.

"No one is making you watch anything. Maybe it's saying something about you that you keep watching." I snap my teeth at Isaac. "It's going to be so hard to make it through dinner when you look this good."

"How hard?" he asks, grabbing my dick.

I rock into his grip. "I think you can feel for yourself."

"I'm still here!" Owen says.

"By your own accord!"

Isaac keeps laughing, but he's still stroking me through my slacks, so I don't complain.

"Olivia is going to be mad if we're late." I lower my gaze to watch myself in Isaac's hand. "I love watching you touch me."

"You and your brother both." Isaac smirks, knowing his words land.

"I'm getting dressed. I can't witness any more of this."

"Again, no one is forcing you to watch. You could have been out of the shower by now!" I grab Isaac's wrist when he tries to release my cock. "You stop when he leaves?"

Isaac grins wider. "You like putting on a show."

"How do you know that?"

"Every window you've ever fucked me in."

I narrow my eyes but don't disagree. "That doesn't mean you can stop."

"And then what? You cum in your pants?" He seems exhilarated by the idea. "Then you'll have to change."

"You're lucky I like my sister, or I'd force you under the table while we eat to service me."

"Is that an option?" Isaac's slacks tent with his hard-on.

I grab it. "You like to put on a show as much as I do."

His cheeks color.

"I'm ready . . ." Owen clears his throat. "And you two are still dry fucking."

"What else do you expect me to do while you force me to wait?" I ask, not taking my eyes off Isaac.

"Why can't I have been born into a normal family?" Owen is suddenly right next to us.

"Because then you'd be poor."

Owen sighs. "I guess if I have to be depressed, it's better to be rich and depressed."

"Remind yourself of that when Mom tries to find you a wife." I detangle myself from Isaac's grasp, giving up on trying to fix my wrinkled clothes.

"She's mental. I can't believe I'm on the chopping block now as the straight kid."

"Be better?" I say with a shrug.

"Maybe be gay?" Isaac adds as we get into the elevator.

"I don't even want to be straight right now. I'm not adding another complication for her to take advantage of!"

We get to the restaurant to find Olivia already sitting at the table.

She jumps up when she sees us, hugging Owen first, then me, before turning on Isaac. "I am so excited to meet you." She hugs him before he can object.

"Hard launch into the family, baby." I use the word back on him.

Isaac wears the biggest smile.

I press my lips to his cheek right next to his ear. "Happiness looks good on you."

"It feels good too." He takes my hand after we sit down.

"You two are so cute!" Olivia picks up her menu. "I hope you like Japanese food."

"I do." Isaac is doing the new boyfriend shy around the family thing.

"When are you telling Mom and Dad?" she asks, closing the menu.

"Never? Is that an option?" I half joke, side-eyeing Isaac to garner his reaction.

Olivia raises her brows, but the waiter comes over, and we all order drinks.

I bring Isaac's hand to my lips when the waiter leaves. "I'll tell them when I get tired of her treating me like the token gay."

"So next week?" Owen laughs.

I groan. "I'm currently living in the delusion it will get better when she gets used to it."

"Can a boomer do that?" Owen says without a hint of a joke to his voice.

"Do not ruin this for me. I need something to hold onto." I pick up my drink the second the waiter puts it down.

Olivia orders a bunch of appetizers. "Is there anything else you want to add?"

"Can we get egg rolls?" Isaac says softly.

The waiter turns, but I ask him to bring me a second drink.

"Bad day?" Olivia lifts an eyebrow.

"Not yet, but there is always time." I roll my eyes and take another gulp. "At least she hasn't tried to marry me off yet."

"No, now she's saying she needs to set me up with someone," Owen grumbles.

"Has she?" Olivia asks, like this is big news. "Maybe she'll get off my dick for a minute."

Owen snorts. "Please. She'll never get off any of our dicks as long as we live."

"Are you sure you want to be a part of this?" I ask Isaac.

He squeezes my hand. "I've never wanted to be part of something more."

"He's smitten!" Olivia is way too excited about this.

"Shh, don't tell him. I want him to stay like this," I shoot back.

"I can hear you." Isaac elbows me but keeps our hands joined.

"Sucks, doesn't it?" Owen mutters.

"Want to walk?" I say when we leave dinner. "It's only a couple of blocks."

"It's cold." Owen tips his head towards the sky like it would open up at any second and start snowing.

"I wasn't asking you." I glare.

"Rude. Not even inviting me for your romantic walk with your boyfriend. I thought we were twins."

"Get in the car, Owen."

He gets into the car, and I meet Isaac's eyes. "Are we walking?"

He nods. "I like the cold."

I kiss his nose.

He laughs, then drops his face to rub against my neck. "It's weird to have you kiss me in public."

"Why?" I ask, hugging him to me.

"I didn't think a guy like you would ever want others to know you were into me."

"You don't see yourself like I see you. I told you the first night we spent together. You're art. I want you everywhere."

His breath hitches for a minute, but he takes a second to collect himself before lifting his head up. "Thank you."

"It's true. You don't need to thank me." I offer my hand. "My sister likes you."

"How do you know?"

"She gets giddy when she's excited." We start toward my building.

"Would that have been a deal breaker?"

"No. Nothing is a deal breaker. That's how I operate."

"What do you mean?" he asks.

"I don't care what anyone else thinks. I want you." I pull him into me as we wait for the light to change. "I shouldn't like you this much."

"No, I think you should."

"Oh? Is that so?"

He nods. "More even."

"You want more of me? I think if you get too much more, you'll get overwhelmed."

"No. I'm greedy. I want it all."

Like Owen predicted it, the sky opens up and giant snowflakes rain down upon us.

We miss the light, kissing in the snow.

Thirty-Nine

Oliver

"I can't sit through another dinner. I'm going to poison the food to get her to shut up."

Owen walks out of his closet with two dinner jackets. "Which one do you think with this tie?"

"Who the fuck are you trying to impress?"

"No one. Why do you ask?" He holds one in front of himself and looks in the mirror.

"Historically, you are not dressed until I threaten to leave without you." I gesture at him. "And for the last three dinners, you're dressing to the nines. What is this?"

"Can't I feel good about myself?" He turns toward me. "Which color?"

"Not when it creeps me out." I take both jackets and hand him back the second.

"And I thought I'm the one who hates change?" He pulls it on.

"It's not change, it's . . ." I don't know what it is. Almost like he's doing a victory lap while I'm suffering. Not that I would ever believe that was Owen's motivation.

"It's not really me. You don't like Mom's focus, even if you've always been the golden child. Olivia had her focus for all this crap." He's hit the nail on the head, finally putting into words what I couldn't.

"I hate it." My phone buzzes in my pocket, and I pull it out to see my mother on the screen. "But you're the golden child. Her favorite and always have been."

"I might be the favorite, but I'm like the broken toy favorite. The one they baby and feel bad for. You're the pride and joy."

I roll my eyes.

"Maybe they'll behave better with Isaac there tonight?" Owen pulls open his watch drawer to select one.

"I doubt it. I don't even know why they invited him."

"Mom feels bad for him. She said she talked to the booster club, and his parents haven't even joined. You know how she is with kids like that. Remember when she mistakenly tried to adopt Prince Nicolas because she thought he was some scholarship kid from an impoverished country, not the literal prince?"

I shudder. "God, every time he came to dinner she'd make him a care package."

"Or when she asked if he wanted to stay with us for the summer so he wouldn't have to 'go back to his country' like the kid wasn't going back to a castle in Luxembourg ?"

"Or when she'd shout at him like he couldn't understand English, as if he wasn't fluent in four fucking languages." I groan. "Isaac is going to have a panic attack when she treats him like a peasant."

"Who's going to treat me like a peasant?" Isaac asks, walking into Owen's room, hair still wet from the shower. I love how he's grown comfortable in the space and willing to just walk into Owen's room.

"Our mother. She's awful."

"Do you not want me to come?" Isaac asks carefully.

"No, you have to or we won't hear the end of it." I step into his space to fix the tie I'd bought for him. "And Olivia will be there to help."

Isaac sighs dramatically. "I know."

"You look gorgeous, boyfriend."

A smile stretches over his face as he looks up at me. "You calling me that will never get old."

"Boyfriend," I murmur into his mouth.

"I love how it tastes."

"I love how you taste." I grab his hips, dragging them to meet mine. "If we didn't need to get in the helicopter in three minutes, I'd strip you where you stand."

"Not in front of your brother," Isaac playfully objects while grinding against my dick.

"I'm like furniture. Don't mind me," Owen says from somewhere behind us. "I'm not even into men."

Isaac's eyes go wide.

I laugh, deepening the kiss. "Fuck, we have to go. Stop making me hard. I can't be hard at dinner with my parents."

"Not even if I'm sitting next to you with my hand on your dick?" Isaac asks coyly.

I bite his lip. "Don't tempt me."

The helicopter ride is uneventful, other than Isaac acting like a giddy schoolboy pointing out all the buildings.

"You're cute," I say when we step out on the rooftop.

"Your parents live here?" he asks, walking closer to the edge.

I grab his hand. "Yes. Wait until you see the views of the park from their dining room."

"I can't imagine waking up to this every day." There is a hesitation to his tone I can't read.

"It's not that much different from my apartment." Sure, the price tag is quite a bit different, but I'd grown up in this building, so maybe it didn't hold the same novelty.

"It's a lot different." He follows us to the elevator.

I want to experience the world from his eyes. Before dating him, I'd never realized how blind I am to my life.

We ride the elevator down and step into my parents' foyer. Isaac gasps as he looks around.

"Is this what it's like having a child on Christmas?" Owen asks under his breath. "Between this and the helicopter, I feel like the fun uncle giving him all his firsts."

I barely hold back a laugh. "Must be."

The butler takes our coats, and Isaac side-eyes me.

"Yes, we have a butler," I say before he asks.

"Who really has a butler?" Isaac turns a slow circle looking at the ceiling art like a wondrous child.

"Lots of people." Probably. At least this entire building. "Come on. My parents will be in the formal living room for before dinner drinks."

He reluctantly stops admiring the ceiling. "It's not too late to run away."

Owen chuckles. "He's not wrong."

"We just have to get through it, then we can go drink ourselves into amnesia."

We round the corner into the formal living room, and I stop in my tracks, never having expected this turn of events.

Isaac's parents sit across from mine, smug as fuck.

Forty

Oliver

Anger sizzles in my veins. "You didn't tell me we'd have guests?"

"Yes, we decided to invite Isaac's parents at the last minute," my mother says easily, like she's not lying.

The pieces come together in my head. All of it is a setup, and there is nothing I loathe more than being set up. But worse than my own naivety, I feel the waves of panic coming off Isaac.

"And why would you do that?" I say, not sure I'll be staying for dinner. Poison returns to my plans for the evening. Would Isaac visit me in prison? I hope so.

I'm jarred back to reality by his mother.

"We asked them to," Mrs. Becker says in her sickly sweet tone, like she's auditioning for a fundamentalist cult. "We just wanted to clear the air with our boys and ourselves. It seems like we got off on the wrong foot with you, Oliver, and we are sorry for that. Parenting is hard, but your parents were so kind as to hear us out, and help us with all the details of being supportive parents."

What is her end game here? I don't know them well enough to guess, and I can't just ask Isaac, confronted like this. My hands are tied without letting my parents know I'm dating Isaac. I have to act like a good captain and accept their apology for the "team's sake" when the last thing I want to do is subject Isaac to a night with his parents.

I can't just walk out without alerting my parents to my games. They have me backed into the corner.

"I'm so glad my parents could facilitate that for you," I say through my teeth. "Anyone need a refresh on their drink?" I ask, needing to pound about five before I can deal with this.

My mother and father accept, but the Beckers decline.

"Will you help me?" I ask Isaac.

"Sure." His word shudders, but he follows.

"I'm so sorry. I had no idea they would pull this." I pull Isaac into my arms as soon as we are out of the room.

"Why would they do this?" He leans into me.

"It has to be because I told them they were shitty parents when I went to go get your artwork. I never in a million years would have expected them to do a one-eighty. Is this like them?"

"No, it's not like them at all. I don't know why they would be here. Why would they just show up? They've disowned me . . ." Isaac is rambling.

I cup his face in an attempt to calm him down. "Could it be they're trying to save face to my parents?" I start to put it together. "Your father is on the board of one of their charities. I didn't realize until I went up there. Did you know?"

He nods slowly. "Yes, but I didn't know it was your family's charity until that night at the gala."

"I must have triggered this by telling them they are an embarrassment to the rest of the fencing parents. I am so sorry. I didn't realize the far-reaching consequences it would have on you. I didn't think it would end in them trying to save face. What fucking douches." I rest my forehead against his. "Do you want to leave? It will look awful if we do, and possibly expose our relationship, but I will if you need to."

Confusion flickers in his expression. "Why would it expose us?"

"As the captain, I can defend you and want your parents to be supportive, but if I don't accept when they are, how does it look?" I know how they'll take it.

Isaac deflates. "Oh."

"Can you stand to put on a brave face? You can leave without me . . . but the optics of that aren't good either. It gives them both fodder to use against you. They will say you're unreasonable and don't deserve my defense."

"How can you foresee all of that?"

"I've played their games my entire life. I know how they think, unfortunately. But I will do whatever you need for support."

Isaac is quiet for a long moment. "Are you ever going to tell them about me?"

"Do you want me to?"

"That's not what I asked," Isaac says.

"I will tell them when we are ready." I make the promise knowing I'll never be ready, but I'll deal with it when we get there. I wouldn't keep him a secret forever.

His face falls, and I can't help but feel like he's upset with me. "Okay."

"Is that a, you're staying or going, okay?"

"Staying. Hopefully, it will end after tonight."

I kiss his forehead. "Thank you, and I'm sorry again."

"It's not your fault my parents are awful."

"No, but I set them off. I take responsibility for it."

He puts on a half-smile. "Thank you."

We return with drinks, and Olivia is there. She is beaming, happy to see Isaac with me, and I offer to make her a drink. She hops up to go with me.

So this is going to be a "conversations at the bar" kind of night. I meet Isaac's eyes in a silent apology as we slip out of the room.

"Why are Isaac's parents here?" she asks. "Mom and Dad don't know, right? They'd never approve of them."

"No, that is a whole other mess." I explain it to her, and she laughs.

"You really put your foot in it."

"Believe me, I know." I make her drink and myself a second to down.

"So it's going to be lit tonight."

"Fuck off." I refill my glass, and she holds hers she's already finished. "Are we both getting plastered tonight?"

"Solidarity. But at least the focus won't be my breakup with Greg tonight."

"Fuck off with that. The focus has been on me for weeks since I came out. I've seriously considered poisoning the soup so I don't have to listen to mother anymore."

She laughs and snorts. "Not right before I move abroad, please."

I roll my eyes. "We have to return. I can't leave Isaac to deal with this himself."

Dinner is shockingly uneventful, and there is only polite conversion, until dessert.

"Oh, Oliver." Mother puts her hand on my arm. "I keep forgetting to mention I invited the Byrons over for dinner next week. Their son is gay, and we cannot wait for you two to meet." Mrs. Becker stiffens, but Mother doesn't notice and goes on.

"Oliver came out as gay a few weeks ago, and we are just delighted."

I grin across the table at Mr. Becker, slowly chewing the French macaron my mother gets from my favorite French bakery.

"It's so wonderful to have a gay son. I feel so much closer to him since he came out," Mother keeps gushing, not noticing or maybe not caring the Beckers are uncomfortable. "I just want him to find the right guy to settle down with."

I'm going to throw myself off a bridge. Is this how Owen feels all the time? Fuck's sake, no wonder he's miserable.

But my will to end my life to get away from my mother is quickly overtaken with the boiling rage I started the dinner with.

They tricked me into this dinner. Tricked Isaac here and his fucking parents orchestrated it all.

I want to burn down their world.

"Speaking of meeting the right guy to settle down with." I shove to my feet and pull my grandmother's ring out of my pocket. "Since this wonderful night has brought both families together unexpectedly, it's the perfect time for what I need to say." I turn to Isaac and get down on one knee, opening the box that holds my grandmother's ring. "I know we had a rocky start, and I'm a prick, but I don't want to be with anyone else. You're different from any person I've ever met. You make me feel, and I know we've barely known each other for six months, but I already know I don't want anyone else. You are everything, Isaac. Everything I didn't know I needed. Will you marry me?"

The room erupts in pandemonium, but I don't care about them. I only care about the brown eyes looking into mine.

Forty-One

Isaac

Oliver wants to marry me?

He's kneeling on the floor in the dining room of his parents' house with everyone shouting at us, but none of that matters.

"Why do you have a ring?" I stare at him blankly. What is he doing?

"My mother gave it to me a few months ago, and I've been carrying it around." He lifts a shoulder like that's completely normal.

"Who just carries a ring around?"

"Holy shit, is that Grandmother's ring?" Olivia asks peering over his shoulder.

"It's your grandmother's ring?" That would explain the huge red stone and antique look of it.

"Yes." He doesn't waiver. He's not joking. "Are you going to answer my question?"

"Yes," I whisper, but I don't think he heard me over the commotion. "Yes! I will marry you."

The smile that splits Oliver's face will forever be my favorite.

He gets off his knee, takes the gold ring out of the box and looks at it. "It's not your style. I planned to have it remade with the same stones, but I didn't expect to do it so soon, so you can help plan it. Okay?" He slips the ring onto my finger.

"Okay," I say, smiling until my cheeks hurt.

Surprisingly, it fits. I know I have small hands, but Jesus.

Oliver lifts my chin, then bends over to place a chaste kiss on my lips. Everyone's eyes are burning into me, making my skin crawl, but when Oliver winks, nothing else matters.

This beautiful, talented man wants me.

"Oh, fuck me," Owen groans, tossing back the last of whatever he's drinking.

Olivia claps and jumps up to hug Oliver, then me.

"Welcome to the circus," she whispers in my ear before she lets go and takes her seat again.

"I guess we will be having a June wedding after all," Mrs. Godfrey says, lifting her glass in a toast to us.

The weight of this ring on my finger is no joke. Both physically and mentally. What did I just agree to? The weight of what will be expected of me, of all the things I don't know, starts pulling me down. What if I mess up? What if I embarrass the Godfrey family? What if I ruin something because I don't know who someone is, and I say the wrong thing?

No wonder Owen is such a mess. How does anyone live under this kind of pressure?

My father is red faced and sputtering, trying very hard to hold in all his hateful comments, I'm sure. Mother is pale and covering her mouth with her hand. I hate that they're here. I hate that they found a way to bully me without actually having to do it. They know I won't make a scene in front of Oliver's family, but I guess they have to behave as well. But where is my brother?

"Where's Noah?" I ask them across the table. Everyone quiets down to listen.

"He's at bible study like the good boy he is," my father says through clenched teeth.

"Isn't that where you should be then?" Oliver lays a hand on my leg and squeezes. With him at my side, I'm not as intimidated by my parents, apparently, but I still can't make a scene here. I don't want to embarrass him.

I take a deep breath and turn away from them. I can't look at them right now, knowing they are wishing harm upon me. Inside their minds are all the scriptures condemning me, saying how I've strayed from God's path and been tempted by the devil.

I can't argue that Oliver isn't temptation in the flesh or a devil.

That idea makes me laugh, and I snort to try to hold it in and end up choking on my macaron.

Oliver pats my back and offers me my water.

"Thank you," I say hoarsely and take the glass. "I'm fine."

"Olivia," their mother begins, and I can all but hear her groan. "Who is your next prospect? The Winifreds have a son about your age who's single, and with Greg out of the picture, you need to do something."

"Why can't you focus on their wedding? They are engaged!" Olivia says, exasperation coloring her tone.

"Are they even allowed to get married? Like legally?" Mrs. Godfrey asks.

"This is New York City," Mr. Godfrey says like that explains everything. "It's been legal since 2011."

Why does he know that?

We make our way back to the formal living room—I guess

that's a thing when you're a gazillionaire—and Oliver puts me in between him and Owen like guards, but now I need to pee. Bad.

I'm squirming in my seat like a child, but I don't want to get lost in this place.

"What's wrong?" Oliver leans in to ask.

"Where's the bathroom?"

"Down the hall, third door on the left."

I stand and bolt for the doorway without caring if it's rude to leave without saying anything.

I find the bathroom that I'm pretty sure is the size of my dorm room and take care of business. Once I've washed my hands, I open the door and find my mother standing on the other side.

She steps inside, shoving me backward before closing the door.

Here I don't have Oliver to protect me. I'm alone, and she knows it if the smirk on her face is anything to go by.

"I can't believe you would shame us like this." She slaps me across the face, jerking my head to the side. It burns through my face, and I can only imagine the mark.

"You are a disgrace." Venom drips from her words, poisoning the very ground she stands on. "We prayed so hard for God to make you understand, to bring you back to us, but you're tainted now. No good woman would ever want to touch you."

The bands around my ribs constrict with every word she spews and take me back to the place I worked so hard to escape from.

"You're a worthless excuse of a child and *his* family will see through you. It's a matter of time." She shoves me back a step, like she doesn't want to be that close to me. "Perverted. Disgusting. Unworthy. They'll see."

A knot threatens to choke me, and tears pour down my face. She's right. I've always known it. A man like Oliver could never be happy with me, not for long, anyway.

"If you really love that boy, you'll leave him to find a good wife."

I curl in on myself and try not to sob.

The ring on my finger cuts into my skin when I cross my arms. I know nothing I do will keep her at arm's length, will protect me from her, but my mind tries anyway.

"The women around here are better at turning a blind eye to a man's indiscretions." She lifts my chin, forcing me to look at her. "Take that boy's ring off and go before you embarrass him and yourself more than you already have."

I work the thick band from my finger and place it on the counter, no longer able to keep my sobs quiet and run from the room. Run from the house. Run from Oliver and the life with him I want so badly.

I don't know how I make it down the street, but with trembling fingers, I find Colin's number and call him.

"Isaac? What's wrong? Why are you calling me? Is someone dead?"

I sob into the phone, slamming my back against the building and sliding down to the sidewalk with my hand covering my eyes.

"Oh my God! Isaac, where are you?"

"God-Godfrey," is the only thing I'm able to get out.

"The Godfrey estate?" I make some noise that he takes as a yes. "I'm on my way. I'll be there in a few minutes."

Forty-Two

Oliver

In the midst of Olivia and Owen gushing over after-dinner drinks, it clicks. Mrs. Becker sits down. But where had she been? Had she excused herself? When? Isaac hasn't been gone long, but I've been distracted by my siblings.

"Where's Isaac?" I barely hold venom out of my tone.

Olivia glances around, not recognizing what's in my voice, but Owen instantly knows.

"Didn't he go to the bathroom?" Owen asks.

I nod. "But where did his mother just go?"

Owen's gaze snaps to her. "What?"

"Cover for me."

The bathroom door is open, and the light is on. Is he lost? The penthouse is massive—my gaze lands on the gold glinting in the light. I pick up my grandmother's ring, and I know.

I storm into the formal living room, boiling over. "Where is he?"

Everyone in the room looks at me.

"Why are you yelling?" my father asks.

"Because they did something to Isaac to make him leave." I spit vitriol, not caring if it upsets my parents.

My parents look at the Beckers, who seem to be clueless, but a tiny smirk plays on the corners of Mrs. Becker's mouth, and it's all the confirmation I need.

"What the fuck did you say to him?" I cross the room to stand over her.

Owen grabs my bicep. "What happened? How do you know he left?"

"He could be lost," Olivia adds.

I hold up the ring. "He left."

"He might have panicked and run," Mother says softly.

"Do you think it was too much for him?" my father is on his feet next to me. "You can't blame his parents. None of us even knew you were seeing each other. How can you know it was them?"

"If the homophobic piece of shit shoe fits." I turn on him. "She left the room when he went to the bathroom."

My father searches my face. He didn't amass the amount of wealth he has without being a shrewd person. He isn't an idiot. "Did you say something to him?" he asks Mrs. Becker.

"We had a brief conversation passing in the hall. I'm not sure why it made him take the ring off."

"Liar," I growl.

Mrs. Becker puts a hand over her heart, faux offended. "Are you going to let your son speak to me like that?"

My father looks at me for an explanation.

"I found the ring on the counter in the washroom. If they were passing in the hall, he'd be leaving, not going in there. Why would he have gone back to put the fucking ring on the counter, and if she'd gone in there to use the washroom, she would have had the door closed and locked."

My father turns back to Mrs. Becker.

"I meant we had a brief conversation in the bathroom." There are daggers in her eyes.

"Why did you shove into the bathroom to confront him?" I press. She purses her lips, but I go on before she can answer. "It's because you're a piece of shit parent who left your son destitute. Do not underestimate the wrath I will unleash upon you if he doesn't marry me. I will make it my life's mission to destroy you and everyone related to you. You will never be free. I will chase you to the ends of the earth to make every single minute of the rest of your lives hell."

Mr. Becker starts to say something, but I'm already out of the room, not giving a single shit about the aftermath or how upset my parents will be. I have one singular focus: to find Isaac.

Forty-Three

Isaac

I don't know how Colin gets to me as quickly as he does, but I also don't care. I'm still a weeping mess when the Uber pulls up and he calls my name. I can't get up. Can't make my body move.

I'm curled into a ball with my back against whatever building I stopped in front of with my arms wrapped around my knees and my face buried in my legs.

"Isaac." His voice is right in front of me, and he clutches my arms. "What happened? Were the Godfreys complete assholes to you?"

"No," I whimper through my tears and lift my face to look at my only friend.

"Jesus. You're a wreck, come on." He helps me to the car and closes the door. I don't bother to buckle my seatbelt, just curl up in the seat and lie my head on his thigh. "Poor baby bird, I've got you."

He runs his hand over my hair in an attempt to soothe me. I don't know where we're going, but I can't go back to the dorms. That's the first place Oliver will look. My mom is right, he needs to find a partner better matched to him. What I want is a pipe dream. A fairy tale.

"Not the dorms," I manage to get out as I stare unblinkingly at the center console in front of me. Tears stream from my eyes, soaking his ripped jeans, but I'm no longer sobbing. I'm almost numb. Maybe I'm going into shock. Feeling nothing would be an improvement to this utter heartbreak. This soul crushing, searing pain.

I almost got everything I've ever wanted. It was in my hand.

But it's better this way. Better to rip the scab off now than to let things fester until he hates or resents me. I hope I didn't hurt him. The idea of hurting him guts me. My Oliver. He's so strong all the time. But he's soft with me. I think I'm the only one he shows those parts of himself to.

Maybe ever.

My phone starts buzzing in my pocket, stops, then starts again.

"Do you want to talk about it?"

I shake my head and curl my arm around myself, setting the back of my hand under my chin. I'm broken, and I don't know how I'll ever be whole again. Not without Oliver.

"Is that your phone?"

Colin digs in my pocket for it and sighs when he sees who's calling.

"I'm going to turn this off, okay?"

I don't respond. I'm sure its Oliver, and he won't stop until he knows where I am. He wants to love me, I think. Or maybe use me to piss off his parents?

But he went and got my drawing supplies. That has to mean something right?

My drawings. Once again I've lost them. I hope he doesn't throw them away or ruin them. I know he'll be angry, but this is for his own good.

Right?

We stop in front of some building I don't recognize but don't pay much attention to it either.

"We're at a friend's flat. He's out of the country and said I could use his place whenever I needed."

I can't imagine what that's like, to have friends who just leave and offer up their house to you. How long is he gone? How is he paying his rent? Is he working?

It doesn't matter. I don't really care. Rich people are weird.

Colin ushers me through the lobby of some fancy apartment building and into an elevator, then down a hallway where he digs out a key.

"Hallways are for peasants," I mumble to myself, another tear falling down my cheek.

How long will it take for his words in my head not to hurt my heart?

Colin leads me to a bedroom and helps me get undressed. Oliver would be so angry if he knew.

"Do you want to get drunk or sleep?" Colin pulls down the blankets, and I sit and shrug. Maybe getting drunk would be fun, but I've never been drunk before, and I wanted to do it with Oliver.

The tears fill my eyes again, and I sniffle.

"Bed it is." Colin pushes my shoulder to get me to lie down, and I don't fight him. He gets me settled, grabs me a water bottle and a granola bar in case I get hungry, then climbs in on the other side.

I want to ask what he's doing, but it doesn't matter. He settles quickly behind me while I stare at the floral wallpaper.

"What do you need right now, Isaac? Do you need me to fuck off? Do you need me to give you a hug? Cuddle? Punch me in the face?"

The last one gets a little chuckle from me.

"Okay fine, but get my left side. My right side is my good side."

I turn to face my friend. The only person I have left.

"Thank you." My throat is dry, and my words crack.

"For leaving my dick appointment to come find you? You're welcome, and you owe me so big." He rolls his eyes. "That guy had a dick like a Mack truck."

I smile a little and shake my head. "That sounds terrifying."

"Oh sweet baby bird." Colin sighs and pats my head.

Without thinking it over, I move closer to him and lie my head on his chest. I need to be held, to feel connected to someone, anchored in the here and now.

He doesn't hesitate to wrap his arms around me and runs his fingers through my hair. It's all I ever wanted from my parents, this acceptance, but I never got it.

As I listen to Colin's heartbeat in a stranger's bed, I think back over the evening and can't figure out how I got here. All I know is I'll never be complete without Oliver.

Forty-Four

Oliver

I take a car to his dorm, but it's empty. Colin must have picked him up. They could be anywhere. Any hotel in the city, or even at Colin's parent's house, and while I have a lot of balls, rocking up to his parents' house at this hour isn't acceptable. No door man in his right mind would let me even speak to them.

I pull out my phone in a last-ditch effort.

> OLIVER: Hey, this is Oliver. Sorry to bother you, but is Isaac there?

> CASSIE: I don't think so.

"FUCK." I sink to a seat with my back pressed against their door.

> CASSIE: Is everything okay?

> OLIVER: I think your brother absconded with Isaac and I'm trying to find him. Sorry to bother you again.

I bang my head into the door. I will level this fucking city to find him. If he thinks he can hide, he's fucking wrong.

My brother and sister are waiting when I step into my penthouse.

I hold up a hand. "I don't want to hear it."

Olivia darts across the room and slams into me with a hug. "What can we do?"

I grunt, but wrap my arms around her. "I need the best private investigators in the city."

"He isn't at his dorm?" Owen asks, bringing me a drink.

"No, and not at Colin's."

"So they are hiding." Owen exhales, opening his phone. "I know Dad has a few private investigators on retainer."

"How were they after I left?"

Owen makes a face. "It was tense until the Beckers left, which they did quickly. You know how Dad feels about liars."

My father might like to keep up appearances, but he hates being misled, which is why I called out Mrs. Becker the way I had. They'd still be mad, but they knew the truth about the Beckers, which is all I care about right now.

"And after?"

"Upset," Olivia says. "They didn't want to talk about it. But it's clear they aren't happy with the whole situation. I don't think they liked that you sprung on the engagement like that. They didn't even know you were dating him."

"I got tired of them trying to marry me off. I'm not doing it. They had to see how serious I am."

"Are you that serious? This isn't just to spite them."

"No one has ever made me happy, not like Isaac does. Or even feel half of what I do when I'm with him. I've known this was different from the moment I met him—"

Owen cuts me off. "I fucking knew it. He made me leave the apartment for twenty-four hours and cover for him at dinner."

"Wait, that's why you weren't at the anniversary dinner?"

"Yes." There isn't a point in hiding it now.

She whistles. "You really have felt like this since the beginning."

"I have. He's always been different for me, even when I didn't want to admit it to Owen or myself." I sip my drink, trying to formulate my next moves. I couldn't let him slip through my fingers. I didn't want him to go through this alone. I just want to hold him. I take a stuttering breath.

Owen hugs me.

"I'm fine."

"You don't look fine," he says and doesn't release me.

"I just need to find him."

I don't sleep, but our efforts are fruitless. We have two private investigators on the case, but there isn't a sign of him. We stakeout his dorm, first class, and Colin's parents' place to try and find them. But they don't show up.

I'm barely human when I make it back to the penthouse to regroup and change before practice.

"Owen?" I call, expecting him and Olivia to be back at any moment.

I round the corner to come face to face with both my parents.

Fuck my life.

Whatever this is, it isn't good. I don't have time for it. I have to be at practice in two hours, and I'm far too tired to deal with bullshit. My give a fuck is also about to snap.

I dead-eye stare them down, crossing my arms over my chest. I won't be the first to speak. I let the silence consume us, until it's uncomfortable.

Finally, my mother breaks it. "We want to touch base on your future plans."

"You mean you want to have an intervention?" I say flatly.

"It's not that. We thought it important to talk to you and make sure you're thinking straight." My mother tries to be soft, but she has never been that parent.

"I've fucked hundreds of people. I'm not blinded by dick, if that's what this is about."

Her eyes go wide for a split second, but my dad looks impressed. Neither has an immediate response to it.

"Anything else? I need to find my fiancé before his lowlife parents do." I don't let my anger out of my tone.

"Speaking of his family, you're tying us to them." Disgust drips from her tone.

"This is not going to go the way you think it will." I meet her eyes.

"What way do you expect this to go?" my father cuts in. "Surely not in your favor either, if you force us into a situation we don't like."

I laugh coldly, without humor. "Fucking say it. You lost the last ounce of control and credibility you had when you brought me a high schooler as a marriage prospect."

"We will cut you out of the will!" my mother snaps, getting a nasty sneer to her pink lips.

"Will you? How will that look? Cutting out your gay son? Would be a shame if every major media publication knew the

Godfrey group acts like this." I lock eyes with my father, cutting out my mother.

"This is a family matter!" my mother says.

"Not when you make it about money." I don't look at her, keeping my focus on my father. "This is business, and you have no one else. Owen sure as fuck isn't taking over the company. He'd have a damn panic attack, that is, if you even have a company after I feed you to the wolves. Don't think I haven't learned from both of you my entire life. If you want to roll in the mud, I'm going to fight dirtier than you've ever fucking imagined."

"This is about who has our family name," he says through his teeth.

"Fine, I'll take his name." I wouldn't, but it's an amusing game to play with him.

Mother gasps, and my father grinds his teeth.

"I'll marry who I want, and you two will stay the fuck out of my love life."

Mother crosses her arms, pursing her lips.

"You need to think about what you're doing, Oliver. He's not one of us. He'll never understand what it is to be a Godfrey."

"I'll burn our legacy down faster than he will if you cross me. I'll sell this company to the Willhams before your body is cold and spit on your grave."

"You'll never inherit." My father is flustered, and I love it.

"Do you think Owen and Olivia won't support me? This isn't going to go the way you think it will. You've played your hand all wrong, and even if you had someone to turn against me, my trust is irrevocable. Good luck fighting that in court. I don't need more money. Give the company to whomever you want. Fuck our name yourself. You can burn your own legacy down without my help." I look at both of them in turn. "This is only going to make me marry him faster and give him the family name right along with Grandma's ring."

They leave in a huff with more empty threats.

I have one hope left. He has to come to practice. He can't lose his scholarship.

I pin my hope on it. But he's not there.

I go through all of practice wondering where he is. I'm barely competent. I shouldn't have a fucking weapon in my hand.

I stop Coach Kennedy when practice finishes. "Where is Isaac?"

"Sick. I told him to keep it to himself and not come in. He sounds awful."

Pain radiates through my chest. I hate that he's pushing me away, but I hate even more he's suffering this alone.

A new plan forms, and I hurry to the locker rooms to corner Colin.

Forty-Five

Oliver

Colin is gone. Fucking bastard. I would kill him. I'm making plans to go to his dorm when I hear my phone ringing in my locker.

The private investigator.

I answer it.

He gives me an address, and I don't bother changing out of my sweats, only taking enough time to toss my gear in my locker before getting in my waiting car. I relay the address and slump back to wait in the traffic.

My personal hell comes in stop lights and taillights. A crawl of cars. Tires screeching and horns.

Time stands still, and I can only hope he's still there when I arrive.

Another red light. We aren't even moving.

I want to scream.

I throw open the door.

"Hey, you can't get out. We are in the middle of an intersection," my driver yells.

"No one's moving. I'm not going to get hit." I slam it and jog the rest of the way to the address. I stop in front of the building breathing hard, ring box clenched in my hand.

I place my card on the doorman's desk and tell him I have an appointment with the resident in six-o-seven. He lets me in without another question. I ride the elevator, not sure what I'll do if he doesn't answer. I get to the right door and knock, but as I expected, there's silence.

I exhale, thinking about kicking down the door. But another idea strikes me. I feel around the plants on either side of the door. Nothing. I lift the mat. Nothing. I slide my hand over the top of the trim, and my fingers find metal.

I slip the key in the lock and hope there isn't a chain. It would go with the hallway. But I'm lucky. No such security device. I close the door behind me and listen for him. Not a single light on. So I search for him in the dark. Finally, I find a lump in a massive bed.

I still in the doorway, seeing the barest flicker of movement with his breathing. I strip off my clothes while I silently cross the room. I slip in behind him, wrapping my arms around him, not even sure if he's awake.

"Colin?" Isaac says weakly.

"He better not be getting into bed with you naked," I reply against his neck.

Isaac stiffens.

I growl.

"He only cuddled me to comfort me. It wasn't like that."

"I'm going to kill him."

Isaac grabs my arm that's around him, like I'd go do it now. "No killing."

"Is that the only reason you want me to stay?"

He shudders in a sob. But he doesn't release me.

I squeeze him tighter into my chest. "What happened?"

He doesn't say a word.

"Do you want me to go?"

He clings to me tighter.

"I'll take that as a no."

I hold him for a long time before he speaks, and when he does, his voice is so raw it breaks my heart. "Did you just ask me to marry you to piss off your family?"

"No, of course not. I'd never do anything I don't want to do." I bite the curve of his neck. "You should know me better than that."

"Are you sure?"

"I'm positive. I'm not unhappy that it's going to make them upset, but I don't enjoy making my life more difficult. But if it does, it does. I don't care what they want, which is why I asked you to marry me. I'm going to do what I want."

"You haven't even told me you love me. How can you know you want to marry me?" Doubt creeps into every word Isaac speaks.

"I do love you. Isn't it obvious?"

He rolls over frowning. "You've never said you love me."

"Do you think I would be with someone for anything less? Do you think I'd deal with your dating bullshit and then dig through the fucking city for a needle in a haystack if I didn't?" Did he think this is normal behavior? I cup his face, bringing my lips to his. "You really must think highly of yourself if you think I'm doing all this without love."

"Say it."

"I love you, Isaac, and I want you to be my husband."

He cries harder, but kisses me back.

"You're not allowed to run away. You said we're together, and that means making it work together. You don't get to hide from me."

"I'm sorry."

"I was really worried."

He pulls back to look at me. "Why?"

"I was worried you'd never speak to me again," I admit, more honest than I've ever been with anyone. He has all the keys to hurt me. "I can't lose you. I need you."

"My mother told me I wasn't good enough for your family and that they will see through me. And she's right. They'll see what I am."

"I don't give a single fuck what anyone else sees. All that matters to me is what I see. How you make me feel." I thumb his lip.

"But they will tell you not to marry me, and I'll fuck everything up for you." He presses his eyes closed, fighting tears.

"They already tried. I told my father if he wants to fight, I'll drag him through the mud. I told him I'd destroy his whole company, and if he really pisses me off, I'll sell it to his competitor and spit on his grave." I grin as I say it, pressing my mouth to his so he can feel it.

His eyes snap open. "What if they disinherit you?"

"I have enough in my trust fund to be fine. And I'm sure I'll be able to find a job after I graduate without any trouble. I'll have to give up the helicopter, but the penthouse is paid for . . ." I trail off when I notice how he's looking at me. "What?"

"You'd risk all that for me?"

"I told you I love you. What more do you want, kitten?"

"I love you too."

"You fucking better."

Forty-Six

Isaac

I haven't showered since Colin picked me up, so when we get back to Oliver's penthouse, he strips me, and we get in the shower.

"You're lucky I'm not using bleach to get Colin off of your skin."

I chuckle. "It wasn't like that. I just needed a hug."

"While sharing the same bed? Absolutely not. You're lucky he's not already dead." Oliver adjusts the water, and I head into the huge stall without prompting. I love his shower. The water pressure, the room, the never-ending hot water.

There are two heads in here so we can shower at the same time, but he doesn't turn the other one on, not this time. Today, I think he needs to touch me as much as I need to be touched. To reinforce to ourselves that we're together.

"No more running," he says against the curve of my neck.

"No more."

"Promise me." His teeth sink into my skin, and I moan, leaning into his body.

"I promise."

Soaping up his hands, he cleans me. Not missing an inch, a centimeter. It's comforting and erotic to have his attention like this. For him to see all the broken parts of me, all the insecurities, and know he still wants me. I don't know how to let him, but I promise myself I'll find a way.

"I love you," I whisper against his lips.

"More than love, I need you." He holds my gaze. "I never thought I would need someone the way I need you. Nothing matters to me like you do. Nothing."

I smile at him and lift onto my toes to take his mouth. "I'm sorry."

I try to show him how sorry I am that I caused him pain because I don't know how to say it. He may not like being vulnerable or showing the soft spots of himself, but they are very much there, and he deserves to be taken care of too.

Oliver grips onto me and pushes me against the cold tiled wall. When my warm skin hits, I gasp and arch into him. He takes advantage of my mouth opening and fucks his tongue between my lips.

His cock thickens between us, and I reach for it, wrapping my hand around him and stroking him until he's panting.

"Let me love you," I say against his lips. "Please."

Oliver pulls back enough to look into my eyes, then shuts the water off. "Anything you want, kitten."

We dry off quickly, and I find the lube in the bedside table, then pull back the blankets on the bed.

"Against the headboard," I tell him, and he gives me a skeptical look but sits and adjusts the pillows. Climbing over his thighs to straddle him, I pour some lube in my hand and stroke him until he's slick.

"What's your plan?"

"You'll just have to wait and see." I smirk and slide my slicked fingers over my hole but don't insert them. No, I want to stretch on his cock.

Grabbing his dick, I slide him between my cheeks, over my hole a few times, then line him up. Oliver tenses under me and grips my hips.

"Isaac . . ."

"Shhh," I moan and lower myself slowly onto him, taking just his head at first and hissing at the burn.

"You're going to hurt yourself." His voice is strained, and he digs his fingers into my skin.

"I can take it." I take a few more inches and tense up, hissing again. He's so big.

"Isaac."

I open my eyes and see the strain around his eyes.

"I need this." I lean my forehead against his. "The burn isn't too bad, and once it settles, it's so good. I'm going slow, I promise."

Oliver cups the back of my neck and pulls my lips to his. I drop the rest of the way, impaling myself on his cock, whimpering into his mouth. He throbs inside of me, and his fingers flex like he's holding himself back.

Keeping my promise, I take it slow and just rock against him at first. He groans, and that sound makes it worth it.

Slowly, I lift up, then lower back down.

"You feel so good, so deep." Wrapping his arms around me, one hand stays at the back of my neck, and one goes to my tail-bone, encouraging me to take him.

Rocking over him has his glorious dick brushing my prostate. I crave it. The explosive, full body orgasm that leaves me weak.

With my arms around his neck, I use all of my muscles to roll back and forth until I'm right on the edge, so close to coming I can taste it, but Oliver rolls us and takes over, thrusting into me like a god. Grabbing one of my hands, he intertwines our fingers above my head and drops his face to my neck where he sucks hard.

I grip his hair in my free hand, moaning and whimpering and desperate to come.

"Come, Oliver, please. I need you."

He shudders and slams into me. Adjusting the angle of my hips until I scream. He smirks into my flesh.

"My greedy little cumslut. You can come as long as you get there before me and don't use your hands."

He latches onto my nipple, and my entire body tightens with the tingling that signals an orgasm.

"Yes, please, don't stop."

I cry out my release, cum splattering up my chest, getting my chin and the pillow next to my head. My heart is going a mile a minute and my lungs are screaming for air, but when the euphoria passes, I'm limp and weak.

"Such a good boy." The strong thrusts don't stop or slow down. "I love you, kitten. No one will ever love you like I do. You're mine."

He buries his face in my neck again and shudders his release into my used hole. I can feel his cock throb deep inside of me, and I manage a lazy smile.

"Yours. Forever."

Forty-Seven

Isaac

I make Nationals in March on my own merit. Kinsey, Leo, and Oliver round out our foil team with Leo being our alternate. Sebastian is pissed, and I may have gloated about it. A little.

Nationals this year is in Michigan, so we've flown on a chartered jet because of course we have. There's four days of competition, training, meetings, teaching. I've never been, so I don't know what to expect, but Oliver has talked me through the ones he's been to.

Of course he and Owen have been.

Colin is here as an alternate for sabre, which I'm also grateful for.

In the locker room, we get changed into warm-ups.

"Even if you have terrible bouts today, remember that you made it to Nationals, and you can go again next year." Leo pats my shoulder as he heads out to start stretching. "And you've done amazing so far."

"Hands," Oliver growls, and I laugh while Leo shakes his head.

"Yes, caveman, I have two. Congratulations on learning to count." He flips off Oliver as he walks out the door and before Oliver can respond.

"I dislike him."

"I like him." I smile up at my fiancé.

"That's okay, I'm plotting his murder in my head. I'll do it before the wedding."

"Maybe I'll make him my best man then."

Oliver grabs my jaw and pulls me up to my toes.

"Watch it, kitten."

I give him a quick kiss, then leave the locker room. Life is so much easier since I stopped hiding, and I have Oliver to thank for that.

"Knock 'em dead," Colin says as he passes.

Nerves are humming in my stomach, but this time, I know I can handle it. I've practiced my butt off, mostly thanks to living with Oliver, and have improved so much the last few months. He even had Owen kick my butt with a sabre, but made it up to me after. And today is the last day of the tournament. I've done well and am proud of myself.

I get stretched out and warmed up with the guys and look around in awe. Part of me can't believe I've made it this far. There are so many people here, twenty-one teams in the US that are NCAA Division I, and we're all competing. Plus all the families and friends who came to cheer us on. I know the Godfreys are here somewhere, and despite them not being very happy about Oliver proposing, they've gotten onboard.

"All right, boys, game faces on." Coach gives us a pep talk, reminds us to stay calm and breathe.

We start the relay against the Vermont Olympians.

Oliver upgraded all my equipment the second I moved into his apartment. Foils, jacket, lame, pants. Everything. Something about his fiancé looking like a peasant.

I'm not ready. I feel like the weakness, and I know the Olympians foilists are focused on destroying me. Knowing the way we pick apart other teams, I just know I am the center of their strategy. I hate being the one bringing the rest of the team down.

I don't want to ruin this for Oliver. It's his last year, and the weight of his last championship riding on my shoulders feels like too much.

I don't want to think like this, but what if I fail him and he breaks up with me?

My thumb searches for the ring on my fourth finger, but it's not there. I took it off for the tournament.

"Do I have to go first?" I ask.

"Yes, you must come out strong. Leo would do it, but they moved their opener to second. So it's all you."

I clasp my hands behind my head, trying not to overthink all the opponent research we'd been going over for days. Their foilist's weaknesses. His strong moves. How to stay out of range of his quick touch openers. It felt like noise I couldn't focus past.

Leo grumbles something, but I don't hear it.

"What?" I lean in so I can hear him.

"Vermont stealing our name, the Olympians, really? The copycats basically stole our name." Leo makes a distasteful sound only a rich guy with a French mother can make.

"They did. They were established five years after us," Oliver says. "They don't even compete on the same level. I can't believe they've held on this long. I'm shocked they beat the Monsters, honestly. Their depth of talent isn't there. They are just wannabes."

Which makes it even more important for us to beat them.

"Riding our coattails," Leo adds. "It will be an embarrassment if we lose."

I feel sick.

I walk a few paces away, bile rising in my throat.

Warm lips brush the back of my neck. "What's wrong?"

"Are you going to hate me if I mess this up?"

"Of course not. Why would you think that?" He wraps his arms around me.

"Because they suck and stole our name, and we'll be the worst fencing team the Gods has ever had if we lose to the stupid Olympians."

Oliver laughs against the back of my neck.

"It's not funny!" I try to pull out of his grasp, but he tightens it, not letting me go anywhere.

"It's a little funny the way your voice turns into a pouty grumble. And as your fiancé, I'm allowed to like it." He turns me in his arms. "Now say it with me. Fucking Olympians."

"Stupid."

"Come on. You can do it."

"Fucking Olympians," I say under my breath.

"Doesn't that feel better?"

I shrug. "Maybe."

"Every shit team has a good day. If they win, they win. I'll be graduated, so I won't have to live with it. You will, but again, it's not the end of the world. We are still getting married, and you don't even have to keep fencing if you don't want to." He rests his forehead against mine.

I stare at him. "What?"

"You will be married to me. I have plenty of money to pay for school, and speaking of. You are changing your fucking major."

I'm speechless. It hadn't occurred to me. "You'd do that?"

"It's our money. We'll be married. Are you kidding?" Oliver's expression is half way between laughing and confusion.

"I don't think of it that way."

"Start thinking of it that way. You're about to be a Godfrey." He kisses my forehead. "We are about to be up. We need to get over there."

I blow out a breath as I step up to the strip. My palms are sweating in my gloves, and my weapon feels unsteady, but I'm not going to embarrass the Gods or my fiancé.

We step to our lines, and I push all the noise out of my head. If I'm going to win, I have to do it my way.

The Olympian foilist jumps at me as soon as the match begins, and I spring back to avoid a quick touch. I parry and attack, scoring the first touch.

He curses under his breath, and we reset. It's a hard-fought round, but I only go down one point in our first leg, putting us at 4-5.

With each round of relay fencing the end is time or five touches, so even a single point has to be made up in the next leg. With nine total legs, a team can go way down heading into the final rounds.

Kinsey takes over and makes up for it, getting us up to 10-7.

They have a new foilist from Russia who's up against Oliver and faster than any human should move. But Oliver wins his first leg, putting us up going into my second leg.

I face my foilist, waiting for him to jump again, but he doesn't. He doesn't move. I move in, but realize it's a mistake and quickly end up at a disadvantage as he ripostes and gets a touch. We return to our lines, and he flèches out of the gate on his next attack.

He wins the round, putting them up 20-16, an impressive comeback. Oliver gave me such a lead, and I blew it. Dread fills my stomach. I'm so disappointed in myself. How am I ever going to fight my last leg and not totally mess us up.

"Shake it off, Isaac," Coach Kennedy calls after me while Leo goes to the line.

We go up and down, and the score stays neck in neck.

I'm going into the final round of three legs.

Coach Kennedy grabs my shoulder when I'm about to step to the line. "They made a change. Oliver, go again against Nicola."

We all look at the line and sure enough, it's the Russian.

"They were trying to trap us?"

Coach Kennedy nods. "They want Oliver tired and for the final round to rely on the two of them."

Oliver is mad. I can tell by the way he holds himself, but what they don't know is he's better when he's mad. He uses anger to his benefit. I'd learned that the hard way.

Oliver keeps us up, leaving Leo with 35-32.

I get ready to take the line, but Coach Kennedy stops me again. He sends Leo up.

"I can't go last!" Panic ices through my veins.

"You're gonna fucking have to!" Coach Kennedy is getting red in the face.

"Stop. He's not going to react well to being yelled at, and frankly, if you yell at him I'll have you fired." Oliver's tone is final. I've never seen him talk to the coach that way.

He drapes his arms over my shoulders, putting us forehead to forehead again. "I believe in you."

"Are you just saying that?" I'm fighting tears, but I don't want him to hear it so I try to keep my voice steady.

"I'm not. You're a much better fighter than he is. You are just in your head. Forget everything we've said and just fight the match. All you have to do is get to forty-five or wait the time out. Play defense. Wait him out. He loves his explosive movements. Use it against him. Wait for him to come to you."

"I thought you said get it all out of my head."

Oliver makes a face. "Right, sorry. Ignore me. Make him play your game. Okay?"

"Okay," I say, hyperventilating.

He slides a finger under my chin, tilting it up. "I love you."

"I love you too."

He brushes his lips over mine. "You're up."

"Wait, what?" Has it been that long? I don't even know the score. I search the board on the way to the line.

40-36. Kinsey had fought well, and upped the divide Oliver created. I have to get five touches or wait out the three-minute clock. It doesn't seem like a lot of time, but on the piste it feels like hours.

My opponent needs nine touches to make up the deficit. Easy right?

He does the same thing he did last leg, standing, trying to force me to come to him. I step off my line, but move slowly. Not letting him get in my head.

He has way more to make up, so taking my time is to my advantage. But somehow he bests me, parrying my attack to get a touch. Only taking ten seconds off the clock.

I start to downward spiral, but I cut myself off. I can't get in my head. I have to focus.

I win the next touch, and then he gets a quick point after me. I can't let him keep getting me two to one. We still have two minutes left.

He springs off the line, coming at me in a flurry of a flunge. I hold my ground, deflecting the attack and then feinting. He falls for it, and I get another touch.

He's mad now, and the time is counting down. I use it, parrying his attack. He retreats, but I go after him instead of falling back.

I need two more, but he scores two in a row, putting him at 43-40. He's making up the deficit.

We come together in a clash with less than a minute left. He backs off and I lunge, barely grazing him, but the board lights up.

One touch away.

He charges and I flinch, my broken foil flashing through my head.

But I defend against his advance and the clock runs out.

Adrenaline courses through me with lightning speed as I run toward my teammates and they meet me on the mat. Oliver picks me up and spins me around, and Leo jumps in to join the hug. I can't believe we won. We're yelling and cheering and celebrating along with people in the stands.

I can't believe my last match is over.

"Congratulations. I knew you could do it!"

"I'm so fucking proud of you!"

I grab Oliver's face and put our foreheads together. "I couldn't have done it without you."

"I love you."

When all is said and done, we take second in overall points. Despite winning the team competition, we couldn't get enough points even with Oliver taking second in Foil, Ryan our epee captain taking third, and Dean Byron our protege taking second in saber, though Owen nearly beat Byron coming in third. The Monsters take first overall, having destroyed in every discipline. taking two of the top three spots in every individual event, while the Olympians take a surprising third over the Guardians.

I'm proud of myself. Proud of us.

We're sweaty and tired but so fired up after the awards ceremony.

With smiles on all our faces, we head to the locker room to change and get out of here.

"I'm so hungry," I whine as I push the door open.

"I've got something you can eat . . .," Oliver whispers in my ear, and I blush.

"I might need something with more . . . substance." I dance out of his reach and end up tripping over a bench, landing on my ass. Colin doubles over laughing at me. I'm laughing too, but Oliver is standing over me shaking his head.

"Feel good about your decisions?"

"Yes," I breathe through my laughter. It's the emotional release I need after the four days of this tournament.

He leaves me on the floor to get changed, and I crane my neck just to watch him walk past me with a shit-eating grin on my face.

"Incorrigible."

"You like it."

I get off the floor, strip out of my gear, and head to the showers. My hair is plastered to my head from the drying sweat and being inside my mask.

We chat while we clean up, talking about the highlights of the matches we played in and the ones we watched. Who did well and who we expected to do better. At this level, all the names are familiar to everyone.

Colin surprises all of us by leaving first.

"You think he wants to jerk one in the locker room before we get out there?" one of the epees asks, and I snort.

"The less Colin's dick is on my mind, the better." Oliver shudders.

Dipping back under the water to rinse the shampoo from my hair, I scream like I'm being murdered when ice water is splashed on me.

"What the fuck?" My voice echoes off the tile, and everyone turns to see what's happening. Colin has a towel wrapped around his hips, on the floor, laughing with a cup in his hand. "I'm going to kill you! You're an ass!'

Colin is crying from laughing so hard. "You screamed like a little girl." He starts coughing, and I can hear Owen sigh before walking past him quickly followed by a few of the other guys.

Grabbing my shampoo, I'm about to squirt it on him when someone yells from the locker room.

"Oliver!" Owen's panicked screech has us tensing. "Oliver!"

"Fuck." He starts toward the locker room, but a ghostly pale Owen appears in the doorway, panting with his phone in his hand.

"Mom is setting me up with Cassie."

Epilogue

Isaac

I f I look back, I don't know how we got here. It was chaos and pain, but it's ours.

It's the night before our wedding, and I'm anxious. Standing in front of a beautiful Catholic cathedral, with its steeples and stained glass, I'm in awe of its beauty.

Even at night, with the sky dusted with stars, it stands out among the other buildings. The white stone that's now more of a cream color, the intricate design and architecture. It's breathtaking, even if you don't believe in the church.

A warm body presses against my back, towering over me, and a hand slides along my waist. I smile, knowing it's my soon-to-be husband. Oliver knew where to find me.

"Not getting cold feet, are you, kitten?"

His warm breath caresses my neck, and he kisses the sensitive spot behind my ear.

"Never."

"Then why are we here? Again."

My head is jumbled, and I'm not sure it will make sense to him. I grew up believing in a higher power, though not the same one my father preached. The more I've learned about the history of Christianity, the more I've discovered that I do believe to a point and sometimes find comfort in a church.

"It . . ." I lean back against him and take the comfort he freely offers me. "It brings me peace."

Oliver kisses my hair. "Have you ever been inside of a confessional?" The low vibration of his tone sends a shiver up my spine. He's not asking because he wants to change the subject . . .

"No," I whisper, my breath catching when his hold turns possessive.

"Perhaps we should visit one."

The idea gets me hard. It's sacrosanct, and what if we get caught? It's a miracle the church agreed to marry us in the first place.

"How did you get a Catholic cathedral to agree to hold our ceremony?" It's the first time I've allowed myself to ask.

"With money? What else would I do?" His nose drags up the side of my neck. "He also owes my father a favor, but we aren't going to talk about that."

"It's a major religious organization. Are you saying you were able to buy them?"

"The Catholic church is pretty down with the queers recently, and it will upset your parents for you to get married in another religion to a man."

He's not wrong. Especially since it'll be splashed in the newspapers and social media because of *who* that man is. My father won't be able to avoid seeing it.

"So, are we going in?" Oliver's hand brushes down the front of my pants, against my erection. "Naughty boy, getting hard outside of God's house. I think you need to repent."

Oh this is not going to end well.

"Oliver, we can't. It's not right."

He leads me inside anyway and straight to the confessional.

"Why am I the one repenting? You're the heathen." I cross my arms and hold his gaze when he turns to me.

"Is that your little game? You want to hear all the dirty things I want to do to you on our wedding night?"

His presence takes up so much space, blocking out everything around us. I force myself to swallow and not melt into a lust-filled puddle at his feet. I'm going to lose this game in the best way possible.

Wait.

"On our wedding night?" My eyebrows pull together in confusion. "What does that mean? Are you not sleeping with me tonight?"

"Sleeping is the only thing that will be happening, kitten, so choose wisely."

Crap. He loves to get me worked up and leaving me wanting, and I have no doubt he'll do exactly that.

Looking at the confessional, I force myself to make a decision. Do I want to hear him tell me all the ways he wants to take me? Yes. Do I want to try to turn the tables and leave him wanting? Absolutely yes.

I reach for the door of the gothic-style wooden confessional, not looking away from him.

"Good boy." He smirks and enters the center stall where the priest would sit. I kneel on the step in front the little lattice window. Trepidation and excitement flutter in my stomach, and my hands tremble as I lace my fingers together and wait.

He loves to make me wait.

I can hear him getting settled into the booth and the little door opens.

"Forgive me, Father, for I have sinned." I try to keep a straight face but fail. I don't know if that's what you actually say in one of these things since I've never actually been in one before, but that's what they say on TV and in movies, right?

"You don't seem to be taking this seriously."

With my head bowed, I look up at him and can barely see his lifted eyebrow. My cock thickens in my jeans until it's painful. It's going to be a long night for me.

"Of course I do."

"What sins have you committed?"

I bite my lip for a second and breathe. "I-I have inappropriate thoughts about another man."

"Why are they inappropriate?"

He's way too good at keeping a straight face. It's not fair at all.

"They're . . . sexual."

My face heats. I'm not much of a dirty talker, it's embarrassing to say things like that, but I love it when Oliver does it.

"In these thoughts, are you doing something to him or him to you?"

Oh good lord. I roll my lips inward and bite them.

"Isaac."

"Both."

"And what do you do when you have these sexual thoughts?"

I lean my forehead against my hands and whisper. "Sometimes I touch myself."

"Touch yourself where?"

I whimper and squirm on the step. It's unfair how controlled he is!

"M-My dick." I can't believe I just said dick in a church.

There's a creak of the wood when he adjusts. Am I getting to him too? I better not be the only one struggling here.

"And what do you do with your dick?"

What the hell, Oliver?

This is torture.

"Stroke it."

"Does it feel good?

"Yes," I whisper. My entire body is hot, lust licking at my veins with an urgency I'm not used to. At least, not when Oliver's hands aren't on me.

I'm throbbing, achingly hard, and unable to do anything about it.

I close my eyes and try to get control over myself but all I'm able to do is beg. "Please."

"Do you cum when you think about these fantasies and stroke yourself?"

He's such a jerk. He's enjoying this way more than he should.

"Every time."

"Tell me about these fantasies. What happens in them? Where are you?"

My breathing is too fast, but I let the words tumble from my lips.

"They happen everywhere. All the time. They consume my waking hours. Thoughts of being pinned, forced to be quiet so we don't get caught, and fucked until my knees give out." I suck in a breath and keep going. "Sometimes I'm on my knees, sucking on his cock until he fills my stomach." The next thought that enters my head is one I've thought about but never spoken out loud. "My favorite one is when he eats me, licking and sucking on my hole until I come."

There's a sharp intake of breath from Oliver, and I smile, despite knowing I'm going to be left with blue balls. It's the principle of it now. Oliver said no sex tonight, so he won't give in, but I'm glad he'll be suffering too. Though that will probably make him more of a jerk tomorrow.

My ass clenches, knowing he'll take me hard afterward. Use

my body until I break and pass out, exhausted but sated and content.

"That's your favorite? The thought of being spread open, vulnerable, and at the mercy of this man to do whatever he wants with you? Your most delicate flesh exposed and used?"

"Yes," the word is breathy, catching in my throat, and I clench my ass cheeks. I want it more than I can stand.

Standing in the bedroom I share with Oliver, Colin is rambling about something while we're putting our suits on.

I'm getting married today.

My hands shake as I try to get my tie straightened, but even after all the practicing I did, I can't.

"For fuck's sake." Colin slaps my hands out of the way, undoes my hard work and reties it. It's perfect, of course.

"I hate you."

He pats my cheek. "Of course you do."

He put product in my hair to make it act right, giving me the perfect unkept look. I spray on Oliver's cologne, and even though it doesn't smell the same on my skin, I don't care.

"Car is here. Let's go, baby bird."

Colin hollers from the hallway, and I squeal in nervous excitement. Today is the day Oliver Godfrey becomes mine.

Tonight, when he takes me to bed, I will be Isaac Godfrey.

The drive to the church is quick, Colin fusses with his hair a bit, and takes a selfie with me in the back of the car.

There are news vans and paparazzi everywhere. I knew getting married to Oliver would be a *thing* but holy crap.

"Come on." Colin reaches for the door, but I grab his arm. "What?"

"There's so many people out there. What if I fall? Or say the wrong thing? What if I spill red sauce on my white shirt? What if I embarrass him?"

Colin cups my face. "Isaac." When I take a breath, he continues. "Don't eat anything with red sauce or drink red wine. That's easy. If you fall, get back up and look down on anyone who laughs. If you say the wrong thing, fuck it, Oliver will fix it. By some twist that no one saw coming, he has a human heart and loves you."

I nod. "Okay. Thank you."

"I've got your back."

When the car door opens, the crowd pushes in against the ropes, but Colin doesn't let me hesitate. With a hand on my lower back, he leads me through, up the sidewalk, and into the cathedral. The sun is shining through the stained-glass windows. There are flowers at the end of every row of pews, ribbons around the stone columns, and at the altar is my Oliver.

I don't want to wait. I just want to go to him. He looks amazing in his tux, standing up there next to his twin brother. Before he can turn to see me, Colin grabs me and pulls me down a side hallway to meet up with Olivia, who is going to walk me down the aisle. She made the trip back from London for this, and I couldn't love her more for it.

Since my family sucks and I'm not particularly close to Oliver's parents, I asked Olivia. Colin is my best man, Owen is his brother's best man, and I wanted her to be involved. I wish my brother Noah were here, though.

Olivia squeals and grabs for me when we enter the little waiting room, wrapping her arms around me.

"Congratulations, Isaac. I can't wait for you to officially be my brother."

Tears well in my eyes as I hug her back. She cups my cheek and kisses my forehead. She's such a lovely woman.

359

"Okay, I have your boutonniere here." She grabs a plastic container off a table and opens it. The white and blue flowers match her corsage and soft blue dress perfectly.

She pins it to my lapel without stabbing me as there's a knock on the door.

Colin answers it, and it's the wedding coordinator. "Ready? It's time."

"I have never been more ready for anything in my life."

Epilogue

Oliver

A flicker catches my eye as I stand near the altar. Isaac arriving. I don't need to see him to know he's in the church. I feel him. Standing up in front of a church full of people isn't intimidating, but I'd been raised for this. I'm worried about how Isaac will handle it, but I breathe a sigh of relief. I didn't think he'd leave me at the altar, but a panic attack is a real possibility. He's here, and my chest is bursting with happiness.

My husband to be. Even rushing to use this spot my sister didn't want for our wedding couldn't diminish this day.

I rather like that Isaac is willing to do this with me not even a year after we met.

All in all, it feels exactly how we should be.

The music starts, and since we skipped all the fanfare of our groomsmen walking down the aisle, Isaac steps out.

A smile captures my face, stretching until my cheeks hurt. I can't take my eyes off him. I took him to the creative director at Alexander McQueen, and it's the perfect choice. Isaac's suit is gleaming in the light shining through the stained glass, catching the hints of sparkle in the hand embroidery stitching. He's an angel. My angel.

I went for a subtler regal look with Saint Laurent, but the two designers worked so well together to work our personalities in the pieces while still having them coordinate for the theme.

I walk down the three steps to meet my sister at the end of the pews to take Isaac from her. I kiss her cheek. "Thank you."

"I love you," she whispers.

I bring Isaac's hand to my lips and kiss his knuckles, leaning in. "You look exquisite. Like a dream come true."

A blush colors his cheeks. "You do too."

"I am the luckiest man in the world."

"Stop. You already got me to the altar." He gives me a playful glare.

"If you think the romance stops there, you're wrong." I lead him to the altar where the priest waits to marry us. As we take our places, I lean over to whisper in his ear. "I hope you know I'll be thinking about the confessional the whole wedding."

Isaac groans and claps a hand over his mouth, glaring at me.

I grin. Not sorry he'll be hard facing the priest. I think it's rather fitting for our nuptials.

Long after the ceremony, we're wrapped together, swaying to the slow song the band is playing, and it's all I've ever wanted.

If you want more, preorder Owen and Colin's book NOW, and turn the page for more.

. . .

To get more Oliver and Isaac join our Patreon!

For a free bonus scene join our mailing list.

The Retreat
Look Ahead

Owen

Twenty-nine hours of flight time, and I haven't slept at all, not even on my family's Gulfstream with my own cabin. I spent the entire trip having a panic attack while listening to emo music. I'm not proud of it, but I am here, and my brother will know what to do.

I barely glance around at the resort when I get out of the Rolls Royce. It seems nice enough, but I'm not here for leisure. I don't have time to enjoy myself in the sun. Or even stop to have a drink. I can't remember the last time I ate, so alcohol is off the table. I peel off my hoodie as I follow the map the concierge gave me.

I flip it around, realizing I am looking at it backwards. Fuck.

I don't have time for this.

I need to find Oliver now.

Before I have my eighteenth panic attack of the day.

Two days? Has it been two days since I'd left Vegas?

What even is time if not a construct to cause me more fucking anxiety?

I need Oliver's advice. He's the only one who can help me out of this situation. I'm not level-headed enough to make adult decisions, let alone ones with life-long consequences. I need a brown paper bag to breathe into. Or barbiturates. I make a mental note to raid mom's fun cabinet when I get back to the city.

Finally, I figure out the directions, since the obvious clue is the entire ocean on one side of the map. I would like to think I'd have figured that out quicker if I wasn't having a panic attack, but I won't worry about it.

I find the walkway to their private villa blocked by a security guard. "Hi Levi. Oliver here?"

"Owen, what a surprise. Is he expecting you?" Levi asks, giving me a strange look.

"I'd like to say because of twin intuition he's always expecting me, but I did call before I showed up."

"Oh, alright." Levi steps aside to let me pass.

I open the door, not bothering to knock. I've seen them naked far too many times to care what I walk in on, and it's been a week. Could they still be fucking? It isn't that fun or exciting.

I wander through the quiet villa, finally hearing them out back. The view is truly lovely, but I can't enjoy it. I can't enjoy anything. I feel like a fugitive.

I open the sliding glass door and turn to find Isaac bent over the back of a sun bathing chair, rather awkwardly.

How does that even work?

"I did a thing," I pronounce when Oliver doesn't notice my arrival.

"What the fuck?!" Oliver doesn't even have the courtesy to pull out as he looks over his shoulder. "What are you doing here?"

"I have to speak to you, and you weren't answering your phone." Obviously. Why else would I be here?

Sometimes Oliver is so dense.

"Of course I'm not answering my phone." He stares at me.

I stare back, not getting his point. "Can you put a pin in this so we can talk? It's rather urgent or I wouldn't have flown twenty-nine hours."

"Never mind the flight. What in the fucking world is so important that you think you should walk into the middle of my honeymoon to tell me?" Oliver's tone drips with annoyance.

Well, I'm annoyed too. "Can you?" I wave at his bare ass.

Oliver groans and turns back to brush his lips over the back of Isaac's neck. "I'm sorry. I'll deal with it." He grabs a towel to wrap around Isaac before turning towards me, hard-on and all. "How did you get past security?"

"Levi? He knows me. He's here to stop criminals, not your brother."

"Clearly I need to re-explain to him his job description. Because when I say no one should disturb us for the next month, he doesn't understand the provided information." Oliver mutters under his breath, but I ignore it. "Out with it then, since you're going to make me wait for my fucking orgasm until you tell me."

Isaac sits awkwardly on the chair, red in the face.

"I apologize, Isaac. This is a crisis."

"What crisis? Did you kill someone?" Oliver asks.

"Worse." I say, barely keeping my tone even.

"What is worse than killing someone? Did you lose all your money?" Oliver acts baffled.

"I married Colin."

"WHAT?"

Preorder The Retreat Now.

ACKNOWLEDGMENTS

Colleen and Kyla — for beta reading!

Bailey— for proofreading.

Sarah — For putting up with our bullshit. Sorry this isn't dino porn.

To all the amazing bloggers who share our novels and help get them into the hands of readers.

And to our readers. You are the best readers a writer could ask for, and why we keep doing this. We're lucky as fuck to have such amazing people supporting us.

ALSO BY J.R. GRAY

Pretty Broken Series

Pretty Obsessed

Pretty Toxic

Pretty Wreck

Pretty F*cked

Pretty Black

Volatile

Working Dogs Series

Scapegoat

Love Equations Series

The Friendship Equation

The Animosity Equation

The Forbidden Equation

Arrowood Series

ALSO BY ANDI JAXON

<u>Darby U Boys</u>

Hidden Scars

Blurred Lines

<u>Bennet Family Novels</u>

Rescue Me

Curves Ahead (MF)

Standalone

Broken

ABOUT J.R. GRAY

Gray is a cynical Chicago native, who drinks coffee all day, barely sleeps, and is a little too fashion obsessed. He writes romance sprinkled with kink, and hot as hell, dark and angsty characters because everyone deserves a happily ever after.

J.R. Gray is Gender Queer and uses He/Him pronouns.

Connect with J.R. Gray online:

Website
Instagram
Twitter - Personal
Twitter - Books
Facebook
Facebook Group
Tumblr
Newsletter
Amazon Author Page
Book Bub
Patreon

ABOUT ANDI JAXON

Sarcastic and snarky, I love to laugh and read dark fucked up shit. I write about tortured pasts and hot sex, a happily ever after that has to be worked for. My stories tend to be a little dark but with some comic relief, typically in the form of sarcasm and usually include two men falling in love though I sometimes dabble in other LGBTQIA stories.

Made in the USA
Columbia, SC
24 July 2024

38629834R00228